The World Ended on a Monday

Darkest Days Series Book 1

By
Tara Johnson

Dedication

I am so thankful to have a loving family that helped this dream come true. To my husband, thank you for taking on so much so that I could finish this book. To my best friend and editor, who read chapters every day and pushed me to get finished. Thank you

The World Ended on a Monday

Copyright 2020 by Tara Johnson. All Rights Reserved.

This book is a work of fiction. People, places, events, and situations are the product of the author's imagination. Any resemblance to an actual person, living or dead, or historical events, is purely coincidental.
No part of the book may be reproduced, stored in a retrieval system, o transmitted by any means without the written permission of the author and publisher.

Chapter 1

The world ended on a Monday, or at least the version we were used to. Why is it that all shitty things seem to happen on a Monday?

As I sat in my home office, desk piled high with papers and reports, I pounded on the send button for the umpteenth time in the last 15 minutes. "Stupid computers!" It had taken me all morning to compose the perfect reply email to my annoying boss's son. Since I worked from home or driving around the country and wasn't under his watchful gaze, the son had decided I needed to account for literally every second of my day.

"Suck it, ya little shit head," I mumbled under my breath, hoping he could hear me by osmosis.

I listened for the satisfying swish sound the computer makes when the email has gone through, nothing. The screen went to black. I hit the on-off button, but still nothing.

"Oh, for fuck's sake! What now?"

I know, or at least *think* I remember paying the electric bill. I grabbed my phone off the desk to look up the company website and double-check I paid the damn bill when the screen was black. Did I forget to charge it? No, I remember plugging it in last night. Huh, what in the fuck is happening?

Oh well, if the electricity is out and my phone is dead, that means nobody will call and bug me. I've always kind of enjoyed being alone with my thoughts. I'm a daydreamer and really kind of a loner. I've never understood why people hated being alone. I want peace while my family is away during the day.

It's just me, Freya, my German Shepard Dog, a sweet, medium-sized mix of unknown origin named Bo, and my six-teen-year-old rat terrier, Skeeter, during the day. My husband, Brandon, works as a builder on fancy pools for the rich and famous. When Brandon and I started our marriage seventeen years ago, we were both in college. Brandon was a chemistry and math whiz, while I mostly stayed safe from all things math-related in my liberal arts building. Our relationship started as fast friends; it continued for about a year, and then we decided to give it a go. I had children from a previous marriage, Kayla, age five, and Connor, almost two, when

Brandon entered our lives. Two years later, we added Max to our happy family.

I entered the workforce at the age of 26 as an Oil and Gas negotiator for major oil companies around the country. Since the job required a ton of travel around the United States, Brandon decided to leave school and raise our children. That was seventeen years ago. Today I was standing in front of a mirror looking at the approaching middle-aged woman in front of me. Long blonde hair went just to my waist, my now slightly overweight frame, no longer a perfect size six after years spent working on computers and answering phone calls.

"That's okay, Tara, let's get you fixed up and then deal with our power issue," I mumbled to myself.

After combing my crazy hair and pulling it into a braid, I picked up my phone and plugged it in, and noticed it didn't make the chirp I was used to. Leaving my newly built ranch style house, I headed next door to my parent's house. Our home wasn't huge by today's standards, but I loved it. Three large bedrooms and three bathrooms are all tucked neatly into a nest of trees. Yes, I'm a middle-aged woman who lives next to her parents; the irony of that isn't lost on me. My grandfather purchased land in the middle of nowhere back in the 1960s. He built a private airstrip for airplane enthusiasts and retired pilots. My immediate and a few extended families have lived on the property ever since. As much as they can drive me crazy, always seeming to interfere with our business at the worst possible times. I love how tightly knit of a family unit we are and wouldn't trade living next door to them for anything.

"Mom, are you here?"

My parent's dogs all ran at me to get all the love they could before the cats ran in and scared them off.
"Hi, guys." I bent down to give head scratches and pats to the beautiful English Shepherds as my parents came around the corner.

My mother looks exactly like me, and my daughter looks like both of us. People get us confused all the time. Hell, Brandon and my Dad get us confused from the back.

"Mom, is your phone working?"

"No, I guess I let the battery die, and now I can't find it," she said as she looked around the kitchen and in the drawers."

My mother was always losing her phone; it amazed me I could ever get ahold of her.

"You've lost it again?" I said with exasperation and an eye roll for added emphasis.

"I know, Tara, I know. I set it down somewhere, and now I can't find it."

My mom, Geraldine Ross, is a badass. We've traveled all over the world and have never once returned with everything we left with. One thing my mother did exceptionally well negotiate. I had never once paid the asking price on any car or good. She just had a way about her. She and I could be in the smallest of random villages, and she would come waltzing up with some weird looking item. She cracked me up.

My Dad stood watching our conversation, amusement sparkling in his eyes because it's the same one we have at least once a week.

"Tara, can I speak with you a minute?" I followed my Dad down to his bedroom.

My parents had slept in different rooms since I was a teenager. My mother is a night owl, and my Dad snores like a chainsaw.

"What's up?" I asked my Dad.

Bill was actually my stepfather but had raised me from the age of three. Standing six foot four, my Dad is a large man who has the coloring and proud demeanor of his Native American ancestors. He continually kept a watchful eye on me while growing up, and still does. Yet, he somehow managed to perfectly balance that watchful gaze while also giving me the freedom needed to learn and grow. I love that about my Dad, and it's a trait I've tried to emulate with my own children. I always thought he was the coolest Dad around. I remember dragging him to a Motley Crew concert when I was only thirteen. There we were, rocking to the song "Home Sweet Home," and I was dying to meet up with my friends and have that small taste of freedom every thirteen years old craves when I look up at him to get the go-ahead-nod. I immediately ran off to stand with my friends in the mosh pit area.

When I looked back to check on my Dad, he had a blonde on each shoulder. That's my Dad in a nutshell: ever watchful, always calm.

"Tara, I've been picking up some weird stuff on the short wave," My Dad was always watching the news and thinking up ways to survive doomsday.

"Like what?" I said as I plopped myself down on the bed.
"The radio is reporting some kind of terrorist attack."

"Daddy, if something was going on, wouldn't there be news or sirens going off?"

"Maybe," he said.

My Dad sat down at his desk and turned the knob on his old hand-cranked short-wave radio. At first, there was just a lot of static, with yelling popping up here and there. Then we heard it.

"This is a message from the Emergency Broadcast System. Today at approximately noon, central standard time, a nuclear weapon was launched on the West Coast of the United States of America. The weapon impacted the area of Los Angeles. A second nuclear weapon was detonated in the New York City area. Lives have been lost, people have been injured, and homes and businesses have been destroyed. All government levels are coordinating their efforts to do everything possible to help the people affected by this emergency (horrific attack?). As lifesaving activities continue, all citizens need to follow the instructions from emergency responders…The instructions are based on the best information we have right now; and will be updated as more information becomes available. The United States Government also believes an EMP, or Electro-Magnetic Pulse device, exploded above the Earth's atmosphere to render our country powerless. Please stay indoors and do not panic. Federal agencies will be in touch with local officials to give more information."

By the time the final beeping sirens had stopped, I knew all the blood had drained from my face. I could feel my heartbeat in my chest and hear a buzzing sound. I had suffered from panic attacks since I was twelve years old, so I bent down and put my head between my knees, knowing full well the drill by now. I did not have time to panic right now. I have a husband and three children to locate. As I slowly got my breathing under control, I looked over at my Dad, hoping to see some reassurance that this would all be okay. Bill, always strong and stoic under any crisis, looked like I felt.

"What do we do now?" I asked my Dad.

Bill stood, not really looking at anything, just staring into space. "Dad?"

"I'm here, just thinking. Tara, do you still have all your gas canisters full from mowing season?"

The Oklahoma mowing season was from March to October, damn near all year. When my grandfather built the first house out here in the middle of nowhere, Oklahoma. He left the airstrip all grass and never really cared to pave over it as other pilots started building homes and hangers for their planes. When he passed away in 2007, everyone voted to keep it grass as it had been for the last 50 years. Between the 12 acres of the airstrip and 6 acres for our immediate family, the mowing season never seemed to end.
"Of course, I have about fifty gallons. I filled them up before winter just in case of an ice storm."

"Good, we're going to need it. With the EMP going off, there will be no more trips to the gas station or running water from our wells without generators to run the pumps," my Dad said as he cranked the radio.

"We need to find out which way the wind is blowing. Fallout shouldn't reach us for a while, and God willing, the wind will be blowing West".

"Dad, it's January; the wind is almost always blowing from the North. Oh my God, I have to find a way to get to Max's high school!" I shouted as another wave of panic started to rear its ugly head.

"Tara, we have time; Max will be in the schools' fallout shelter."

My son, Max's school, was thankfully built during the Cold War when fallout shelters were commonplace; the school system currently used it for a tornado shelter. Living in Oklahoma was a bitch during the storm season because living in Oklahoma during storm season was not taken lightly. It seems like we are always under some kind of storm watch. March through June, and you never knew when or where a tornado could pop up, demolishing entire neighborhoods in its path of destruction. I knew my Dad was right, and Max was safe, but it sure as hell didn't make me feel better.

"Where are the other kids?" My Dad asked.

"Kayla is at work in the city today, and Connor is outside working on the tractor."

My middle son, Connor, stayed in a mobile home out on the back of the property. I dreaded explaining what was going on to him; he tended to panic in any kind of emergency. I would always sit him down and calmly explain what was happening and how there was no need to panic. Funny, half the time, I was panicked, but I could never let it show on the outside when he was around. I tried to protect Connor from the world, but it looked like it wasn't going to work this time.

"Let's get together in about an hour and go over all of our supplies and any vehicles we might be able to use."

"We have Max's truck!" I said.

Max, my almost six-foot-tall son with wavy brown hair and bright blue eyes like his Dad, would be turning sixteen in a few months. He had been fixing up an old Chevy truck for the last 6 months in preparation for the big day he could finally get his license. He was so proud of all the work he had put into it no one had the heart to tell him it was the biggest jalopy we'd ever seen. Girls wouldn't be lining up to take a ride anytime soon, but we let him dream the dream anyway and snickered when he wasn't in earshot. Max is a fantastic kid; he never asks for anything and is sweet, polite, and handsome.

I left my parents' house. I know I needed some time to myself to think and decide the best way to proceed. I decided to leave my Dad to tell mom the news in private. What in the hell was I going to do!? My husband and daughter are at least 30 minutes by car from me, and now my car wouldn't even work. My daughter Kayla had recently moved in with her boyfriend, Carlos, about 30 minutes away from us, too, so all I could do was pray they'd make it back home safely.

"God! I've got freaking braces on my teeth! I'm going to be stuck in braces forever now." My brain was starting to spiral.

I started hearing loud booming sounds going off in the city. I couldn't see anything, but I was starting to smell smoke. I had read books on electromagnetic pulses before. I knew there was a high likelihood of planes immediately dropping from the sky. Thankfully all of the aircraft on this airport was built sometime before the Carter administration.

"Shit shit shit," I said as I walked towards Connor.

I needed to reign in my thoughts before I found him.
Connor was sitting on our old tractor, trying to get it going. He loved working with his hands and was fantastic with old machines, somehow managing to always get them to start up again. I watched him move his too long auburn hair out of his brown eyes while he patiently tinkered with some piece of engine part I couldn't name if my life depended on it. Connor was a big kid; he stood about five feet ten inches and was a bit overweight, thanks to the holiday season and his love of all things baked goods. The holidays had hit both of us hard. When it came to sweets, Connor and I both overindulged. He loves to lay on the couch next to my recliner and watch movies with me while we share a big tin of Christmas cookies.

"Connor, can we go to your house a minute?"

"Sure, mom, what's up? I think I've almost got the old tractor running!"

"That's great, honey." Connor and I walked through the field and onto his porch.

"I wasn't expecting company, so it's kind of a mess today."

My children all knew how I felt about a messy house and had all grown up with Sunday cleaning days when they lived at home.

"Its fine, kiddo, let's just get inside."

Connor's house was a mess. Dishes in the sink and dirty clothes lying around. I looked over and saw Connor blanch.

"It's fine, it's your home, and you can keep it any way you want," Connor looked at me like I just told him he was from another planet.

"Sit, Sit, please." "Mom, what's going on?"

"About an hour ago, a bomb went off in California, L.A. actually, and another one in New York City. The bombs were nuclear and have killed a lot of people. Now, what we need to worry about is getting Brandon and your brother and sister home." I saw the look on his face go from amusement to worry in about two seconds.

"Do we know who did it?" Surprised, I hadn't even thought about who did it; I had only been worried about finding the family I said,

"No, I don't think so, at least if they have, I haven't heard yet," I watched as he took deep breaths, the color draining from his face.

"Hey, hey, now is not the time for panic, now is the time for action. You're almost 20 years old, and I'm going to need your help to save our family." He slowly looked at me and nodded.

"I want you to gather your stuff. Grab all your food and first aid supplies, and go up to my house."

"I have lots of books on survival; grandpa gives me new ones every year for Christmas."

"Excellent, bring them all with you," I said.

I left Connor's house and began the walk through the fields back to my house. I mindlessly cranked the radio in my hand that my Dad had handed to me as I left my parents' house earlier. I turned it on as I walked, flipping the knob, looking for any sign of news. I found what I thought may have been an afternoon radio show taking calls from panicked people. Still, nothing gave me any new information about what was happening in the rest of the country.

"What should I do about my children and family? Should I leave to find my children?" a frantic lady was saying. On the other end, the man told her the government said if your children or family are with you, stay together. If your children or family are in another home or building, they should remain there until you are told it is safe to travel. You also should stay where you are…schools have emergency plans and shelters.

I could feel the woman's panic over the radio. It matched my own only a few minutes ago. It's hard in any situation where your children may be in danger. I reached my door and was greeted by all the dogs at the door, tales wagging. I sat on the floor in my entryway and hugged them, Letting the tears out. Animals always have a way of comforting people when they're sad. I squished their little faces to mine and got doggie kisses. I sat that way for a few minutes, just taking in all the crazy that had happened in the last 30 minutes. Looking at my oldest dog Skeeter, I knew what would happen; he was doomed without his heart medication twice a day. I brushed my tears away and stood. Damn it, I have plans to make!

Okay, first things first, I told the dogs. I went into my bedroom, where all my supplies are stored. My Dad and I started doing the "prepping" thing back in 2009 when the recession hit us extremely hard. Brandon and I ended up out of work early in the year and had gone through our savings in only three months. We looked everywhere for a job and found nothing; it took months to get back on our feet. Once we were back on our feet, we began to collect things we would need to survive if it ever happened to us again. We started slow, an extra can of something here and there, and before long, we had tons of food, ammo, and camping gear. Brandon and I both loved camping, to the utter disgust of my technology addicted children. For my part, I loved collecting medical supplies. Do I have medical training? Nope! I have watched many YouTube videos, though, so I guess we'll just have to see how my Dr. YouTube training turns out during all of this. After about ten minutes, my parents came through the door. They looked rough; my mom brought in bags of supplies, then the dogs, followed by the damn cats. My Dad looked broken; I could see the stress lines on his face. I have two sisters, one brother, and we have no idea where they could be.

Connor came in the door next, dragging an old trunk full of books, clothes, and all the food from his house.
"Okay," he said, "according to the books, we need to line the windows and doors with plastic, then all of our outer clothes need to be taken off and thrown away. We'll also need to take a shower, but no heavy scrubbing with anything that could tear the skin. That will keep some of the radioactive material from coming into contact with our bodies. Then we just have to wait until it's safe to go

outside. The books say it should take about 24 hours for the dust to settle"

Chapter 2

I popped up at that news. "Twenty-four hours? I can't leave our family out there for twenty-four flipping hours!" I said.

"No, Tara, he's right. I know you want to go get them, but you need to make a plan; first, you can't just go running around outside in the damn apocalypse!" my mother said.

"We need to get the generators hooked up and running before the radiation has time to settle into the groundwater," my Dad said.

"I'll help," said Connor.
I turned to my mom then.

"How are you doing with all this, I asked while nervously running my fingers through my hair? I'm freaking the hell out."

"I know, honey, I am too, but I know you'll figure it all out."

"Tara, I wanted to talk to you about something else while everyone is outside working." I plopped down on the couch next to her.

I was amazed by her level of calm. I could tell she was mildly upset, but nowhere near was the level of crazy I headed towards. "Tara, I've been on heart medication for about six months now. It's been too high lately, and the doctor said as long as I continue to take it, I should be alright". She said.

"Jesus, mom, why didn't you tell me? That's awful. Did he change your diet? Is that all he said......?" The thought hit me like a brick to the face!

My mom needed medicine, the medicine we were no longer able to get... At the age of forty-two, I sat stunned. I had never before really thought about not having her with me. Living next door, doing movie nights, and bitching about random things that bothered only her. Like the year, she complained about my Christmas lights being uneven; or that my car is always covered in dog hair.
"How many pills do you have left?" I asked. Mom turned to face me, "I have about 90 days' worth of pills left. I'm not sure if I have the full 90 days or if I want to try and cut them into halves. I worry a half dose won't be strong enough, though. I'm on a pretty high dose."

"Shit, mom, what does dad say about it?" I asked.

"He hasn't said anything; at the time when I got the prescription, I honestly forgot to say anything about it. It's high blood pressure; people get it every day; you pop a pill and go on with your life. I can honestly say I wasn't exactly prepared for the apocalypse."

"I just thought you and Bill had a type of PTSD from the recession when you two started doing all of the prepping. Your Dad filled the entire house with random crap."

"So what now, are you going to tell him? I asked.

"I will, but let's try to get all the family home safe first. Bill has more than enough to worry about right now, and so do you. I just wanted to let you know so you'd be ready if anything happens." She said.

I wanted to say more, but Connor and my Dad rounded the corner of the living room just then.

"I've got the industrial-sized tanks in the shop building filling up. I'm hoping by late this evening, we'll have them filled up. We also have all the water in the pool we can use for other stuff, but not for drinking. Thankfully this happened in winter while the cover is on. Hell, I'm not even sure about that water. I'm going to have to do some reading up on radiation and fallout." He said as he paced around my living room.

I noticed he had made a "to-do list." I love to make lists; it was one thing I got from being raised by him—my love of lists.

"Okay," he said, looking at his list.

"Next, we need to get off all of these clothes and get rid of them, just in case. I don't think any radiation has made it this far yet."

"Damn it," he said. "

"I always thought the market would bust, and we would have an economic breakdown. Why didn't I do more research on a nuclear bomb blast? I've got the generators hooked up to the water well pumps. Everyone needs to hop in the shower and wash up, but no more than five minutes. Connor, you and I get two minutes; we don't have hair down to our ass." My Dad laughed as he walked away.

The next hour went by pretty fast. While one of us was washing up and disposing of our clothes, the others were hanging and taping plastic sheeting on the windows and doors. When I came out of the shower and looked at my home, it looked like one of those pandemic movies. Plastic and duct tape covered everything. My mom sat combing out her waist-length hair, and the guys were nose deep in books. We were coming up at three o'clock. It was now about three hours after the bomb fell. Looking around my house at my family, it felt like it should be midnight. I started cleaning out the refrigerator; we would have one hell of a feast today with leftovers and the lunch meat I had in here. I had some hamburger thawing out for dinner. Without power, risking exposure to the radiation outside where the grill was, was a lost cause.

We all sat and ate in silence while we read our assigned books on survival. The book I was reading talked about "duck and cover." In the 1950s, the United States Government suggested this oh so not practical method of protecting yourself in a nuclear attack. This was intended as an alternative to the more effective target/citywide emergency evacuation. I had to roll my eyes at that. Okay, kiddies, duck and cover your ass under the school desk or with a textbook, as if that will save you…snort. This brought back memories of our old elementary school tornado drills. My school would have us line up in the hall, squat down and hold a book over our heads.
My thoughts drifted to Max; was he okay? Did the school evacuate everyone into the fallout shelter? I wasn't comfortable leaving my child's safety in the hands of anyone but myself and my husband. What about Brandon? Where was he? I knew he was working at some mansion in a ritzy neighborhood in Oklahoma City called Nichols Hills, where most of the "old money" chose to live. Would the homeowners have let the workers in or left them to fend for themselves? My daughter Kayla and the boyfriend, were they safely locked up tight in the dentist's office? All I had were fucking questions, and I hated having no answers to any of them.

My daughter's best friend and old roommate, Jalyn, and her two boys were at the daycare she worked at. Jalyn had become like a daughter to me in the years she lived next door, sharing a house with Kayla. When Kayla had moved in with her boyfriend, Jalyn and her boys stayed next door. I thought of her two small boys like my own grandbabies. Brandon and I spoiled them rotten. Now they were stuck at daycare. Jalyn was a hard-working single mother.

The boys' father had run off as soon as he discovered Jalyn was pregnant with their second child. I knew if there was a way, I need to get to her and the kids and bring them home with me. At least the daycare was outside of town. I had to hope that would keep them safe until we could get to them. Shit, I was driving myself crazy. Seeing my obvious signs of approaching crazy woman panic, my Dad walked over to me and sat.

"I think I have a plan to at least get Max, Jalyn, and the boys." I started to speak, but he cut me off with a hand.

"I know you're worried about them all, but Brandon and Kayla are only about a mile from each other, and If I know Brandon, he will be making his way to her as soon as he can," he said. I nodded; I had considered this too.

My husband is an amazing man; I'm not sure I could live if something happened to him. My chest squeezed as just the thought of something happening to him. I took a deep breath and looked back at my Dad.

"Okay, what's the plan?" I asked.

"Okay, I have two. We have Max's truck; it's old and doesn't have any computer parts, so I doubt it's been compromised in any way. This issue is getting through all the cars on the road and reaching the daycare and high school. We've talked about disasters enough; you know there will be many crazy and desperate people. If they see a running vehicle, they will want either a ride or worse, to take it from you." He said.

"Now, plan two is a little bit more dangerous than even plan one. We can ask the neighbor to fly us in the old 71' Cessna 172 Skyhawk. It's small, and we could fly in and look for a place to land near the high school or, worst-case scenario, land at the airport in town. If we have to land at the airport, it's still at least a three-mile walk to the school, and God only knows what conditions will be like." He said.

I had thirty-three hours of training and was still terrified of flying it. My sweet elderly neighbor had been my flight instructor. He was always very calm and relaxed while I flew white-knuckled around Oklahoma City. I was almost done with my flight training when we had to complete a "dead drop." A dead drop was when you fly to about seven thousand feet and shut down the engine. The pilot in training is then supposed to calmly restart the plane and go on about their merry way. Unfortunately, I panicked for my flight instructor, grabbed him by his little jumpsuit, and screamed more cuss words than he had ever experienced while we plummeted to the ground. Thankfully for both of us, we only fell about two thousand feet before he managed to pry my hands off of him and recover the plane. I stepped out of the little Cessna that day and NEVER got near it again. Boom, just like that, I was no longer a pilot in training. My Dad must have seen my face pale.

"It's okay, we'll ask Keith if he will take us to town, but if he can't manage it, you will have to fly us. You know he's been sick and on chemo. There's a possibility he won't feel up to flying us. You have more than enough training in that plane to get us to town and back without a problem." He said, sitting down on the couch to think.

I need to get to high school. God, there were too many people we needed to find and bring home and things that needed to be done, and I had very few ideas on how to accomplish any of them.
After a few hours of snacking and reading, we finally decided to draw up some plans to get everyone here to the house. Where in the hell was I going to put all these people in my three-bedroom place?
I started to drag out old radio equipment I had purchased after the crash in 2009. After the crash, my best friend and I had decided that we would never be caught up in something like the economic crash and left with nothing again. To that end, we had been preparing as a kind of hobby. People thought we were kind of crazy, but we didn't care. Alicia and I had both got our HAM radio license. Now I just had to hope I could get ahold of her. Alicia lived with her psychiatrist husband Mike and their two boys Sean and Joseph, about ten minutes south of us. After getting everything set up, I called and called but couldn't reach her on the HAM. I just had to hope they were okay.
We all stayed up visiting and trying to come up with plans to get everyone home for hours.

After a long-heated conversation, tomorrow we would go next door and ask for a ride, or God help us all, to borrow an airplane so I could fly into town on my own.

I was startled awake at five am. I looked over to see I was the last one to wake up. Connor had his hand stuck in a box of Frosted Flakes, and my parents were making coffee with my French press. I figured we had about two hours before sun-up. I needed to pull myself together today and focus on finding my loved ones. After a quick cold breakfast and some even colder coffee, I set off to get dressed and ready. I pulled on my old hiking boots, worn from years of summer hiking with Brandon, and a bunch of bitching kids, to our favorite campsite. Brandon and I both loved hiking and fishing; but, once the kids had gotten older and started to pull away into their own adult lives, we didn't go as much. There was just something sad about it. The first time Brandon and I had gone alone, we spent a lot of time talking about the old days with the kids. Kayla's tent was always leaking, and Connor was still bringing the wrong hot dogs. After that first trip by ourselves, we just stopped going.

I opened a hidden compartment in our bedroom where we kept our firearms. When we built our home in 2015, we decided we liked the idea of having hidden areas around the house. It made us feel safe to know we had a firearm an arm's length away in every room. You would never know to look around our house how many things were hidden in the walls if you didn't know where to look. I took out my Glock 19, a full magazine, and a box of ammo. I prayed I wouldn't have to use it, but our world had just gone to shit, and I'd rather be prepared than have regrets should something happen while I was out. I holstered my weapon, grabbed an extra just in case, and headed back into the living room to talk to the family.

"Okay, let's go over and talk to Keith about using the plane," I said.

I had spent most of the previous night thinking over my options. Driving the truck would mean taking all the back roads and praying I didn't hit any roadblocks or traffic jams. Then, like my Dad had said, getting beat up or gunned down for it once people saw me driving down the street. The plane, as terrified as I was at having to fly it, would be the better option. The little town of Guthrie, Oklahoma, where we lived, has an airport right in the middle of it. I could put the plane down and walk through town to the high school. Jalyn and her boys were only a few blocks from the airstrip, so I decided to start with them. I hoped Jalyn would take the boys to the plane and watch it while I hit the high school.

My Dad was strapping on his shoes and also bolstering his gun. "Keith should be up by now; we need to check on him anyway." After a long night of reading as far as we could tell with the north winds, we should be okay to go outside today without fear of contamination".

My Dad and I set off for the short walk across the runway to Keith's house. I was remembering how many times I had made this walk. Keith and his late wife had been like grandparents to me after my grandparents had passed away. I loved them and felt a pain in my heart anytime I thought of Keith's late wife. When I knocked on the door, I was met with a 20 gauge shotgun pointed in my face.

"Damn Keith, it's Tara and Bill from next door," I said as I darted out of the way.

"Sorry, sorry, Tara, with everything that's happened, I'm scared there will be looting. I brought out the shotgun to make sure nobody got inside."

"I think we're okay for now. We live far enough away from the town I think we have a few days before the looters get this far. I hope anyway." I said.

"What can I do for ya?" he asked as he led us into the kitchen.

"I wanted to ask about possibly you flying me to Guthrie to get Max. I also have our neighbor and her kids at the daycare. I'd like to pick up if it's possible." I asked.

I looked at Keith; he was an eighty-six year old, maybe five-foot six-inch man, ninety pounds soaking wet. Cancer had done a number on the sweet little old man. As we sat down at the kitchen table, his large tabby cat Scooby jumped in my lap and commenced that strange thing all cats do, the massage of claws on your leg. I wasn't a massive fan of cats, but for some reason, this one loved me. Anytime I visited the house, Scooby would jump in my lap and purr like I was one of his favorite people. I enjoyed fetching and walks. Cats just laid around, looking like they were plotting your death all day but to each his own.

"I think you could handle the Cessna on your own. I know you haven't flown in a while since the "incident," he said with a smile, but it will all come back to you once you get inside."

"But Keith," I started.

"Now, now, if you are planning on bringing people back with you, I'd just be taking up an extra seat and adding extra weight." He said.

True, as that statement was, that didn't mean I was comfortable entrusting the lives of my son and the others to my own flying prowess, or lack thereof. Keith led us outside to the hanger, and there she was, the Cessna of doom. Keith and I did a full pre-trip on the plane, checking the oil, gas, and wings for any damage. Once finished, my heart started to race. It was almost time. Keith looked at me and smiled.

"You were a fine pilot; you had one close call. Don't you think I've had hundreds of close calls in a lifetime of flight?"

"Now, once you get to the airport, talk to Jacob Brown. I'd bet you a hundred bucks he's holed up there. Jacob is always hanging out at the airport, hitting on the pretty widow that runs the snack shop. He can help you keep the plane safe while you're looking for Max and the others." Keith then tossed me a handheld radio.
"Here," he said, "I kept a few of these in a safe place. It won't have a super far range, but it may come in handy," He said.

I hugged my Dad.

"Please be safe, I wish I could go with you, but Keith is right. To bring everyone home means no extra passengers on the plane," he said.

"Dad, please keep yourself, mom, and Connor safe for me. I love you." I said.

"I love you too. Fly safe," he said.

"I'm wondering if it wouldn't be better for you and Connor to take the truck and go for Jalyn and the boys. The daycare is far enough on the outskirts of town that I think you could get there, taking only back roads. It's less than a mile off a dirt road." I said.

That was one thing I always like about where we lived. The countryside was full of dirt roads. Some so small they were only one lane.

I heard a bark on the other side of the hanger and walked out to find my mother trying to hold onto Freya's leash. Freya was having none of it. Mom finally dropped the leash, and Freya bolted straight for me. She sat in front of me, her large almond-shaped black eyes looking at mine.

"She's refusing to stay quiet. The second you left the house, this dog went crazy, trying to follow you." My mom said.

"Personally, I think you should take her with you. A woman walking with a large dog is less likely to be jumped." She said.

"I agree," said my Dad.

I looked at Freya; I could almost read her thoughts just looking in her eyes. I bent down, and she licked my face.

"Okay, I'll take her with me. It will be nice to have the company for the flight and the long walk to the school through the middle of town." I said.

Freya seeing that she had won this battle, jumped into the co-pilot seat as soon as I opened the door to the plane.
I jumped in the plane and put on my headset. It had been a long time since I had sat in this plane. I looked around, checking all of the gauges before finally starting up the motor. I made sure to close off all of the outside air vents. It would get cold without engine heat and the air vents to circulate air; being in a stuffy plane was still better than possible radiation that may seep through the vents. With a deep sigh, I taxied onto the runway. Slowly bringing up the engine, I prepared for take-off. Freya sat in her co-pilot seat in full attention mode, like flying an airplane was something we did every day. I wasn't sure if I was more scared of the plane or the journey that awaited me only ten miles away. I guess we'll find out. With increasing pressure on the wheel, I lifted off the ground headed north to find my baby.

Chapter 3

I slowly reached an altitude of about three thousand feet. The first thing I noticed as I got a good look at the landscape was the smoke. At this altitude, I could see forever. Fires were burning in all directions. It looked like homes and businesses burned in the larger and more populated cities.

"Wow," I said as I looked first to the town from the south, then banking the plane more towards my little town of Guthrie.

"I can't believe in such a short time it's gotten this bad!" I quickly picked up the radio Keith had given me and turned it on.

"This is Cessna to base. Do you copy?" I asked as I depressed the buttons. I was hoping Keith would answer. I didn't want to use any names if I didn't have to.

"I copy," I heard Keith's voice come over the radio.

"You need to take precautions; it looks like the town to the south has fallen and is on fire. Please be aware and prepared." I said.

"I copy; thanks for the update, be safe and high enough to evade small arms fire."

"Copy," I said with a wince. I hadn't even thought about that.

I put the radio down between the seats but left the volume on as loud as It would go. The tiny plane was noisy, even with the large headset in place. As I flew north, I started seeing the same kinds of fires in my little town. My heart broke; this small town that closed school for homecoming games and had an annoying amount of parades was on fire. I'd spend most of my childhood running around on those streets, spending all my allowance money at a little candy and antique store. My friends and I would skip school and spend the day in the park, just talking and smoking stolen cigarettes. Before modern technology had advanced, it was easy to run to a payphone and call in as a parent. There was no caller I.D. back then. Poor kids today can't get away with anything, I thought with a chuckle. Even now, the childhood memories made me smile with the world seeming to have gone to shit.

The closer I got to the town, the more I raised my altitude. I wanted to fly around the outskirts of town to get a lay of the land; it looked like a small war zone. These people were shop owners and farmers. I wouldn't believe it was going as feral it looked.

I headed to the edge of town that housed the high school. It looked locked up tight. No fires and no people were running around acting crazy. That was a good sign. I just hoped they hadn't allowed the children to leave the safety of the school.

I flew alongside the highway. I-35, the major highway running North and south through Oklahoma's entire state, was at a complete shutdown. Cars, as far as I could see, were stranded on the road. People stood around like they were waiting for someone to come save them. Several people waved their arms around like they were trying to get my attention. As I looked over the horizon, I could see fires.

As I headed back, I flew closer to downtown. I knew it was a risky move, but I wanted to see what I was in for. It was then that I saw a group of men running with what looked like homemade torches. They were all wearing matching orange jumpsuits.

"Fuck!" I swore.

The jails were all electronic. I now understood all the fires and terrified townspeople running around. I would have to risk a confrontation or take the much longer way into the high school. I reached between the seats and tried the radio.

"Cessna to base." Nothing, just static.

I was out of range of my little radio. I wanted to tell Keith about the escaped prisoners. Where were the guards? Had they killed them? Had the guards left the prisoners to find their own families? I'm not sure our small-town police department and sheriff's office could handle that amount of prisoners. I thought back to when the entire town pulled together to update our old jails. We had all voted for a bond issue for the upgrades. Now I was kicking my ass over it.

I circled the town, looking for any other small planes. I was always super paranoid about a mid-air collision. It had almost happened once. I was flying along, looking around, when Keith yelled, "do you see that plane?" Keith had grabbed the controls and put us in a deep dive. I was scared to death. I looked everywhere but never did see the plane I almost hit. I rolled my eyes at the memory. I was always something when I was learning to fly. Twice I had nearly hit deer trying to land on the runway. Oh, the airport workers got several laughs at my expense. I slowed the engine on the plane to prepare for landing; I hated landings because I sucked at doing them. The Cessna was a taildragger. This meant I had two tires under where I sat and one small tire on the aircraft's tail that I had to control with foot pedals. For some reason, the foot pedals were always hard for me to handle. People would come out of their homes, or in the case of this airport, they would come out of the tower to watch me try and land with big smiles plastered on their faces. People always knew who was landing without even seeing the plane numbers. I would swerve around on the runway like a drunk driver.

The moment I dreaded even before I took off was here; it was time to set her down. I lined up the plane with the runway, put down my flaps, and held my breath. Freya whined next to me. What does it say when even a dog is nervous. I touched down on the pavement and started hitting my brakes. My wings tipped side to side like they would hit the pavement. When I finally stopped the airplane, I took a deep breath.
"One of my better landings if I do say so myself." Freya gave me the side-eye.

"Geez, you survived, didn't you?' I huffed.

I taxied off the main runway, still swerving like a drunk, but managing to at least stay on the paved taxiway. I jerkily pulled the plane by the gas pumps and turned off the engine.
The airport was exactly like I remembered it. It had old and shabby looking hangers where the pilots kept their planes. The old control tower still looked like a good strong wind could knock it down. They were grey, every single building and the tower was a deep grey color. I understand colors could be distracting, but, damn, all the same color had always looked so sad and old to me.
 As Freya and I jumped out, Freya jumping over me to get out of the plane, I heard a man's voice say

"Stop right there!" I slowly raised my hands and told Freya to sit and stay.

I looked over to see Jacob Brown. , a tall African American man. Now in probably his mid-sixties, incredibly handsome for an older man, he stood tall with a massive smile on his face. Jacob loved to tease me about my lack of flying skills. Anytime I landed on the town runway, he would run out to get to Keith. He loved to be first to hear how many embarrassing mistakes I had made on my flight lesson that day. Jacob was such a happy and outgoing guy. Today, however, behind the smile, I saw the lines of tension around his handsome face.

"I knew as soon as I saw that landing who was in the driver's seat. Sorry for the gun, but I had to make sure it was you." he laughed.

"Personally, I think it was one of my better landings; the wing didn't hit the ground this time," I said with a huff and a smile.

"Where is Keith? Is everyone okay?" he said in rapid-fire questions.

"It's okay, everyone is okay, and Keith stayed home so I would have enough space in the plane to bring Max back with me," I said.

"I flew over the area before I came in; prisoners are running free with homemade torches!"

"You're lucky you flew in when you did. I've been hearing gunfire all night," he said.

"If they get any further this way, I might have to leave. I've been coming to this airport since I got home from Vietnam," he said sadly.

"When the original bomb went off in L.A. I was here doing some maintenance on a few of the birds. I went in to talk to widow James, and she's the one that told me about the attack. Hazel has one of those HAM radios, and she's always talking to her sister out west on it," he said.

In her mid to late fifty's, Hazel was a pretty woman with long beautiful red hair that fell to her back in waves and only a few strands of grey starting to weave their way through it. I had talked to her anytime I came into the control tower for a coffee. Hazel was always talking about government conspiracies. She always thought the government could listen to you on your cell phone. She had refused to own one.

"That's how they get ya!" she would say anytime she caught me checking text messages or using my phone to call Brandon. Jacob and I made our way to the door and knocked. Hazel had found wood and boarded up the doors. Smart move now that the town was in chaos.

"Who's there?" Hazel asked in her usual gruff voice.

"Hazel damn it, I was only gone for two minutes, and I've got Tara with me. She flew in with Keith's plane." Jacob said.
Hazel opened the door just a crack to look at the two of us before opening the door.

"Isn't she just the best woman ever?" Jacob said with a dreamy voice.
I just rolled my eyes and moved inside with Jacob and Freya.

"So, I'm thinking this was the Russki's," she said as she made her way back behind her snack counter.

"Do you want some coffee? I've got an old outside heater for power outages I used to heat it up. It's not that Starbucks you kids live on, but it's warm." Hazel said.

"Oh my God, yes," I said.
Hazel handed me a cup absently, sat down a bowl of water for Freya, and then returned to the HAM radio.

"Have there been any more updates? I haven't heard anything since yesterday, right after the bomb went off." I said.

"Only smart people that kept their radios in Faraday cages are left now," she said while spinning the knobs of the radio.

"Nothing from the government big wigs, just a bunch of people speculating who attacked us. I'm still betting on the Russians," she said, but I wasn't so sure.

Over the last month, the United States had been in a battle of wills with the Iranians. The U.S. had killed one of their prominent war generals in a drone strike. General what's his name, I could never remember names that long, had been supporting another government's coup attempt, and ordered an American embassy destroyed. I kept these thoughts to myself. I wasn't going to do any good to argue with Hazel.
Hazel's coffee shop was the only bit of warmth and color the little airport had. She had decorated for Christmas and just left everything up.

"So," said Jacob.

"How are you going to get to the high school from here with all those escaped prisoners running around burning shit to the ground? "He said.

I shrugged, "I'm going to try to make my way along the east side of town. It's further than straight through the middle, but hopefully, I'll run into less trouble.

"I'm going with ya," they both said almost simultaneously.

"Guys, the town is in terrible shape. Not to mention someone has to guard the planes. It would be a long walk back to my house if someone steals, or God forbid, lights the dame plane on fire." I said with a shake of my head.

Jacob looked at Hazel.

"Hazel, you're a better shot than me, plus you know how to work the HAM radio. It just makes more sense for you to stay here and guard the airport. I just really hate the thought of leaving you here." he said.

"Don't go acting like I can't, and won't, kick somebody's ass, Jacob!" Hazel said.

"I'll be just fine; I've got my shotgun and enough rounds to blow up anyone wanting in this building," she said with a grin.

"Now, you two need to get going. You're going to need to hurry if you plan to make it back here in time for Tara to fly back," she said, looking at me.

"Tara, I'm guessing you still haven't mastered the art of flying in the dark?" She said with a full smile this time.

"Arg," I said, "does everyone know how much I suck at flying?" I asked as Jacob and Hazel both burst into laughter.

"Oh, yea," Jacob said as he snort laughed.

"Your flying lessons are legendary around here," he said, hanging on to his belly.

"Fabulous," I said as I was starting laying out my plans.

A good thirty minutes later, with a paper map in hand, Jacob, Freya, and I set off for the high school. Instead of even trying to get near the road, we would take to the wooded area surrounding the airport and head East. We had only been walking ten minutes before we heard gunfire. We both ducked down and began to run hunched over. I knew what we would see before we even reached the strip mall. People. Hoards of townspeople in groups yelling at shop owners that could no longer run debit cards for goods. In today's modern society, nobody carried cash with them. Money is dirty and easy to lose.

The EMP had knocked us back to the dark ages in only a matter of seconds. Desperate people become dangerous people. I looked at Jacob, he just shrugged. We slowly made our way through the wooded area that surrounded the strip mall and the Walmart. As we made our way closer, we heard a gunshot followed by glass exploding.

"Sounds like people were tired of negotiating for food and water," I said.

Jacob just nodded. Jacob and I peeked through the trees as twenty or so people ran into Walmart. Personally, I thought going into that store would be all kinds of crazy right now. I bet it looked just like Black Friday in there with people pushing and shoving to reach the few items left that were advertised at excellent prices. I've been hitting Black Friday with my best friend Alicia for over twenty years now. Alicia and I love to watch from a distance; people go insane over something as stupid as a game console or television. We would laugh and watch as the people fought, cursed, and shoved. It kind of reminded me of watching rugby. As we made our way past Walmart, I saw a couple of people carry out T.V.s.

"That's just sad," I said to Jacob as we walked.

"Idiots," he said.

Thankfully our small little town had plenty of wooded areas to hide in. We had only walked a couple of miles past the Walmart when we heard hoots and yelling. I couldn't see who was making the noise, but Jacob pulled me to the ground and held his finger up to his mouth. I nodded, understanding that my running commentary was not welcome at this moment. We laid as still and quiet as possible. Freya laid still on the ground, but her ears stood straight up. She knew, the way all dogs do somehow, that trouble was close. I could tell she was stressed out. She was panting with her mouth open. I ran my hands through her fur, soothing her until she quieted.

Chapter 4

My holstered gun on my belt was digging into my side, something awful. I slowly reached down and pulled my Smith and Wesson out of its holster. As I did this, I could hear just snippets of conversation, a conversation that was way too close for comfort, in my option.

"Capped his ass, and fuck that dude." was being yelled by some guys in the street.

I couldn't see them, but I guessed it was some of the town's escaped prisoners. The three of us laid there a good ten minutes after we heard the voices melt away. I was okay with the wait; I'd rather not take any chances in a world now gone crazy. We walked for what felt like hours, it was probably like thirty minutes, but I was getting excited at the thought we were only about a mile from the school. Jacob looked at me as we entered a neighborhood.

"Okay, we have to cross through this neighborhood. If we follow the sidewalk, it will eventually take us to the high school. Keep your eyes and ears open." he said.

I just nodded. I hated the idea of having to walk through a neighborhood. What if crazy people or anyone looked out their window to see two armed people headed towards a high school? This neighborhood was your average lower-middle-class neighborhood. You had the elderly who had all grown up in town, that really loved and took pride in their homes and community; then you had the houses with grass up to your knees that were slowly falling down around them. We'd be lucky if we aren't shot dead in the street.

We rounded a corner to see an elderly man standing in his yard with an old rifle. He pointed it at us as soon as we came into sight. He had great reflexes for an elderly man.

"Stop right there!" he said as he lifted the rifle to hit us center mass.

"Sir, I'm trying to get to my son; he goes to the high school up the road," I said.
He looked at me with a raised eyebrow then let the gun barrel point down.

"Crazy ass people been running all over! Starting fires and breaking windows. I'm going to shoot anyone that tries that shit on me," he said.

I slowly approached the man; he was still wary but let us come up to him.

"Things in town aren't good. They've burned down a lot of the downtown area and are making their way into the neighborhood areas. You need to be careful. The prisoners escaped the jail and are raising hell. I haven't seen any police since I've been in town." I said.

The old man's skin paled as he kind of slumped.

"I knew it was bad when the power went out, but I had no idea how bad," he said in a defeated voice.

I knew how he felt. The bomb had dropped a little over twenty-four hours ago, and it felt like the end of the world. In a way, I guess it was.

"I need to pass by your property and through the neighborhood to reach the high school. I mean you no harm; I just really need to get to my son, Max." I said.

The old man nodded and walked into his house. As we passed by and made our way down the street, I heard a shot go off. I didn't look back, and neither did Jacob. Freya perked up her ears but didn't bark. It seemed like none of us wanted to think about it.

As we made our way through the neighborhood, I saw people looking out of the window, accessing us to know if we were a threat. This was a large neighborhood, and the longer we walked, the more it seemed to stretch on. Then I saw it—the top of the school. I picked up my pace, Jacob and Freya jogging behind me when I heard a scream. My blood ran cold, and I froze in place. Freya let out a bark, but I silenced her. She paced around me in tight circles, ready for a fight.

A small man in an orange jumpsuit walked between the compact homes. I figured him for about fifty-five or so; he was balding and had a potbelly. I couldn't imagine him as a dangerous criminal. He was huffing and puffing while he tried to run. I was more worried about watching him have a heart attack than giving me problems. He glanced up and looked at Jacob and me but mostly kept his eyes on Freya.

I had to guess it was a K-9 unit that arrested him in the first place. I kept hold of Freya's leash; I didn't want this guy doing something stupid out of fear of the dog. I thought it was kind of funny, he had two grown adults, both armed, and he's looking at the dog. I wanted to roll my eyes but refrained.

"What do you want, and who did you hurt? I heard a scream." I said.
His eyes finally met mine at that point.

"Nobody!" he said.

"A lady saw me in my jumpsuit and screamed when I ran through her yard. I didn't hurt anybody, promise," he said.

I stroked Freya's head; she was as still as a statue. I honestly doubted she would hurt the guy, she was too much of a sweetheart for that, but she was extremely intimidating.

"Can I please go now?" The guy asked.

"Fine, go," I said in my most aggressive voice.

The guy glanced at Freya once more and took off running in the other direction.

"I hope we did the right thing by letting him go," I said.

"Me too, but I don't like the other alternatives." Said Jacob.

We took off walking again. As we crossed onto the school parking lot, we noted something odd. Children were in every window with weapons. Some had baseball bats, some had golf clubs. The kids were geared up for war. The school had been doing active shooter drills for years; I guess they were running with that training. Guthrie high school was built in the late '80s and was one of our nicer and more modern schools. It was a substantial brick structure, with a lot of large windows overlooking the student parking lot.
  I slowly made my way through the cars to the front of the school.

"Who's there?" A loud yell came from a side window.

"My name is Tara Johnson; I came to pick up my son Max Johnson. He's a tenth grader." I yelled.

Then I waited. I'm not sure what was going on in the school, but clearly, in only twenty-four hours, these children had come up with a strategy, or gone all lord of the flies on us, who knows. I leaned on a car and made small talk with Jacob for about ten minutes before I heard him.

"Mom?" I spun around to find my son standing with a massive smile on his face.

"You came!" He said.

"Of course, I came for you. I will always come for you!" I cried as I hugged my son.

Max was quite a bit taller than me, but I almost lifted him in the hug. Freya was jumping all over him like a puppy until he finally bent down to love on her. Max stood back up and was looking around me.

"Mom, where's Dad?" he asked.

"He was at work when the bomb dropped. He will get Kayla and Carlos and bring them home with him. It will probably be several days before they can make it on foot." I said.
Max just nodded.

Besides, Max stood a couple of kids. One I knew, Dillon. Max and Dillon had been best friends since kindergarten. The two would spend full weeks at each other's homes during the summer, locked in bedrooms playing the Xbox. Personally, I would have been bored to death after about an hour, but not these two. I would have to force the boys outside some days to swim or just be in the sunshine. If not, they would have been paler than any vampire ever thought about being.

"Hey, Dillon, how are you, honey?" I asked as I leaned in for a hug.

"I'm fine," he said with a sad half-smile.

"You sure don't look fine. I'm sure your parents will be here as soon as they can. I flew here; that's why I was able to get here as soon as I did." I said.

"My parents took the baby to Texas to see my grandma. I made a big deal about getting to stay by myself for two days, and now I'm worried I'll never see them again." he moaned.

"It's okay, Dillon, you come home with us, and we'll find a way to get to your house and leave them a note. I imagine they would go there first before heading to school," I told him.

"Thanks, I'd like that," he said in a sad but reassured tone.

"Mom," said Max,

"This is Jess; her parents live in the farmhouse down the road. Do you think we can take her home with us?" he asked.

"Max, if I came for you, I'm guessing her parents will try to come for her. It's not safe to be traveling right now. If we take her and her parents were hurt or something trying to get to her, I'd feel awful." I said.

"My parents work on the farm Max, I'm sure they'll come for me. We have horses they can use to get here. It's okay," Jess said.

There was something in her face that made me wonder. Almost like she was soothing, Max. Jess was a cute girl with short brown hair that hung just off her shoulders and super bright blue eyes, the sky's color on a cloudless day. She was quite a bit smaller than the boys, maybe standing five foot two inches. Her slim frame made her too large, and bulky clothes seem like an odd choice. I didn't know Jess or her parents. I had seen them dropping her off at school and loading up on beer at the gas station on the weekends. I wasn't sure what to think.
"Jess, if they don't come to get you in a week, I want you to take all back roads and make it to our house," I said.
I hated to think of this little girl walking on the roads in our new society of "anything goes," but I wasn't sure what to do.

Max, Jacob, and I walked over to talk to the adult I had seen. It was Mrs. Berryman. This woman hated me. All three of my kids had been in her classes, and she hated all three. I had been fighting with this woman for ten years now because of the spacing between my kids. I took a deep breath and made my way up to her. She looked the way I imagined all of us looked, tired and a little beaten down.

"Mrs. Berryman, thanks for watching out for the kids until the parents can get here," I said.

Mrs. Berryman squinted her eyes at me, giving me the "I'm pretending not to know who you are" look.-I despised this woman! "

"Oh, hello, Mrs. Johnson, I'm glad you were able to make it." She said in her usual snippy tone.

 God, I simply despised this woman! I gritted my teeth in an attempt to not pop off with something snarky and schooled my features into a polite smile.

"Yes, I was able to fly into the Guthrie town airport. It made the trip much shorter". I said.

"I'll be taking Max and Dillon home with me. The town is hazardous right now. It may be hard for parents to get here. I think Jess is anxious about her parents, not coming." I said. Mrs. Berryman snorted.

"She needs to be. Her parents are probably lying around her house, drunk. They're horrible people, and if I'm being honest, they probably could not care less that she's missing." She said.

Berryman was a bitch, but at least I got the information about Jess. I kind of figured it might be something like that, but I hated to speculate about anybody's child-raising.

"Hey, Jess?" I said and waved her over to me.

"Yes, Mam?" She asked questioningly.

"I think maybe you should go with us. It's only about a ten-minute walk to your house from mine. Let's get you as far as my place, then we can walk over. If we missed them, I could always fly you back." I said.
Jess looked at me with a look I've seen before. I had known the children of alcoholics before. It was a rough life that usually left the kids to raise themselves.

"Are you sure, because that would be great?" She said, her eyes lighting just a little.

"I'm sure, do any of you need anything before we leave? I need to try and make it back to the airport before it starts getting dark. I've never done any night flying, and besides, the lights on our runway will be out. It's too dangerous to head back in the dark." I said.

I looked down at my watch; it was just after two o'clock. Crap, it had taken us much longer to get here than I thought. We were going to have to push it to get back in time, or we'd end up spending the night in the airport control tower.
Max, Dillon, and Jess hugged some of their friends and made their way to where Jacob, Freya, and I stood.

"Now," I said, looking up a Jacob, "We just have to make it back."

He gave me a wink, and he set off into the neighborhood again. As we walked, we quickly and quietly explained to the kids what had been going on in town. All three of them just nodded and kept walking as they had already seen it for themselves. I didn't ask if they wanted to share what had gone on in the school. I figured we could do it at home, not in the middle of what was quickly turning into a war zone. We walked in a single file line. If anyone saw us coming, we hoped we would look less menacing. I lead the group, and Jacob brought up the end, keeping an eye out for any trouble that might come up behind us.

We had only been walking for about thirty minutes when we heard the screams start. I motioned to the kids to hide. We darted behind a house and got down low, making sure we couldn't be seen from the street. Jacob and I both leaned around the corner of the house to see the jumpsuits.

"SHIT!" I cursed under my breath.

Chapter 5

"What now?" I whispered to Jacob.

"It looks like they have hostages," he whispered back.

We could both hear the yelling and screaming of a couple in the backyard of a house two houses down from our hiding spot. telling the prisoners too

"Take whatever you want, just don't hurt us," I heard a male voice say.

"What do we do?" I asked Jacob.

"Mom, you have to help them!" Max all but whisper yelled at me. I gave him the mom look, and he immediately got quiet again. I looked back to Jacob,

"He's not wrong, you know. "We have to do something."

"Okay, let's get a closer look and see how many guys there are," he said.

I looked back at Max and handed him the Glock off my belt. He wasn't a great shot by any means, but I wasn't leaving the kids unarmed just in case.
I had taken Max to the gun range with the other kids before. Kayla was an excellent shot, nothing but heart and headshots. Max and Connor struggled to hit the target. This, of course, pissed Max off to no end because
"I'm so good at this in my game!" I would just roll my eyes and let him try again. Apparently, hours and hours of *Call of Duty* just wasn't enough training for the real world. That thought made me smile to myself as Jacob, and I signaled to the kids and crept around the side of the house. The men were two houses down. The homeowners were lying in the grass, holding each other. I don't think any of us lived under the illusion the prisoners were just going to rob them and let them go. If I had to guess, they would kill the husband and take the woman with them. To me, that would be a fate worse than death. I would never want to be at the mercy of a group of guys unarmed.

"We need to see how many of them there are. I want to go through the yard along with the house and see if I can look in the windows," Jacob whispered in my ear.

Jacob was out of sight in just a few seconds. I waited, hoping the people could survive long enough for us to do recon. I peeked around just as a booted foot smashed me in the nose. Blood exploded from my face as I fell back and onto the grass.

"Hey Butch, I found an old lady, a pretty girl, and a couple of kids hiding back behind the house," the prisoner said with a sneer.

Freya jumped at the man and bit him on his side. Teeth were going deep into his flesh. The man screamed like one of the hounds from hell had him. I guess, in a way, one did. I would never know the prisoner's name because Max shot the guy right between the eyes. It was a perfect shot. He fell on top of me, his weight pinning me to the ground. I was almost free of the dead weight when I heard another shot go off. I struggled free and looked out from under the man's torso. The gunshot had not been fired by any of my kids. It took forever to pull a reluctant Freya off the guy; she was still growling, with long strings of spit dripping down on the dead man.

Just then, Jacob yelled to us. "It's okay to come out. I got the second guy."

I stood up, looking back at the kids. Max stared at the body, but I'm not sure if he was even seeing it. I walked over to Max, slowly taking the gun out of his trembling hand.

"Mom, I killed someone," he said in a quiet voice.

"I know, baby. You protected me and everyone here. That man would have done horrible things to all of us if you hadn't shot him," I said.

I thought Max may have been in shock as I pulled him along with me, and the other kids followed, looking like they, too, were going into shock. I slowly led them along the house's side until we reached Jacob and the homeowners that were being attacked. They stood, hugging each other. Watching this little bit of intimacy was like a knife in the heart. I was so worried about Brandon and Kayla. I could only hope people would help them along the way if they need it.

"Tara, this is Ed and Jackie; they live in this house," Jacob said. I nodded my head to them.

Jackie jumped into action, "Oh my God, your face! Just a second, I have first aid stuff in the house," she called over her shoulder as she darted in the house.

"I can't thank you enough," said Ed.

He was in pretty bad shape. Looking at him, it looked like he had been beaten much worse than I had.

"What happened? How did they know you were here?" I asked.

Ed looked at the ground and kind of shuffled his feet. Whatever it was, you could tell he knew it had been a colossal mistake.

"I opened the blinds to get some light and had the old grill fired up outside. I'm pretty sure the smell of meat brought them looking. Then when they got here, they saw Jackie in the front window. It was so stupid. I wasn't even thinking about attracting anyone. I was in the back yard when those two guys kicked in our door and went after Jackie. I tried to get my shotgun ready to fire, but it was jammed. I hadn't even tried to fire it in years. The one guy over there on the ground used it to beat me in the face." Ed said.

Ed and I both looked over at the dead man lying on the ground. He was a tall white man with a shaved head and a face covered in tattoos. Someone you would avoid if you saw him on the street. He just looked like a jackass. Jacob's bullet had hit the guy center mass in the chest. Blood had made a massive pool in the grass where he lay. I had seen tons of dead bodies in my life. My family was, unfortunately, all older and unhealthy. I had been attending funerals for as long as I could remember, but I had never seen one like this. I had to look away. I glanced over to the man that Max had shot. I couldn't see much detail, just some tattoos on his now pale face and the blood that encircled him on the ground. The man was probably in his mid to late '20s. I was guessing by the tattoos on his face that he probably wasn't the best of guys, but I still hated losing a life.

Jackie came out of the house, holding an extensive first aid kit. She was a very plain-looking woman, maybe fifty, but seemed full of life and pep, even after what I'm sure was a terrible ordeal. If she was anything like me, she would wait until she was alone to sit and think about what had just happened in her home. Jackie started to wipe the blood off my face. I was drenched in blood. It looked like the "*Carrie* prom scene" movie.

Noses bled like a bitch. Once enough, blood had been removed to assess my condition, Jackie grimaced.

"The nose is broken; if you sit still for a second, I'll set it for you," Jackie said.

"Do you know how to set my nose?" I mumbled through my quickly swelling mouth as I leaned slightly away from her.

"Yes, Ma'am, my mom was a registered nurse; I've seen it done tons of times. My brothers were always getting into fistfights when we were kids," She said with a grin as she leaned a little closer.

"Okay, I guess," I said.

Jackie grabbed hold of my nose, and I'm pretty sure she tried to rip the damn thing off! I heard a sharp crack in my face, and she let go.

"There ya go, good as new, kind of," Jackie said, moving quickly out of my reach.

"Mother Fucker! Ouch! Wait, what do you mean "kind of?" I said, "Awesome."

"You're going to have two black eyes for a while, but you'll heal," Jackie said with a grin.

I looked over at Jacob then. He had been reticent after the commotion was over. He sat in the grass and looked at his lap. I got up and walked over to check on him. I don't think he heard me approaching; if he did, he didn't look up.

"Jacob, are you hurt?" I asked.
He looked at me with tears in his eyes,

"I killed a man, Tara. He was a bad man, but I'm not sure how I'm supposed to feel about that."

I glanced over at Max; he murmured to Jess and Dillon but seemed to be handling it okay.

"Jacob, nobody ever *wants* to kill a human being, but all of us were at risk of death, or worse," I said, "You saved not only your life but the lives of all these people."
I looked around and saw everyone looking at us, nodding their heads.

"I know," he said, shaking his head, "I thought once I got home from Vietnam, I would never have to take another person's life."
I put my hand on his shoulder and left him to his thoughts.

"Ed, what are your plans now? Are you going to stay in the house?" I asked.

"I think we might try for my sisters in Edmond, it's only about twenty miles, and I have a ton of camping gear," Ed said, shrugging.

I nodded and started rounding up my group to leave.

"You're not leaving now, are you? I thought you could stay for dinner. Ed and I are so thankful for everything you've done. There's no way I can ever repay you." Jackie said, running over to us.

"Thanks for the offer Jackie, but I've got to get everyone home. We need to get going. You guys stay safe," I said.

Jackie ran up to Jacob and wrapped him in a hug. I saw tears running down her face as she whispered, "thank you." The group shook hands, and we set off again. The way this day was looking, we may all have to crash with Jacob and Hazel tonight at the airport.
The days were always short during the winter, and we still had miles to go before reaching the airport.
Thankfully the rest of the walk through the neighborhood was uneventful. We carefully darted from house to house the closer we got to any main roads. To get across to the more wooded area, we still had to pass the main road. Noble was one of our two main roads that crossed through the entirety of the town. If we were going to run into trouble, it would be in getting across one of them. Looking to the right and down the streets, the streets were empty; looking left, I saw why.

The sheriff's department had set up a roadblock. I had to guess it was to round up the prisoners, but I wasn't sure. I didn't need to be hassled about my guns or my son and friend carrying guns. Yes, this is Oklahoma, where most everyone owned at least two or three guns, but something made me pause at that barricade. I looked back at Jacob, who gave me an emphatic shake of the head. I just nodded. To cross the road unseen, we would have to either go through the heart of town and face off with God only knows what, or make our way much further out than we wanted too. It became apparent quickly we were not making it home tonight. The sun was already starting to set. If we took off now, we could just make it before the real dark. Unfortunately, we were only a quarter of the way back to the plane.

I started thinking about the plane. I was beginning to worry about Hazel being able to hold down the airport tower. If random people showed up at the airport, I had no worries she'd be able to run them off, but what if cops showed up wanting to take the planes to use for the force? I wasn't so sure. It was nothing for law enforcement to seize and control anything they wanted in a martial law situation.

I needed to shake off all these thoughts and concentrate on getting these kids back home. Jacob led the way through the deep brush and trees on the outskirts of town. The kids walked as quietly as possible, but we still sounded like a heard of elephants crashing through the forest to my ears.

After a good hour of crashing around, we stopped for a break. I was sweating and huffing and puffing from exhaustion; being overweight in the apocalypse was just not going to work for me. We stopped on the edge of the creek. It had some water in it but wasn't clean by any stretch of the imagination. Freya all but dove into the stream and began drinking up the water. Jacob and I had stocked up on water and other rations in small packs before we left the airport, and thankfully, we had also included Lifestraws. Life straws are a unique survival tool in that you can drink anything, and the straw will filter out all the contaminants. I took a couple of long pulls through the straw and passed it to the kids. By the looks on their faces, you would think I had just drunk poop.
I grinned as I said, "It won't taste great, but it's safe to drink," handing it over to the kids.

Dillon took the straw, finally, and gave it a try, "It tastes kind of like chemicals."

"I promise it's fine. The straw filters out all the contamination. Without it, you'd get sick, and I'm guessing none of you want to deal with crippling diarrhea on the trip home," I said.

"MOM," Max said as he handed the straw to Jess, cheeks flaming from embarrassment. Jess repeated the process and passed the straw off to Max.
With that fun bit of entertainment over, I reached in my small pack and tossed everyone a granola bar.

"Eat up; we need to get moving," I said.

I looked over at Jacob; I could tell he was getting nervous about leaving Hazel alone as he kept glancing in the direction of the airport.

Chapter 6

We had already been gone longer than we had hoped. We were just getting our wrappers put away in the bag when we heard a shotgun cock.

"Well, shit," I said as I slowly went for my Smith and Wesson.

"Lady, you draw that gun, and I'll shoot at least two of you before you can get a shot off," said a man as he stepped out from behind a copse of trees. He was dressed in camouflage head to toe with a gillie suit on over that.

"What are you doing on my land?" the man said as he came closer.

"Sir, we walked from the south side of town to the high school to get my son and his friends. We are trying to avoid the roadblocks the sheriff's department has set up back on Noble Street. I was scared they might confiscate my firearms. Plus, we had to shoot and kill two of the escaped prisoners, and it's not a good time for us to have to deal with any law enforcement," I said.

I knew the prepper world and all the trigger words he would want to hear to believe my story. "We mean you no harm; we were just taking a small break then moving on towards the south," I said.

"I KNEW THEY WOULD SET UP ROADBLOCKS! Assholes," he grumbled.

I told the man the exact location of the roadblock so he could avoid them as well.

"Can we please pass through your land? We need to make it south, and it's already a long walk without having to detour any further out," I said in an almost pleading tone.

"I'll tell you what, I will escort you off my property to the south. I'm not up for random strangers being on my land and me not being there," he said.

"That's fine with us; we're also trying to stay away from the Walmart area. It was a crazy mob scene of looting and fighting when we came through that way," I said.

"Yep, those are the actions of the unprepared!" he said with a head shake.

"People go through life every day like nothing was ever going to happen. Look at them now, fighting like animals. I knew this would happen someday. I didn't know how, but I knew!" he said, puffing his chest out.

"Can I ask your name?" I asked, doubting I would get an answer. He looked a little dubious but finally answered after a couple of minutes.

"It's A.J.," He said.

"Hi A.J., I'm Tara, and this is my friend Jacob, my son Max, and his friends Dillon and Jess. It's nice to meet you," I said.

I noticed everyone else was perfectly content to let me deal with the crazy redneck. A.J. took the hood off his gillie suit. I could see he was about my age, forty-two to forty-five or so. He was shorter than me, about five foot six, with a scruffy beard and long wild hair. He looked like a character out of one of the apocalyptic stories I read.
We walked along for what felt like hours, A.J. moving to the front and guiding us to the more accessible pathways through the brush.

"I'm at the edge of my land, so I'll leave you here. I need to get back and check my traps," he said

"A.J., thank you so much for helping us get through there. If you ever need help or get run off your land, you're welcome to join us at the Myrick Airport. We're a long way from here but way out of town," I said.

"I'll be fine right here on my land, but thanks for the offer," he said as he turned away, pulling the gillie suit hood back up and disappearing into the woods.

"Wow, mom. He's kinda weird. Are you sure you want him around our house?" Max asked.

"Yep, I think he would be a wonderful addition to our group," I said.

A.J.s property was a lot bigger than I had first guessed. We were only about half a mile away from the airport now. It was already getting dark, and hard to see where we were going. We didn't dare pull out flashlights. This was not the kind of world you wanted to be noticed in anymore. Thankfully A.J. had led us far around from Walmart and the crazies looting televisions that would no longer even work.

We just had to make it around to the west now. We would be entering the town's airport from the east. I looked at Freya then. Her tongue was hanging out of her mouth. I knew the water she drank out of the creek earlier wasn't enough, and we were going to have to make our way around and down the runway to the tower. We walked single file, all of us tired and dragging ass. As we finally reached the airport tower, Jacob made some random bird call noise. I looked over at him like he was freaking crazy. He just laughed.

"I make that noise all the time; I'm hoping Hazel will hear it and not panic and shoot all of us," he said.

I grinned up at Jacob; those two were meant to be. I heard a shotgun cock and stopped. The rest of my tired group smashing into the back of me. Even Freya kind of stumbled.

"Identify yourself. I've got a gun on each one of you," Hazel yelled from inside.

"Not unless you suddenly multiplied, and in which case one of you needs to marry me," Jacob yelled back. The door to the airport tower was flung open to show Hazel with a big ear-splitting grin plastered on her sweet face and relief apparent in her eyes.

"Oh my God, I've been hearing gunshots all day. I was so scared you guys wouldn't make it back!" exclaimed Hazel.
She quickly got all of us inside and shut and locked the door.

"Jesus, girl, what the hell happened to your face?" she asked, looking at my busted nose and bloody clothes.

"That's a long story Miss Hazel," I said as I dropped in a chair.

Freya ran to her water bowl that Hazel had gotten out for her before we headed out this morning while the rest of the group plopped down on the black and white checkered diner floor to rest. Freya laid down and was sound asleep before the rest of us were even settled. I knew exactly how she felt. I was overweight, out of shape, and I was going to have a hell of a time getting any rest tonight; by the way, my legs felt. I had never been big on exercise, and I knew I'd be paying the price for all the activity we had today.

"I've had a couple of people come by today looking for pilots. People are wanting someone to fly them to different towns. I told them that none of the pilots had made it to the airport, and I doubted they would. People were so mad! They would hold money up in the air like it's worth anything. The damn world's gone crazy. I stayed up at the top of the tower so I could see all around. I saw several idiots going by carrying stolen T.V.'s," Hazel said, tossing her hair back and rolling her eyes.

We spend the next hour or so telling Hazel all about our trip. Hazel's eyes went wide when we reached the part about the prisoners.

"I can't believe how bad it's gotten in only two days. Jacob, we can't stay here," she said, looking at Jacob with pleading in her eyes.

"The both of you are welcome out at my place. I'm sure Keith would love the company, and we could always use the extra help. Jacob, is your plane here?" I asked.

"Yes, Mam, but are you sure about us coming out there. We don't want to take away from any of your resources," he said.

"Jacob, good people are as much important a resource as food or water. That's why I invited that A.J. guy. I don't know how to set traps," I said with a giggle.

"Okay, tomorrow morning, let's gather up everything we could use and load it in my plane. I'll follow you to your runway," Jacob said.

Hazel looked at us with relief. All of us settled down in the airport chairs after a snack and some water. The airport had a small but cozy seating area. I looked around at the kids. Even after the day they had, they were sound asleep in minutes. I laid on the floor next to Freya and stroked her soft fur. She was growling and sleep running. I whispered in her ear until she quieted. I thought once I laid down, I would go straight to sleep, but I didn't. I tried to put the day's events out of my mind and thought about the rest of my family.

Did my dad and Connor manage to get Jalyn and the boys? Was my mom, okay and taking her pills? I was going to have to deal with my mom's heart problem, and soon. Finally, I wondered if Brandon and Kayla were safe tonight. They were going to have to walk through a terrible part of town. I was terrified at the thought of losing one or both of them. I wish, more than anything, I had a way of getting in touch with them. If I had to guess, it would take them around seven to ten days to walk home. If I hadn't seen them by day ten, I was going to panic. For now, I just had to trust they were safe.

We awoke to a grey and cloudy day. The wind was blowing somewhere in the 20 miles per hour zone, a light breeze by Oklahoma standards, but not ideal for my flying skills. The smell of rain hung heavy in the air with the remains of smoke from yesterday's fires. I had been startled awake by gunshots a couple of times in the night, but thankfully for us, if not for someone else, they were from the middle of town. I walked around the area I had bedded down for the night to find the kids in a pile. Hazel had moved all the tables against the doors, so we had a place to stretch out for the night. I grinned, thinking that they kind of looked like a pile of puppies. I wish I had access to my long-dead cell phone camera to capture the moment. The kids slept deeply, breathing softly. I could only hope they were dreaming of better days, school functions, or summer, not about what happened yesterday. I wandered through the airport tower until I got to the snack shop. Like yesterday, Hazel had made a large pot of strong black coffee off a small camp stove she had in one of the storage rooms. I would have cut the coffee with some creamer to thin it out in years past, but I felt I would always want the strong stuff now. I needed a bit of caffeine for another long day. While I poured my cup, I wondered if every day would be a fight to survive now. Would my family and friends always be in danger from the likes of escaped prisoners? Or bad people no longer having to hold back now that the laws had pretty much been erased?

I sipped at my coffee while I went in search of Jacob and Hazel. I was wanting to get packed and in the air. Just because trouble hadn't come looking for us last night didn't mean it wouldn't show up today. As I walked around the corner, all thoughts of quick movement stopped. Jacob held Hazel in an embrace so tender she might have been made of glass. As I stopped short, the two pulled apart the way two teenagers would after being caught by their parents. I gave a broad toothy smile and made a cheers motion with my coffee cup.

Jacob recovered first, "Uhm, good morning Tara. Did you manage to get any sleep?"

"Yep, I'm good and ready to get moving towards the house. I'd like to get away from the airport before any of the townspeople know we're here and come pestering." I said, sipping my coffee as I watched a blushing Hazel try to squeeze by us without being noticed.

I gave Jacob a huge smile and held my fist out for a bump. Jacob rolled his eyes but bumped my fist with a grin.

"Let's get the kids up. They can help Hazel and me to load what we can inside the plane," Jacob said as we both made our way back around to where the kids were.

Freya had been sleeping beside the kids like they were her puppies to protect. I appreciated the gesture more than the sweet pup could ever know. I bent and stroked her back while she thumped her tail.

"Good girl," I said.

The noise of my speaking and Freya's now wildly beating tail started to stir the kids.

"Come on, guys, let's get home," I said.

I let the kids get up and around while Freya and I went outside to take care of her morning needs. When I got back to the front of the tower, I walked over to Jacob. He was hauling around a hug hose with some kind of gadget at the end of it.

"Hey, whaddya got there?" I asked, hurrying to try and help with the dragging process.

"This is a manual gas pump I made a couple of years ago after an Ice storm. We needed to fuel a couple of planes, but the power was out. I made this baby after that," he said. I looked dubious but held up my end.

"I think we should take the brakes off the planes and roll them to fill them with fuel. If we turn on the engines and someone hears them, we might not have time to take off before we're jumped on," he said.

Jacob and I spend the next few minutes dragging and hooking up the hoses to the ground gas tanks. When Max and Dillon came out of the tower, we instructed both boys on how we would slowly roll the planes into position at the tanks, fill them and roll them out again. Jacob and I would then start both engines simultaneously and take off seconds apart from each other. We decided we needed to gain as much attitude as possible to be out of range of small arms fire. It would be a gamble, but one we both knew we had to take. I was already stressing the climbing attitude before we even got gas in the planes.

There was an "incident" early in my flight training. I needed to recover from a stall on the engine. If I went too high too fast, I would stall, and since I panicked and freaked out last time, I wasn't sure how to recover from the stall before crashing to the earth as a fireball. If I didn't move fast enough, though, I would be a sitting duck for any assholes around here that would just love to shoot me down.

Taking a deep breath to try and center myself just made me choke on gas fumes. So much for that Idea. The two boys managed to push the plane to the gas tank. Jacob was using his weird hose contraption, pumping it up and down. It was using suction to move the gas right into the tank.
"Jacob, you're a genius! I said, happily strolling over to watch.

After Keith's plane was rolled out of the way and the boys had moved Jacob's aircraft into position, I did a full and too long pre-check of the plane. Checking and inspecting every inch for any issues that might cause me to have problems in the air. By the time I was done with Jacob's exhausting task, the boys had finished with the other plane. Hazel and Jess were filling the aircraft's back seat with supplies and clothes that I guess Hazel kept around here for some reason.

Jess look better today than she did yesterday, her short brown hair blowing in the breeze as she followed Hazel. I didn't see how anyone looked that happy and content on a day like today, but the enthusiasm was kind of contagious. After a few seconds of watching Jess, I even felt a little better.

Chapter 7

After everything was loaded, my heart raced, knowing it was time. When I left my home yesterday, it was mine and Freya's life on the line, and I was okay with that. Any mistakes I made would only end in disaster for the two of us. Today I would be risking not only mine and the life of my dog but my baby and his friends. I think Freya could sense my fear; she was whining and bumping my leg with her head. I rubbed her silky ears and tried to slow my heart.

"Okay, you get in and open your window. Your plane is in front, so you've going to give the countdown to start the engines. When I see you hold up a three, we will start the engines together. As soon as that engine is warm, you slam on the gas and get the hell out of here. I will be right on your butt. We need to climb as high as possible as quickly as we can. I don't want us flying under three thousand feet if we can help it. Are you ready?" he asked.

I nodded, not letting him see my fear. "Let's go."

The little plane was kind of cramped. Dillon, Jess, and Freya all piled in the two-person backseat while Max sat co-pilot. With my arms shaking, I reached one hand out the window and placed the other hand on the key. One, Two, and three. The engines started, and the blades began to whirl. I adjusted my flaps and put the hammer down. As my speed increased, I felt the plane begin to lift. As I climbed higher, I changed the flaps again and began to rise. I kept my plane much more level during my climb than I'm sure Jacob was going to. The wind was making the plane lunge from side to side. It was like being in a speed boat going over choppy water. Max yelled at me when Jacob and Hazel were in the air to let me know they had made it off the runway without any issues. I took a deep breath and set myself for three thousand feet.

The air was heavy with water at this height. The rain beaded and rolled off the windshield. I looked back at the kids to see them all looking out the windows. Between the engines' sound, rain coming down in sheets, it didn't do much good to try to talk to any of them. I looked around the plane to see how the kids were handling the flight. The wind was blowing our little plane like a flag in the wind.

I saw Max reach for the air sickness bag. I was proud he had gone this long. The ten-minute flight was thankfully uneventful, other than Max throwing up. I saw the airstrip as I started the descent out of the clouds. I HATED landings. I had tried so many damn times to land this plane without looking like a drunk driver and had never once pulled it off. At least the people on the ground would know who was flying the plane. We landed hard, with a bump. Freya yelped as she hit the roof of the aircraft. Max thankfully held on to his barf bag. I'm pretty sure we all would have lost our breakfast if that had spilled on us.

"Sorry, sorry," I said as I made what had to look to onlookers as a sliding stop.

I dipped my head; I had got this plane back on the ground with everyone alive. People could make fun of me all day if they wanted. I had done it.

"Uhm, Mom, shouldn't you get out of the way for Jacob?" Max said with a grin.

I turned the plane around and got out of the way just as Jacob and Hazel touched down in a perfect landing.

"Show off," I said to no one in particular.

My parents, Conner, Jalyn, and the boys came running out of the house. My sweet little grandbabies were safe and happy. I burst into tears and hugged everyone until the snot from my stuffy busted nose started to drip. My mom wrapped me in her arms and held on.

"It's okay, honey, it's okay, you're home now," she crooned in my ear.

Keith met us up on the runway as the rain started to taper off. He shook hands with Jacob and gave Hazel a big hug.

"Hey Keith, I told them they could stay with you at your place," I said.

"Yes, Maam, I'd love that!" he said in an excited tone.

I knew he had been lonely at his place. Having two new roommates would give him, and that cat, all the company he needed.

After helping to unload Jacobs's plane and storing both aircraft out of site in hangers, we helped get everyone set up and comfortable.

I went into my room, where I dropped my "go bag" on the floor and kicked off my boots. I sank onto my bed and allowed myself a few minutes to just breathe. My legs throbbed from all the walking I had forced on them. My face hurt, and I felt like I was just about frozen to death. The last twenty-four hours had been as crazy as the twenty-four before that. I turned my head, looking towards the window, when I saw a picture of Brandon and me at the beach. It was one of my favorites. Brandon, the kids, and I had all been vacationing with his family in Florida. We had this fantastic house that sat right off the beach. I woke up extra early every morning just so I could sit on the deck and drink my coffee, watching the sun come up over the ocean. I took my camera out on the deck each morning and took pictures of the sunrise and the birds flying around. It was truly amazing.

On the third day of our trip, I was on the deck sipping my coffee when I heard Brandon's voice from behind me say, "do you know what's even more beautiful than the sunrise this morning?" He was grinning ear to ear, bare feet shuffling on the deck, knowing he had just aced the only smooth pickup line of his adult life.

He took the camera out of my hand and set the timer. We took several shots that day, but his one picture of us stood out to me. The happiness in the photo just had to be printed out and framed. Then like the lovebirds we still were after all these years, we had walked hand and hand down the beach, picking up seashells and flicking water at each other. If I thought hard, I could still remember how his face looked bathed in the morning light. I could smell the ocean and hear the waves that crashed onto the beach. Looking back on that picture today made me cry. I would do anything to go back and relive that day. I had no idea where the love of my life and my only daughter were. No idea if they were okay or safe. All I could do was hope and pray.

I allowed myself about ten minutes of self-pity for my situation before I dragged my ass off the bed and went out to face the others. My mom brought me a cup of coffee and eggs she had made on the camp stove. Jacob, the kids, and I took the next hour to tell our story, starting with how we found each other. I watched my mom get paler and paler as we recounted the story. It wasn't a nice story. At one point, my mom had to get up and leave the table. She said it was to check on something for dinner, but I'm guessing our tale of the run-in with the prisoners was more than any mother could handle hearing about. I kept looking at Max to see how he was taking the retelling. His eyes were downcast until Jacob informed the group Max had saved us all from certain death, or worse for Jess and me, at the men's hands. Max puffed up his chest a little at being called a hero. I knew what Jacob was doing. Having had to kill in the war, Jacob knew better than anyone else what Max was feeling by taking a life. Later, I would ask Jacob if he could talk to Max. To be honest, I think they both need each other after the last day or so.

I walked into my spare room that now looked like our command center. A HAM radio and other gadgets sat around on the desk that used to be in Max's room. My dad sat by the desk, hunched over and turning knobs.

I reached over and touched his shoulder, which made him jump. "Sorry, I didn't mean to scare you. Have we heard any updates on the radio?"

"Not really. I've spoken to people North and East of the "hot zone." That's what the people have been calling it.
From what everyone can tell, no FEMA trucks have shown up yet. Nobody knows if maybe the blast took them out or what. Also, what's weird is the President should have made a statement by now. I know he's in his bunker, but he's got to get information out to the United States people. It's his job!" my dad said, pounding his fist on the desk in frustration.

"I did finally get ahold of Alicia. I guess Michael was down the street picking the boys up from preschool when the blast went off. Alicia said he ended up carrying both boys for a couple of miles back to the house. They got lucky, Tara. Thank goodness you and Alicia made those Faraday cages for the radios too. We might never know what happened to each other. If Alicia or Michael would have been in the center of town and not so close to the house, they could have been in big trouble. Alicia said she would radio in tomorrow morning," he said while running his hand through his thinning hair.

I sank in the chair next to him and looked into his dark brown eyes. His eyes were sad; something other than the radio had upset him.

"Dad, what's going on? Did something happen on the trip to get Jalyn and the boys?" I asked.

"We saw a truck with men in the back. They were driving around with shotguns. I think they might have seen us when we left the daycare. Thankfully, Jalyn and the boys were the only ones at the daycare. A couple of parents had walked in from the surrounding neighborhoods and picked up their kids yesterday before we got there. The guys followed us after we left the parking lot for a while. Not chasing us exactly, but not letting us lose them either. Connor drove, I held Ryler, and Jalyn held Brody. I had Jalyn get down as low as she could and stay out of sight. That poor girl was hunched almost in the floorboard of the truck. I had Connor drive the long way around and double back a few times. I think we got away mostly unseen, but we need to step up our security if not. Maybe do watches around the clock, and I'm sure people saw or heard the planes coming in. We just need to be careful," he said with a sigh.

"I agree, we also need to be careful with our cooking. The couple whose house was busted into by the prisoners, the husband said it might have been the smell of grilling meat. I'm not sure how we're going to cook without making a smoke or smells and without killing ourselves with carbon monoxide," I said.

"Let's call a meeting tonight and see what everyone thinks about doing patrols in shifts from now on," I said, making to stand, but my dad reached out and touched my arm.

"Your mom told me about her blood pressure medications. She only has the ninety-day supply, and I can't lose her," he said, eyes wide with fear.

"I know. I've got some ideas about that. Come on, let's go look at our defenses," I said as I lead him out of the room.
Jess and the boys were sitting with Body and Ryler, trying to keep them entertained while my mom prepared dinner.

"Hey Jess, are you ready for me to run you home?" I asked.

Jess looked at me and shook her head. "Uhm, it's getting dark. I don't want my dad to shoot someone pulling up the drive. Maybe tomorrow would be better?" she asked with a hopeful look.

"Sure, I guess," I told her.

Something was wrong. I knew Jess's parents were heavy drinkers, but they still had to be worried sick about her. Jess was probably right; driving up to a farm that now housed one of the only transportation modes wasn't a great idea. Tomorrow I would load

Max, Dillon, and Jess in the truck, and we would drive the short distance to her family's horse farm. Max squeezed Jess's arm and got up to join in our meeting.

I wanted to tell him to go back to playing, this was a grown-up meeting, but after yesterday with the shooting, I figured I was the only one that thought of him as a child. The group gathered in my living room. Keith and his new house guests sat across from Connor, Max, my parents, and myself.

"Okay, now that we know what happened to California, we need to be careful about radiation contamination. We live roughly eleven hundred miles from the blast zone, but the winds could shift at any time. I think the best thing to do is keep the plastic sheeting up on the windows and doors. The wind changing from North to East can happen at any time. If it does, we need to make sure we decontaminate any time we come into the house. The dogs could just as quickly bring it in on their fur; we need to set up a clean water soap station. We also need to have a spare set of clothes set out for changing after we shower. For now, water is not an issue, we have plenty in our underground storage tanks, but we still need to conserve all we can. I'd prefer it if we gathered in just the two houses because of security. We've all heard Tara and Jacobs's story about the craziness going on in town. Now, I was talking to Tara, and I think we need to start security patrols.

Each of us could take a turn with another to walk the property and watch out for problems. People will start to try to make their way off the highways and out of the towns soon. We need to be ready for that. I spoke with Alicia and Mike earlier tonight. I think we need to be each other's bug-out place, and they agreed. If our house is overrun, we bug out to their home and they to ours. Alicia and Mike have a large garden and are willing to share the fresh food produced. They already have the garden covered to shield the food from any radioactive fallout. Together between Tara's house and my own, we have food for one year for seven people. As of right now, we have twice that amount of people," he said to the group.

"I had just done my monthly shopping when the lights went out," Keith said

"Hazel and I brought all the food and supplies we could find in the airport tower. It wasn't much, but it's something," Jacob said.

"That's all fine, but we do need to start thinking about ways to gather more supplies. I'm not saying rob people's houses or anything," I quickened to say, 'I'm talking about bartering for the things we need.

Brandon and I, as well as my parents, invested in silver several years ago. This should hopefully be enough to trade for anything that comes up. I would also like to ask for volunteers to make a trip to town to do some bartering for medications," I said pointedly, *not* looking at my mother.

Chapter 8

Everyone's hands went up.

"I need a couple of meds to keep my strength up," said Keith.

"I need a few things too, and we're all going to need some vitamins," I said.

"Okay, tomorrow we head to town with some silver and see what we can find. Everyone that's going needs to have a gun of some kind concealed. I don't want us to get jumped if we can avoid it. We'll start at Jess's house tomorrow when we drop her off, then hide the truck just outside of town and hike in. Everybody needs to get some sleep. Keith and I will take the first watch, with Jacob and Tara on the second watch if that's okay," my dad asked, looking around the room. When everyone nodded, I got up and made my way to my room.

"Can the boys and I sleep with you?" Jalyn asked.

I looked down at those sweet little faces and scooped up Ryler. He was only two and much lighter than his six-year-old brother, Brody.

"I don't know…Do you want to come to sleep in GiGi's bed?" I asked, looking at the boys with a big smile.

Both boys nodded and ran to jump up on my giant king-size bed. They had spent many nights staying with GiGi and Papaw, which were the names the boys had chosen for us. I loved the terms, and I loved and adored these boys and their mother. Jalyn and I used some water on a rag to wipe the dirt of the day off the boys, then letting them brush their teeth with a shared glass. From the surface, it all looked perfectly normal, like nothing was happening outside these walls. I fired up an old oil lamp I used in my room for power outages and watched the flames dance. Jalyn, the boys, and I all climbed into the bed and got still. The boys were out in five minutes. It had been a long day for me; I couldn't imagine what it looked like through the eyes of a child. I laid in bed, running through how I wanted tomorrow to go in my head until Jalyn spoke.

"Thank you for coming for us. I don't know what I would have done if you hadn't,", Jalyn said with her eyes full of tears. "I tried to stay strong and act like nothing was happening since the lights went out. The boys kept asking questions that I had no answers for.

Like, when can we go home, and why are we spending the night at daycare. I was terrified," she said with a sniffle that turned into a full out a sob.

"Hey, it's okay. You're home now, and the boys are fine. You had to know I would never have left you at the daycare. I will always come for you and the boys the same way I would come for my children," I said. She stopped sobbing, but I heard sniffling until I finally got myself to sleep.

That night I dreamt of Brandon and Kayla. They were running through gunfire. I could see the exact path for them to take, but they couldn't hear my screams. They ran, Brandon, dragging a crying Kayla behind him. I saw one of the prisoners Jacob and I had faced off with when we were in town. He pointed a rifle, fired, and I saw my husband and daughter go down. I tried to run to them, but I couldn't move. I was crying as I tried to reach them but to no avail.

"Tara! Wake up! It's okay, it's okay," Jalyn was leaning over me, shaking my arms with tears in her eyes. I sat up, drenched in sweat with tears running down my face and my throat raw. I had been screaming out for Brandon and Kayla in my sleep.

"Oh God, I'm sorry, kiddo. I didn't mean to scare you, honey," I said as I sat up, trying to shake the rest of the dream off.

I looked between us to see both boys still sound asleep. This made me grin slightly; those boys can sleep through anything. Checking the clock, I saw that it was three forty-five, only fifteen minutes until I was supposed to start my patrol shift.

"Go back to sleep; it's going to be another long day. It's best to get all the rest you can," I said to Jalyn as I rose.

I used a washrag to clean my sweat-soaked skin the best I could and stared at myself in the mirror. I had brought my small oil lamp into the bathroom with me and closed the door; I didn't bother Jalyn any more than I'm sure my blood-curdling screams already had. I looked like a ghost in the mirror. My hair was long, down to my hips, but stringy. I had dark shadows under my eyes. The last night I had gotten a good night's sleep was last Sunday, and that felt like a lifetime ago. It was only Thursday. How was I ever going to keep up at this pace? How was I going to help all the people I loved and cared about? I gathered my hair into a ponytail and grabbed a pair of scissors and stopped. How stupid to be worrying about something as silly as my hair at a time like this.

I met Jacob in the middle of the runway between our houses. Then we walked to our agreed meeting area to meet my dad and Keith. The guys walked up to us, looking half frozen to death. I could see both of them had pink cheeks and were bouncing around to try and keep warm.

"Did you see anything?" I asked them.

"Around midnight or so, we saw a group of people walking down the main road. We stayed down out of sight, but they never even looked our way. So far, we've been lucky to not have strangers coming up to the house. They would have walked right in front of Jess's house, though. We need to get over there and make sure things are okay," my dad said as he bounced.

"Okay, go get out of the cold. We'll leave in about four hours, so that gives you some time to rest," I said as I checked all my guns.

I slung my rifle strap over my shoulder after checking the ammo clip. I saw Jacob doing the same as we spilt up to walk the area. It was still pitch black as I walked. The damn moles had dug so many holes over the summer months, I just knew I'd probably fall and break my damn neck. I walked to the end of our property. I could smell smoke, but not seeing any fire and not being willing to venture out of my area, I turned back towards the house.

"Do you smell that, Jacob?" I asked as we came back together in the meeting area. "It smells like smoke. That group of people my dad and Keith saw either stopped to get warm or set something else on fire."

"I think it's far enough away for now. If we smell it later, we might walk over and see if those people set up some kind of camp. I don't like people being that close to us," Jacob said with a shiver.

"Shit, it's cold out here!" I said as I bounced up and down to try and warm up.

"Let's walk down to the main road and see if we hear anything. People from the highway could have come this way looking for shelter," Jacob said.

Jacob moved as only a former military man can. He was so quiet when he walked; it seemed otherworldly. I watched his movements and tried to step exactly in his footsteps, and damn it if I didn't make constant noise. We reached the end of the property. My side of the runway was about twelve acres, and a lot of that was heavily wooded. We got set up in the trees and sat in perfect silence. After about an hour, we were just whispering about getting up to walk the perimeter when we heard what sounded like a weed eater. Jacob and I both gave each other a "What the fuck?" look. We slowly walked the property line until we were almost to the driveway of the house. I saw what looked like a hunk of grass riding a four-wheeler with a wire basket on the front. I had to laugh out loud at the site. Inside the wire basket was one pissed-off mangy cat. Jacob and I stepped out in the road as A.J. pulled into the drive.

"The assholes ran me off my land! The cops came with guns and told me everyone needed to report to the elementary school. They said we all had to live there now!" A.J. said as he swung a leg over the bike to stand with us. "This is Agenda 21! I read all about this online. I'm not moving into no damn school with a bunch of weirdos!" he mumbled as he adjusted the large pack on the back of the four-wheeler.

"Crap, we all wondered what was going to happen when the cops got the town back under control. Did they catch the rest of the prisoners?" I asked.

"The people around town are saying they got all but one. I stopped and talked to a crowd walking towards the school. A man in the group said they shot all of them they found, execution-style, but didn't know if they got them all. At least we won't have to be worrying about them running loose anymore," he said.

I instructed A.J. to drive the four-wheeler up to the house and hide it around back. Jacob and I laughed as that damn cat hissed every time we looked at it. Where the cat had fur, it was gray with black stripes and a good ten pounds overweight. A.J. got parked and started to pull stuff out of his pack.

"Thanks for inviting me to come to stay here. I never thought I would have to leave my land. My family has owned that land for generations, and now it's just all gone. Government takeover! That's what it is. When they came and told me to go, they took every gun they could see out of my little house. Jokes on those fuckers! I have cashes of guns and food all over that property. I knew someday this would happen. I've been ready, so don't be worrying about Scratch and me," he said, motioning to the hissing cat. 'We have a tent, food, and can hunt. We won't be any bother," he said.

I looked at Jacob, then back to A.J.

"Hey, what about setting up your tent in my workshop by the house. It will protect you from the elements a little more, and we have a hell of a mouse problem in there that Scratch could help us with," I said, pointing at the large workshop next to the house.

"That's nice of ya. Scratch and I just about froze ourselves to death last night making this trip. It'll be great to get out of this wind," he said as he unloaded.

"When you get done setting up, come in the house and meet everyone else. We're making a run later, looking to barter for some medications we need. I could sure use the backup if you feel up to it," I said, walking back to the house. Jacobs and my shift was over, finally! I was freezing my ass off out here. I walked into the house to find everyone awake and curled up in blankets.

"I have a gas stove in the workshop. Has anyone tried the gas to see if it's running? "I asked.

"A broad high altitude EMP attack over the continental U.S. probably shut down not only electric but also the other infrastructure elements like water and gas. Plus, I already tried your gas stove," my dad said with a grin. 'We can hook up some portable heaters to the generators tonight to try and take the main chill out of the house," he said while writing on his notepad.

"Also, who is the strange guy in the gillie suit you just moved into the workshop?" He asked.

"His name is A.J.; he helped us navigate through his property when we were on our way to get the kids from the high school. He's interesting, but I feel like he can help us. I told him to come to the airport if he had problems with his land," I said.

I spent the next several minutes telling A.J.'s story about the cops taking over the town to the group.

"He might not be that far off base about the Agenda 21 thing," my dad said as he wrote his notes.

"What's agenda 21?" Asked Max

"It's a totalitarian plan to subjugate western society in the name of Godless socialism. The U.N. run everything after they've taken away all our guns," A.J. explained as he came through the door.

A.J. Looked over at me. "Don't the schools teach anything to kids anymore?" he shook his head and made his way over to the table.

Max and the rest of us just stared at him for a few seconds.

"What?" A.J. asked.

"It's true. It's about applying Martial Law in the U.S., just like the cops did in town. The ruling government will kill you if you disagree with their orders. The police and military are given total power over the citizens," he said as he opened an M.R.E. he had brought into the house with him.

"Okay, let's decide who's going on the trip to town today and how we're going to pull it off without being shot or robbed," I said.

"I'm working on that now. Alicia called on the radio a few minutes ago. Go, make sure she's okay," my dad said as he finished his notes.

I used a particular channel Alicia, and I had set up a few years ago. "Hello, are you there? Over," I said into the receiver.

"Oh, my God! I was starting to think I would never get you on the radio! Over," she said.

"How is everyone doing over there? You have a fireplace, so at least I know you're staying warm. Over," I said.

"I've got two people over here that are dying to talk to you. Over," she said.

This made me sit up straight in my chair. "Alicia! Did Brandon and Kayla make it to your house? Over," I said, my heart beginning to swell with hope.

"They did. The two ate and are in the back of the house, getting cleaned up and changing clothes. We're still worried they might have been exposed to radiation. Mike and I gave them extra clothes. They'll be back inside in just a minute. I'll have them call you," she said.

I yelled at Max and Jalyn to come into the room. I waited, my heart pounding.

"Mom, are you there? Over," Kayla said.

I burst into tears with giant sobs that shook my chest. I could hardly breathe as I depressed the button on the radio. "I'm here, honey. Are you okay?" I asked, trying to mask my crying.

"We're okay," she sobbed back at me. 'It was horrible in the city! A plane crashed only a couple of miles from me. Everything was on fire; people were running and screaming. Carlos and I hid in the dental office until Brandon came. Carlos left to check on his mom. I don't know if he made it. I don't know anything," she sobbed.

"Will you please come and get us?" She asked. 'Just a second, here's Brandon," she said as she clicked off.

"Babe, are you there?" I heard his voice say.

"I'm here, honey, are you guys okay? I've been worried sick," I said.

"Kayla and I are fine. It was a rough walk. Thank God I had random things in my truck to have as weapons. I walked with my crowbar and gave Kayla a piece of metal pipe. We looked badass, but we were terrified of walking through town. I was surprised we only ran into trouble a couple of times. I'm guessing you got to Max," he said.

"Yes, I got him. I'll tell you all about it when you get home," I replied. 'Let me talk to my dad about a plan to come to get you guys. We were getting ready to take Max's friend Jess from up the street home; then try to go to town to find some medications," I said.

"I don't know if I would try going to town. The further North we walked, the crazier people got. We had to cross the highway to get here to Alicia's. We saw big groups of people fighting on the road. I heard a couple of gunshots, so we ran," he said.

"Shit, we need to get some meds for Keith and my mom before everything is gone. I'm guessing all the meth heads have already robbed all the pharmacies of opioids. Maybe they've cleared out now. We need mom's blood pressure medicine and Keith's pills he takes. Without chemotherapy, I'm not sure what's going to happen there," I said with a sigh.

I left Max to talk to his dad while I went into the living room to speak to mine. It was decided we would go to Jess's house to drop her off, then to Alicia's house, taking only back roads. My mom protested the trip saying it was too dangerous for us, but nobody listened. There was no way we would just "hope for the best" when her medications ran out. We would definitely by making a run to find her pills.

The next morning just after sunrise, we piled into the truck cab. My dad was driving, Jess and I sat in the front seat, leaving Jacob, Keith, Max, and A.J. in the back. My mother had packed us all some rice and beans from the night before. It wasn't bad, but the rice and bean diet was going to get old quick. I had passed out everyone's portions through the back window. I tried to switch places with Keith, knowing it had to be freezing in the back of the truck, but he was having no part of it. Keith was an old southern gentleman. I loved him for it but was fearful of his heath. With everyone armed to the teeth, we pulled out of the drive.

Chapter 9

We pulled up to Jess's gate in about two minutes. Thankfully she lived close. The gate was electric, so Jacob and I got out to help her open it manually. The three of us were walking side by side. I wanted her parents to see her the second they looked out the window. I was hoping this would keep us from getting shot. I looked around as we walked down the long path to the farmhouse. As a child, I had wanted this house every time we drove by. It was like a storybook farmhouse—a large two-story, white with green trim and a large wrap around porch. Next to the house were large red barns that held the horses the family boarded. Horses milled around all over, none of them wearing the usual blanket jackets I had seen in previous years during the winter.

Jess and her family had moved in only about a year ago after her grandmother had passed away and left the farm to her son, Jess's dad. Jess's grandmother had run the farm for as long as I could remember. At Christmas time, her grandmother had strung lights all over the house and the barns. As a kid, I always thought it was magical. I would make my mom stop on the road so we could just look at the lights. Jess's parents hadn't bothered to hang the lights this year. I hadn't thought much of it at the time, thinking maybe Christmas just wasn't their thing, but as I looked around at the unkempt house, I started to wonder. I looked over at Jess to see she was wringing her hands together and had an almost pained look on her face.

"Jess, is everything alright?" I said, slowing my pace. Jacob had also noticed Jess and slowed down, rifle at low and ready.

"It will be fine, Mrs. Johnson. You can go if you want. I can walk the rest of the way alone," Jess said while never breaking eye contact with the house.

"On no problem at all, Jess, let's make sure your parents are home. We can look for food for the horses and get some water out of the creek for them," I said, trying to reassure her with my tone of voice. I had a bad feeling but kept my gun down at my side, trusting Jacob would cover me if Jess's mom or dad started shooting.

A loud slam of a door had me drawing my weapon. I looked up to see a man I guessed to be Jess's dad standing in the doorway. He looked like shit. His clothes were dirty, and he had what appeared to be vomit on his shirt and a large piss stain on the front of his worn jeans. He held a twelve-gauge shotgun in his hands across his body.

"Who the fuck are you, and what are you doing on my property?!" he shouted in a drunken slur.

"Dad, it's me, Jess," she said, looking embarrassed.

I remembered what the teacher at the school had said about her parents being drunks, but damn this was much worse than I could have imagined. I heard footsteps behind me but didn't dare take my eyes off of her dad.

"Is everything okay, Jess?" Max asked as he came up behind us.

"Hell no, boy, everything's not alright! That damn girl just ran off and left us here to starve to death. Ain't nobody been cleaning or cooking. Hell, the damn horses are all going to die cause she won't fucking go take care of them. What about your mama and me? Huh? Your momma had to walk to the liquor store because you weren't around to go for her, and the truck wouldn't start. That was two days ago. And my daughter didn't pay the damn light bill. Her momma and I can't even watch television! Does that sound like everything's all right, boy?" he yelled at Max as he staggered around the porch.

"Jess, honey, I want you and Max to go get back in the truck and get warm. Okay?" I said, looking over at Max.

Max gave me the nod and took Jess by the shoulders. Jess never even looked back at her dad. That told me she didn't care if she never came back here.

"Sir, how about I run-up to the liquor store for ya and pick up your wife when I see her," I said in a friendly tone.

The man looked a little taken back but nodded at me and stumbled back into the house. Jacob looked at me like I had just grown a second head.

"I'm taking Jess back to our house, then we're going for Brandon and Kayla. I'm not going to pick a fight with the gross drunken redneck," I said in a whisper as we walked off. Jacob issued a snort of laughter as we walked back to the truck.

"Jess, is it okay if you just ride out the apocalypse with us?" I asked with a smile.

She looked at me with huge eyes getting ready to spill over with tears. "Yes, Ma'am, I'd like that. Thank you," She whispered.

"Not a problem, let's get you back to the house," I said.

As we pulled back into our driveway, mom and the others spilled out. I pulled mom aside and explained the situation. As we loaded back up in the truck, I looked in the mirror to see my mom wrapping Jess up in a hug.

"That poor kid!" I said to Jacob. 'Who the hell would treat their kid like that?" I said in disgust.

"You realize the mother is probably gone for good, and the dad will be dead within a week or two from starvation, exposure, or withdrawal, right?" Jacob said in a low voice.

I hadn't thought that far in advance. I just knew I needed to get Jess somewhere safe and away from her father. I couldn't bear to think of all the things that child had endured. I just nodded at Jacob.

We headed east, our plan to avoid any main roads altogether. Keith sat next to me. He looked so small sitting next to my much bigger form. He was hanging forward over the heater. I knew looking at him, we were going to have to come up with a much better solution to heat our homes if we were going to survive the winter. Oklahoma was a hard state to live in. One day it's seventy degrees, and the next day is twenty degrees and snowing. The running joke had always been if you didn't like the weather in Oklahoma, wait twenty minutes, and it would change. Unfortunately for us, it had been a solid month of cold this January, only letting up a few days. When we got back from our medication run and picking up Brandon and Kayla, I would talk to my dad about the heat issue. Surely, between all of us, someone would have an idea.

The trip was long; we took all the backroads, winding around all we could before crossing onto a major roadway. Alicia's house was only ten miles away by highway, but since that wasn't an option, we were having to go far out of the way. Thirty minutes later, we finally saw the main road that would take us by Alicia's neighborhood. I couldn't exactly bring the HAM radio in the truck with me. Alicia and I had never thought of getting handheld radios because we lived so far away from each other. I had no way to "call ahead" and tell her we are almost there. Alicia's neighborhood was a huge gated lake community that is fully walled off to the lake in both directions. I had no idea if we would even be able to open her gate. Jess's entrance had been electronic, but it was tiny compared to Alicia's. There had to be a way to open it. Surely the people inside didn't just stay home if the power was out.

We were only about two miles from Alicia's when we saw the first signs of life. There was a group of people staying in a field off the road. They had a massive fire going, and all looked to be heavily armed. Why in the hell would all these people be standing outside? Then it hit me, they have the same problems with the heat we did. Without a fireplace, we had no way to heat the homes that wouldn't have us all dead from carbon monoxide poisoning. We slowed the truck and came to a stop. The guys jumped out of the truck and came up to the cab. My dad and I jumped out, letting Max and Jacob get in the truck cab to get warm while we all talked.

"Well, what do you guys think? We can try driving by and risk getting shot, or we can double back and try a different route," my dad said as he started rubbing his now cold hands together.

"This is the only road on this side of the lake. There's no other way in," I said.

"Let me go up and talk to them. I'll see if they're friend or foe." A.J. called from the other side of the truck where he was relieving himself.

"Yuck!" I thought to myself as I shuddered with either disgust or cold; I wasn't sure which.

"Do you think that's safe, just walking upon a group of armed men and women?" I asked while averting my eyes at the still urinating A.J.

"Only one way to find out," A.J. said while zipping up and reaching for his rifle.

"Invite the weird redneck home with you, you said. He'll be a great addition to our group, you said…" Jacob mumbled in a mocking tone as he started walking to catch up with A.J. The rest of us stayed with the truck.

My dad, Max, and I sat in the cab, guns ready just in case A.J.'s "let's go talk to the guys with the guns" plan didn't work out. I had Max turn around in the seat so he could keep an eye out for anyone who might be sneaking up behind us. I started wearing an old motion winding watch that I remembered putting in a keepsake box of my grandpa's things when he passed away. I don't remember ever owning a watch that didn't require a battery, but it sure was coming in handy now. I hadn't worn a watch in twenty years, or at least since I started carrying a cell phone. It still kinda bugged me to wear, but I figured I'd get used to it soon enough. I had been checking the time for what felt like forever, but it was probably only ten minutes when my dad thumped my shoulder.

"Here they come; they've got another guy with them," my dad said, sitting up straight.

Max tried to turn and look, but I gave him a stern look and whispered, "DO NOT take your eyes off our six. You got me? People could sneak up when they think we're not looking."

Max blanched but got his eyes back to look behind us.

I saw through the windshield Jacob, A.J., and another man walking towards us. None of the guys looked upset or angry. They were just walking and talking. The guys finished walking to the side of the truck. My dad had rolled down the window to speak with them.

"Bill, Tara, Max, this is Mike. Mike's family and a few of his neighbors have decided to move down to the lake. They have tents and are hoping to live and hunt," Jacob explained as he introduced us all.

"Hi everyone, it's nice to meet you," Mike said.

"Mike has asked if we could take the women and children to the entrance of the lake so they won't have to make the walk. We go right past it on our way to where we're going," Jacob said.

"We won't bother you even if you don't. I just figured it wouldn't hurt to ask," Mike said with a hopeful look in his eyes.

He looked half-frozen. I could only imagine what little kids looked like living outside like this. I looked over at A.J., and he nodded at me. I took his nod to mean the guy was okay. I have no idea why, but that nod put me at ease.

"Dad, is that okay with you?" I asked in a sweet tone. He looked a little wary but nodded his head.

"You guys jump in the back; we'll give you a lift to your camp and help you load up the kids," I said, looking over at Mike. Mike nodded, and all the guys climbed in the back.

"You're playing with fire doing this," my dad hissed.

I had already been thinking the same thing, so I just ignored the comment. Max kept his eyes on the back of the truck as we pulled up alongside the fire. Mike jumped out and began explaining what was going on to his group. Several women jumped at the chance for a ride and began gathering up their children and belongings. Others looked at us the same way we were probably looking at them. Suspicious and guarded. It was only day four of the apocalypse, and already social niceties were gone. In the end, only three women and seven children decided to ride in the truck with us. I sat in the back with them. Not only because I didn't trust anyone, but because I wanted to ask what they had seen and if they had any run-ins with bad people.

A woman sat across from me in her mid-twenties. She was heavily pregnant and looked miserable. She had a toddler sitting next to her. I'm not sure if it was a girl or a boy. He, or she, was wrapped up in so many coats, hats, and scarves that it reminded me of the boy in the Christmas story that couldn't put his arms down. I almost grinned, looking at the child but didn't want the lady to think I was making fun of how she was taking care of her child.

"I'm Mary; thanks for taking us to the lake entrance. It's getting harder to walk and carry Jordan," she said, but not extending a hand for a shake.

This didn't bother me as much as it would have a week ago.

"Not a problem Mary. Have you guys seen any cops putting up roadblocks or anything? I left Guthrie, just north of here, a few days ago. The cops were setting up roadblocks, taking away guns, and making everyone move into one area," I said.

Mary looked puzzled. "No, we haven't seen any cops. We ran into some people now and then. Still, nothing bad," she said as she gathered the little stay puffed marshmallow baby of unknown sexual orientation in her arms.

"That's great, we're looking for my husband and daughter. I'm hoping to find them at a friend's house a few miles down the road," I said.

Alicia's house was only about a quarter-mile from where we were dropping Mary and the others off, but I wasn't about to tell her where we were going.

"When's your baby due?" I asked conversationally.

"Any day now, a great time for an apocalypse, huh?" Mary said with a roll of her eyes.

That made me giggle. We slowed down before the entrance of the lake. I knew it had to be a good mile walk down to the water from the gate. I felt terrible, but the gates were locked up at the entrance for the winter season. There was nothing I could do.

Mary looked back at me while everyone else unloaded. "Thank you, Tara; I've been terrified to talk to any strangers since this happened. It's nice to know there are some decent people left out there," she said.

"Same," I said with a smile.

Mary and her group began climbing and handing children and supplies over the gate. I waved my arm as we drove on. We pulled up to Alicia's neighborhood no more than five minutes later. The gate was closed and locked. A.J. jumped out of the truck to look at the locking mechanism to see if he could detach it, allowing us to drive through.
A loud blast of a shotgun went off. I saw the guy; I'm guessing he was the homeowner closest to the gates.

"Sir!" I yelled to get his attention. 'My sister lives here on Nandina Circle. She knows we are coming. Please, sir, don't shoot," I said as calmly and reassuringly as I could muster with my heart pounding.

My group put all their guns in a ready pose but did not aim at the man as I spoke.

"The gate code is 3962 pound," I said as I walked towards him with my hands up. 'My husband and daughter got here last night. We are just coming to pick them up. We mean you no harm. Do you know Alicia and Michael Sawyer? They live at the end of Nandina, by the lake."

"How do I know you're not here to cause trouble?" The man asked. He was about eighty, wearing designer outdoor gear.

"Sir, you can come down the street with me and verify with Alicia who we are. Please, I haven't seen my husband or daughter since the bomb dropped on Monday," I said.

"Fine, but you'd better not be up to any trouble, or I'm coming down there," he said, waving his arms and heading back into his home.

"Hell of a guard dog they got," A.J. said in a whisper.

It took A.J. about ten minutes to get the gate open. My dad drove the truck through and stopped. We closed the gate behind us and pulled down the road. I had the door to the truck open before we were even at a full stop. I ran to the door and knocked.

My sweet little nephew Sean threw the door open, making it hit the wall. Sean was four years old, skinny, and tall with blonde hair and brown eyes. This kid is going to be a heartbreaker when he grows up. I heard at least three people yelling, "NO SEAN!" behind him.

"Aunt Tara!" he yelled as I reached down for a hug.

"Hey, guys, it's just me!" I yelled from just inside the door.

Alicia's house was warm and cozy due to her having a large fireplace. Brandon rounded the corner then, and I ran to him, throwing myself into his arms. I let the tears I had been trying to hold for days run down my face. Brandon ran his hands into my hair, and I'm sure he was saying sweet things, but my ugly sobs wouldn't let me hear any of them.

"MOM!" Kayla yelled as she rounded the corner carrying my youngest nephew, Joseph.

Joseph, who was only two, probably weighed as much as his older brother. He had dark brown hair and bright blue eyes. How the two children came out of the same DNA, we would never know. He waved his chubby little hand at me. Kayla wrapped us all up in a group hug. I'm not sure how long we stood there together, but Alicia must have seen the group of other people I brought with me on her stoop and let them in to warm up.

Chapter 10

Kayla pulled away, setting Joseph down to play. She looked good; she was out of her usual work scrubs and wearing one of Alicia's t-shirts. Kayla was small, standing only five foot three, with long blonde hair just like mine and my mother's, and light blue eyes. This was the first time she had seen my face for more than the second; I grabbed her and began kissing her head.

"Oh my God, Mom, what happened to your face?!" She asked as she reached up to poke my wound.

"Ouch, and it's a long story. Let's go sit down," I said while grabbing Brandon's hand.

"I'm guessing the other guy looks worse," he said with a chuckle.

"What about you? I really thought it might be over a week for you to make it home," I asked.

"It would have been, but we met a lady the first night that was leaving the city. So give us a ride to the highway. It was only a few miles to walk after that. The city was a nightmare. People were shooting at each other in the streets," He said.

"Max shot the man that did this to me in the face on the way back from the school. He seems to be handling it okay, but you should talk to him," I said.

This stopped Brandon in his tracts. Brandon was only two inches taller than me. He has brown hair that he always covers with a ball cap. I think he would sleep in it if I allowed it. He looked at me and pulled me in for another hug. I heard the other people making introductions and decided I had better get in the living room.

Brandon pulled me aside to ask who in the hell some of these people were with us. Brandon had never flown with Keith and me; he always said he "valued his own life too much." I gave Brandon the back story on Jacob and how we had come to meet A.J. in the woods. We spent the next hour telling our stories of when the bomb had dropped and the EMP had hit. Alicia even had hot cocoa and was serving everyone gathered around. We might need to ride out the apocalypse here, I thought with a laugh.

"So, what are your plans?" Michael asked.

Michael looked a lot like Joseph to me. He was about five foot seven, a bit stalky. I told him and Alicia about our medication issues and how we would have to make a run to see what we could find and barter for.

"That sounds dangerous," Michael said with a worried look on his face.

I could see Alicia didn't look too excited at the thought, either. Alicia and I had been best friends for so many years; we had been together longer than we had been apart. Alicia and I shared a weird kind of instant bond. There wasn't a friendship building period like most people have. The day we met, we were just best friends from that day on. Alicia and I had very similar builds, and features, except Alicia's blonde hair was short, while mine was long. So many people would ask us if we were sisters, which eventually, we just said yes.

"Mom has blood pressure issues. It's dire. Without the medications, we will lose her. I'm not willing to let that happen without one hell of a fight," I said.

"I understand," Alicia said.

"I'm trying to plan a way to get my mom here. With her living in the middle of the city and having COPD, I'm not sure if it's something I can do," Alicia said quietly.

"I have my grandpa's old Cutlass I can take." She said with a determined look.

"Okay, get a plan together, and we'll go," I said, hugging her. Brandon gave me some side-eye over my declaration but wisely stayed silent on the matter.

"I'm going to get home and see how in the hell we're going to warm the house. I hate having to be dependent on the generators, and the gas isn't going to last forever," I said.

"Wait, let me look in the outbuilding for a second," Alicia said as she started layering up to go outside. It had been about five minutes or so when I heard her yell, "Yep! Tara, come look at this!"

Brandon and I walked outside to the building. Alicia had recently lost both of her grandparents only a few months apart. She had hired some movers to move all their belongings into an outbuilding on their property until she had time to go through it.

"Isn't this an old wood stove?" Alicia said with a big smile.

"I just remembered my grandparents heating their house with it during the winter when I was a little before they got central heat and air. Grandpa never threw anything away. I had a feeling it would still be with his stuff," she said, laughter and tears welling up in her eyes.

"You are a LIFESAVER!" I yelled, hugging Alicia for all I was worth.

The wood stove was old and cast iron. It would be perfect. So many people these days depended on only modern conveniences. Those people are likely in trouble now that none of them work anymore. It would be people like Alicia's grandparents and the preppers that survived now. That is until people got desperate and decided to invade other people's homes to get what they needed. With that thought entering my mind, it was time to go.

"Please let me know as soon as you get done, making the medication run. Don't you dare make me come out looking for you!" Alicia said, hugging me, fiercely.

"I promise I'll let you know. If we leave tomorrow, it could be an overnight trip, so try not to panic until at least Sunday if you don't hear from me. Okay?" I said.

"Okay, Sunday," She said. Michael and the boys waved in front as Alicia gave hugs to the group.

We pulled out of the neighborhood, crazy old guy watching us the whole time. The stove Alicia had given us would be easy enough to install, I hoped anyway. I'm guessing Brandon and my dad will disagree about the best way to get it done. Basically, things would be status quo in my house again, assuming you didn't count all the people living there now or the seven dogs and an angry cat.

I drove the truck with Kayla and Keith sitting shotgun. The guys had all chosen to ride in the back, holding onto the stove. I looked in my rearview mirror to see my husband and dad talking and waving arms around. I was guessing the plan for the installation of the stove was already up for debate. This made me grin, it had been almost five minutes of driving, and they were already fighting about the best way to do things. Even the apocalypse was no match for macho pride.

I slowly drove by the lake entrance but didn't see any of the women and children we had dropped off there. They must have managed to get over the gate. I hope Mary and the others made it to where they would set up camp. I decided to take the same roads back to the house we drove on the way here. I kind of wanted to stop and tell Mike the women and children had made it safely to the lake. I went down the back road where I had last seen the rest of their group but didn't see any of them.

"That's weird; I don't see Mike or any of the group. Do you, Keith?" I asked, looking to all sides. I couldn't imagine missing them.

"Tara, stop!" Keith yelled at me.

I had no more brought the truck to a stop when all the guys started pouring out of the truck.

"What the hell?" I yelled as they headed to where Mike's group had been. 'Kayla, move over into the driver's seat and keep the truck running," I said as I slipped out to the ground.

Max thankfully remembered his post and stayed turned around in the bed of the truck. Eyes were looking behind us for trouble. I walked quickly to catch up with the guys.

"What the hell are we……?" my voice cut off when I saw a body lying half behind the fire pit.

It was Mike, and he was in really rough shape. I could smell the coppery scent of blood, mixed with the smell of the fire now. I stood with my gun in hand, looking around. Near the edge of the clearing that Mike and the group stayed in, we saw that bloody drag marks were heading into the dense brush. A.J. crouched down to get a good look at his wound.

"It's a gutshot; there's nothing we can do for him," he said as he slowly rolled him over.

Mike was losing a lot of blood. Without real medical attention, we knew he wouldn't make it. Gut shots are painful; it can take a while for them to bleed to death. A.J. ripped his shirt off over his head and placed it on the wound.

"Mike, can you hear me, bud?" A.J. said, patting his face lightly, trying to bring him around.

Mike opened his eyes slowly and then went into a full panic as if we were the ones that had shot him. He yanked his body away from A.J.'s hold.

"This is your fault! You did this! They followed YOU here," he yelled with fear. Tears fell from his eyes as he began to slump back to the ground. Mike was clearly out of breath and almost out of time.

My dad bent down to him then. "Mike, who did this to you? Did you see them? Did anyone in the group getaway?" he asked gently.

"Don't you already know?" Mike asked as he spat in my dad's face.

"No, Mike, we don't know. Your group is the only one we've seen since the bomb dropped," he said, using his shirt to wipe the spit off his face.

"A group of men came by about ten minutes after you; they said they were friends looking for you. When we wouldn't tell them any more about where you had gone, they started shooting. They took all the women and shot anyone that tried to run. I don't know why, but they drug the bodies into the woods over there before they left. They left me here. I don't know why," Mike started to sob, his whole body shaking.

"Did you tell the men we had taken most of the women and children to the lake?" I asked, terrified for their safety already.

"No! We didn't tell them shit; that's when they started shooting. They wanted to know who you were and where you were from. Something about airplanes," Mike said.

Mike laid on the ground. Blood was now coming from his mouth. A.J. Tried to shake him gently, but he was gone.

"Shit!" I yelled as I kicked some ash near the pit. 'What the fuck are we going to do now? If whoever did this manages to get a map, they could easily find our place. And what about the women and children we dropped off at the lake? Do we warn them or hope they will hide if they hear someone coming. If they hear a motor, will they think it's us and come out to look only to be snatched up by jackasses?" I said, turning and starting to walk back to the truck.

The rest of our small group headed back to the truck. If the guys were looking for us, we would have to up our security as much as we could, post more guards, add more weapons. Shit, we were a group of mostly retired pilots and teenagers. How the hell were we going to fight off a group. Who knows what is coming after us.

We decided to drive all different roads on the way back. We made it just before nightfall, hopefully without being seen. Everyone, including the dogs, came running out of the house. Kayla ran into my mother's arms and stayed there. I walked into the house, leaving the two of them to sob and comfort each other. Once inside the house, I could smell cooking rice. My mother had agreed about fires and how cooking anything on the grill would put off any kind of smoke or smell. I looked in a pot on the old camp stove she was cooking on. She had been boiling some type of meat. I knew the freezer would start to thaw no matter how tightly packed it was to preserve the cold. Looking in the pot, I saw she was boiling a whole chicken. Next to the chicken was a large pot of rice. None of us had eaten anything since the little beans and rice my mom had sent with us this morning, and this simple meal smelled like heaven to my grumbling stomach.

After dinner, we warmed up water to fill the bathtub, taking turns rinsing off and cleaning up the best we could. We were going to have to come up with a better system than this for bathing. By the time the last person got in the tub, the water would be cold and dirty.

As a group, we gathered in the living room to talk about the day and tell the others everything that had happened. The room was deathly silent when A.J. related all Mike had said as he lay dying.

"We need to talk to all the other airport lot owners. We are going to have to let them know they're in even more danger than they thought. We also need to ask everyone to drag their airplanes out of sight. Hopefully, if whoever those people are don't see airplanes, they'll pass us by. We also need to take down the Myrick Airport sign at the end of the drive," Keith said as he slowly rose.

It was time to walk patrol. Tonight was Keith, Max, my mom, and Jess's turn to walk the acreage. I worried about Keith doing the patrol after being out with us all day. We would have to come up with a way to get more rest without letting him realize what we were doing.

While we were out today getting Brandon and Kayla, the rest of the family had been busy moving mattresses and filling my large three-bedroom house. Max and Dillon were sharing Max's room with Jalyn's boys, Brody and Ryler. My parents had a bed in what used to be my dining room. Kayla, Jalyn, and Jess shared the "Radio Room," and Connor was on the couch. Add in six dogs, A.J., and that crazy-ass cat Scratch in my workshop, and my house was coming apart at the seams.

I crawled into bed next to Brandon, and he folded me in his arms. We fell asleep like that, never letting go. Usually, Brandon had his side, and I mine with two or three dogs between us. I don't think either of us would ever want to let go again.

I woke up to the smell of coffee; Brandon had put a cup near my head on the nightstand. He had done this every morning for years. I can never decide if he does it because I'm grouchy without my coffee or if he's just being a sweetheart. Probably a little of both, but I always lean toward the grouchiness reason. Kayla came in as I took my first sip, flopping down on my bed and causing me to spill coffee all over my sleep shirt.

"Oops, sorry, mom," She said with a pensive look.

I just rolled my eyes. Kayla and I were both accident-prone. If there was a way to fall, one of us would find it. I had broken my ankle three times in as many years just from walking. Once, I had asked Brandon to please fill in the holes the dogs had been digging in the yard, but he kept putting it off, a typical move for most husbands. I needed to get something from my car, and when I stepped off the porch, just like that, I fell in a hole and broke my damn ankle. I own multiple walking casts and braces for next time. It's terrible when you're so clumsy you own your own collection of casts. I just take them to the hospital with me when I go so I don't have to pay for a new one.

"Mam and Tupaw are up and eating breakfast, and Max is outside with the weird guy and his cat," she said, sitting up next to me.

My children referred to by parents as Mam and Tupaw instead of Grandma and Grandpa. My mother heard me call one of my friends' grandmothers Ma'am when I was a kid. She thought I was just being polite; however, that was just the lady's grandmother's name. Grandparents pick out the strangest of names to be called. My dad, or Tupaw, had been called Tup as a child. The nickname stuck so naturally Tupaw was chosen as his grandpa's name. Brandon and I were Gigi and Papaw to Jalyns boys. It was going to get confusing fast with all of us in the house.

"Kayla, will you round everyone up for a meeting in about thirty minutes? We need to figure out what we're going to do for security. We have a ton of stuff to do today," I said as I finished off my coffee and put my cup back down on my nightstand.

I've been leaving my favorite coffee mug in my room. Ridiculous not to share such a stupid thing, but it was my favorite. It says "ray of fucking sunshine" on the side. It just described my morning mood to a tee.

Chapter 11

After brushing my hair and securing it into a tight, but greasy braid, I brushed my teeth and headed to the living room to face the day. Within twenty minutes, everyone had gathered. My dad was leading the meeting today. He looked so tired, his brown eyes looked dull, and his face seemed to have more lines as he spoke.

"Okay, we need to get a plan together. Even IF the guys that attacked Mike's group doesn't manage to find us, it probably won't be long before someone does. I don't mind helping people. I want us too, in fact, but we can't ignore the fact that someone is out there looking for us. They might want the planes, but more than likely, they will also want the pilots. They took the women in Mike's group that didn't go with us to the lake; there's no reason to think they wouldn't do that to any women they find here. I think we should think of ways to beef up our security. We have about three guns per person, and I've been counting our bullets. We have about twenty thousand rounds for the 9MM, but only about seven hundred 12 gauge shells. As a group, we also have lots of long rifle shots. We need to conserve as much as we can. Keith, I need you and Jacob to go door to door on the runway and talk to the other pilots. They know you better than us and are more likely to listen to you. Geraldine, can you and Hazel do an inventory of all the food we have between the two houses? Tara, I want you to be on perimeter duty with me. Jess, you stay inside and listen to the radio. If you hear anything from the government or information, we might want to know, come get one of us. A.J., would you try and make as much room in the workshop? We might need to bring other people into the fold, and we'll need as much room as possible. Brandon, I need you to try and install the stove we got from Alicias. I'm going to put the boys with you to help until dark. Then they'll need to be out on perimeter duty with us. Okay, everyone knows what needs to be done?" He asked as he marked off the checklist he had in his hand.

A chorus of "yep" and "yes" filled the room from the rest of us.

A.J. spoke up then. "I've got a ton of ideas on how we can start to fortify the property if you want to hear them."

"Yes! I'd like to hear them. We need all the help we can get," My dad told him.

"Okay, I'll move stuff around in the shop, and move my tent into a corner, then come see you," A.J. said as he hurried out the door.

As we started out the door, there was a loud squawk from the radio. I was guessing Jess had already started spinning dials looking for information. I turned around along with everyone else and jogged to the radio room.

> "This is WKLS, coming to you from Washington, D.C. The government is reporting President Thompson, as well as Vice President Webb, have been assassinated. The report says they were shot and killed from within our government. More information is not known at this time. The Speaker of the House has just been sworn in as the president. Newly sworn-in President Jackson will be delivering a message to the people of the United States this evening at 8 pm eastern time. Repeat, the President and Vice President..."

Jess turned the volume down on the radio and turned to look at us. We all stood in stunned silence. I guess now we finally knew why the President hadn't addressed the nation about the bomb or the EMP released on US soil. The whole time that we had been cussing him for ignoring us, he had probably been dead. I couldn't see how this was even possible! Who in the hell could have been high up enough on the government's food chain to get close to the president during what was probably a lockdown? At the first sign of trouble, the President and Vice President are moved to separate bunkers; at least I thought so anyway. Unless there were two shooters, maybe they could communicate some kind of orders to each other. I just didn't know. It was only 8 am; we still had twelve hours of work ahead of us before finding any answers, so I grabbed my radio and headed out the door.

The sun was shining today. It was a nice day in January and a vast relief not to be freezing my ass off while on patrol. We had about 12 acres to walk and check for intruders or problems. As a mildly overweight woman, I had to stop and sit a few times. I very seldom did any kind of exercise. When Jacob and I had gotten back from getting Max and his friends, my legs burned like fire. During the trip, I had so much adrenaline pumping through my blood that I never noticed how much my body hurt. I continually asked it for more or to go faster, and it was catching up to me now. I staggered over and sat on a rock, pulling my rifle over my head, placing it on the ground next to me. This spot allowed me to see a mile down the road but still be hidden by trees. My radio squawked to life then, scaring the holy hell out of me.

"Hey, Tara, anything going on up your way? Over," I rolled my eyes at my jumpy heart and answered my dad.

"Nope, I can see about a mile down the road, and I haven't seen or heard anything. Over," I said.

"Come on back to the house. I want to show you some of A.J.'s plans for our security. I don't want to talk about them over the radio in case someone can hear us. Over," my dad said.

I slowly made my way across the acreage back to the workshop.

A.J. had done an excellent job moving stuff around. He had cleared out a large section of the shop that could be used to set up tents for other survivors or be used to put together the new booby traps A.J. had drawn out on paper. After spending the last few days with A.J., I was kind of expecting him to have drawn out a set of booby traps with paint cans and rope ala *Home Alone* style. Still, I was surprised to see real plans drawn out with written notes next to each drawing. The techniques were pretty simple to execute but were going to be time-consuming, to say the least. First, we would take our non-working vehicles and roll them down the driveway to block cars from pulling in. Next, we would run some twine around the trees bordering the property, attaching a device he had made to the trees. If we had an intruder, they would trigger the device to set off a bullet alerting everyone in the house. While half of our ever-growing group worked on those things, some of us would be building sniper nests in the trees and on top of the house, allowing us to have cover while we fired our weapons.

After a quick lunch, finishing up the bread and cheese we had left in the house, we set off outside to work on our new security measures. My house sat at the top of a hill, looking out on the majority of the acreage. I had huge mature trees in my front yard that had been on this property as long as I could remember, and now they were going to have some kind of treehouse set up in them. The only issue I could see with this idea is that it was January. The trees were bare and looked dead this time of year.

My house sat on the spot my grandparents had lived for the last forty years of their lives. They had lived in a tiny two-bedroom house that had been built using gun crates from World War One.

The elderly couple who had owned the property before my grandparents had used those crates symbolically. They took these boxes, once used to defend their country, and now used them to build the home that would protect their family. I loved the story of the little old house as it was just so unique. I had spent thirty years visiting that home, eating ice cream with my grandfather, and making paper dolls with my grandmother. After my grandparents passed away, leaving the house and land to me, I had to make a difficult decision. This little house, built with gun crates, was full of termites and falling down around the seams. I knew it needed to be torn down, but my heart just couldn't fathom it not being here. So, I sat in this crumbling house by myself a few times a week, sometimes for hours. I relived all the wonderful childhood memories it held and cherished the smell of my grandfather's cologne that lingered in his favorite chair. After doing this for an entire year, I knew it was time.

I cried for days after we demolished the house. I watched the machines tear down my memories and haul them away. It took me another six years to build my own home on their spot, and I kept the area's landscape as close to what it had been as possible

Now I looked up in my tree to see a jackass in a gillie suit hammering away at the old branches. Why was he even wearing the gillie suit? There wasn't one damn leaf in that tree. A.J. looked like a giant clump of fungus while he hung off a branch. I rolled my eyes and walked to the road to help move the cars into positions blocking the drive.

Thankfully, the day went quickly for all of us; the temperatures were mild today, around sixty degrees. This would have been the perfect day for spring cleaning or planting flowers in pots for the coming spring. I had already purchased some pots and starting pods of dirt for the coming spring. Now they would be used to plant food. I had always tried to plant gardens in the past. They were expensive failures every year. I would get tired of messing with them and let the grass take them over. This year those plants would be the difference between life and death for our little group.

My mom and Jess called us all in the house around sundown for dinner and bathing. I glanced up at my mom when I walked into the house and stopped. My mother had cut her hip long hair into a short bob. I guess I looked at her with a look of shock, mouth hanging open because she patted her hair self-consciously. I quickly shut my mouth.

"Wow, mom, that looks great! What made you decide to cut it all off?" I asked.

"Well, we have to be careful about how much water we use. Plus, this will use less soap and be easier to care for," she said, patting the bob into place again.

"Good idea. Will you cut mine?" I asked with a hopeful expression.

"Mine too," Kayla said as she pushed me out of the doorframe.

I did not want a haircut. The three of us have had hip-length hair for well over ten years, only trimming it if it got longer than our jeans' waist. Hair wasn't important now that the world had ended, I kept telling myself as my mother cut my hair to my shoulders. Secretly, If I ever found out who nuked us, I was going to kick their ass! After my hair had all been cut off and washed, I left the room. Hair was such a stupid thing to be concerned about; why was it bothering me so damn bad? It was just one more change in the past week of constant changes.

Keith, Jacob, and Hazel joined us for the new Presidential broadcast. As a group, we sat around in the radio room. I sat on the bed next to Brandon, holding his hand, waiting.

"Do you think the new President will say who nuked us?" Max asked, plopping down next to Jess and handing her a piece of candy with a grin.

I knew Max liked Jess. It was pretty clear to all of us. As his mother, I was going to have to watch them. The last thing we needed in the apocalypse was to learn how to birth a baby. The thought made me think about Mary and the other women and children at the lake. I wondered if she would go looking for Mike and the others. Would she try to make the walk back to their campsite only to find Mike and the others dead? Even worse, would she think we did it? I needed to speak to the group about maybe driving back to the lake to check on them. Mary had the right to know about what had happened to the rest of her family.

At 8:00 pm, we turned the radio up and waited. The loud emergency beeps started, nearly blowing out our eardrums.

Jess smiled sheepishly, face turning beet red, "Sorry, I wanted to make sure we didn't miss anything." I smiled at her and gave her a wink.

> "This message is being broadcast by the Department of Defense of the Republic. Please stand by for the President of the United States."
>
> "My fellow Americans, as you by now know, nuclear devices detonated in Los Angeles and the New York City area on Monday morning, followed by a nuclear detonation above earth's atmosphere causing an electromagnetic pulse. As I will now refer to it, the EMP has caused much damage to the nation's power grid, but we hope to have it back up and running in the coming weeks.
>
> Suppose you are currently in California or as far East as Wyoming, Colorado, and New Mexico. In that case, we ask that you remain indoors until we can determine the spread of radiation. We also ask that the people of Oregon and Idaho also remain in your homes. The government will provide information on when it is safe to leave your homes. If you live in the New York State area, please also seek shelter from the fallout in your homes. Please do not try to leave your homes until the fallout settles.
>
> The United States government will send aid as quickly as we are able. We currently have thousands of FEMA trucks rolling out of Washington, D.C., full of food and water. Please, upon seeing the FEMA trucks, do not fire at them. To receive aid from FEMA, we are asking for one firearm per box of food and water. We, as a nation, need to rebuild together and lay down our arms. Our nation has been attacked. Many are dead or lay dying. We need to work together to get through this current crisis and the many rough months ahead.
>
> I can now tell you it was Iran that launched the nuclear device at the citizens of Los Angeles, California, and New York City, New York. The United States has responded in kind, destroying their capital city of Tehran as well as the nearby cities of Karaj and Qods. The United States of America is at war. I am asking for all enlisted men and women currently on leave from any military branch to please return to your base immediately. I am asking for able-bodied men and women who wish to join us in

defending our nation to please report to your closest military base.

I am instituting martial law for all of the United States. This is a difficult time in our nation's history, but we will face these times together! I will be posting the local National Guardsmen in all states to give further instructions. Please follow the orders given so that we might begin to rebuild this great nation.

Thank you, and God bless America."

We sat as a group in complete silence while the loud beeps signaling the emergency broadcast's end.

"What does Martial Law mean?' Jess asked

"It means we are screwed," A.J. said as he stormed out of the room.

Jess looked at me with wide eyes. "Okay, Jess, it's not that bad. It means the President has given all authority to the military. The local cops are outnumbered and outgunned. The military will come in and take over. Depending on how the military handles things, it could be okay, or it could be a shit show," I explained. I looked over and saw Max and Dillon whispering in the corner of the room.

"Don't even think about it! We need your help right here. I'm not letting either of you go sign up for war at the age of 16, so you can just forget it," I said, pointing my "mom finger" with a look twenty years in the making at both of them. Both boys looked sheepish but nodded their heads.

I left the room as everyone else started to discuss the broadcast. I walked to the porch and sat on my steps next to A.J., "We are so FUCKED!" I said after a minute of silence.

A.J. just looked at me and nodded.

Chapter 12

I don't think any of us slept that night. Keith and his group went home in silence, and the rest of us just sat there. Tonight's broadcast had been a lot of information to take in. I knew America would respond to any threat by retaliating for the nuclear strike. I wasn't surprised at all by that news.

"Why didn't the new President say anything about the assassination of the President and the Vice President? It doesn't make any sense. Also, he said we're at war. Is he worried about a ground assault on US soil?" I asked.

"I would like to say that was impossible," my dad said as he began to count off reasons on his fingers. 'The US has Allies in NATO, an armed attack against one or more members, in Europe or North America, is considered an attack on all of them. Plus, this is the third-largest country in the world, surrounded by two oceans. As far as I know, the US has the best army in the world. The United States is said to have over three and a half million guns, and any invading force would be met with militias."

"Then why are they asking for our guns? People are going to start getting desperate for food and other things. They're going to start turning in guns as soon as FEMA rolls up," I said as I stood up.

I was siding with A.J. in the area of martial law. I went to my dark bedroom, leaving the rest of them to talk it out without me. We needed to make our trip to town for the medications we needed before the military descended on our cities. It was going to be extremely dangerous, but it was a trip we had to make. I also wanted to check on Mary and give her the news of Mike and the other's fate. I also kind of hoped she would let me take her to Alicia's husband, Michael, for a checkup for her baby. Michael was a shrink but had done an obstetrician rotation in medical school. Michael was going to have to be an "all in one" doctor from now on.

Tomorrow I would radio Alicia to check on them and see if Michael would take a lake camp trip with us. Then we would go to town to get the medications we needed. It was going to be another long day.

I started my day at 3:00 am for my turn on watch duty. Brandon was with me this morning, and we paced around for hours, not hearing or seeing anything. By the time I made it back to the house at 7:00 am, both houses had gathered for our morning meeting. It had been decided after I left the room last night that Keith, his housemates, and all of my house would meet every morning at 7:00 am to determine the things that would be done that day. This was fine with me because I had my proposal to make this morning.

I waited while my dad droned on about the importance of making check marks on his list for what seemed like forever before I cut in. "Okay, thank you, dad. I was wondering if I might have the floor for a minute?" My dad huffed a little but sat down, holding that damn clipboard full of lists.

"I want to ask for volunteers to run to the lake. I want to tell Mary about the rest of her group, so they don't try walking back to where the rest of them were. I also would like to take Michael Sawyer with us to check on her welfare. Mary said she was due any day now, and the baby has a much better chance at life if she has a doctor with her, or at least knows how to get to one once she goes into labor. Then I think it's time we make our medication run.
If we want to find anything useful, it would be best to get to the stores now. It's been a week, so the tweakers should have cleared out with all the painkillers by now and be stoned or dead somewhere else. I understand this means using our only vehicle and some of the gas stores, but it needs to be done," I said as I sat down to wait for the reactions of the others.

A.J. stood up immediately after I sat down, followed closely by Brandon, Jacob, and Keith. "I agree we need to check on Mary and the others. I can't stand the thought of all those women and children being out in the cold with no protection. I don't know if you saw any, but I only saw one gun between them when they rode with us over to the campgrounds," A.J. said, retaking his seat with the others.
"If everyone is okay with the idea, I'd like to ask them to join our group here. It's not safe out there. Hell, it's probably not safe here after what happened to Mike at their camp, but at least we have numbers on our side here," I said, turning to everyone slowly.

"Tara, I understand you want to help them, but where will we put them, and how will we feed them?" Jalyn asked, speaking up for the first time in a meeting. 'I need to go look for inhalers for Ryler, so I'm going too," she said, leaving the room—her boys in tow.

"We can get the food from my house," Jess said, looking at the floor.

"I doubt my father is still alive, and it would be nice to get the horses and bring them here if we can. We can't drive the truck forever; we're going to need the horses. Plus, if things get really bad…" she said, trailing off.

I knew where she was going with that. If things got as bad as they might, we would have to kill and eat the horses.
"Okay, Jess, let's hit your house first and see if your father is still there. If not, we will clean out the food and load it up. You, Max, and Dillon can bring the horses back and put them in the neighbor's fence," I said.

The closest non-related neighbor we had was Edward. He shared the back pasture with us. He had purchased the home only recently as his retirement from his job as an engineer in L.A. I felt terrible that this was the first time I even thought about him since the E.M.P. went off. I had only seen Ed a handful of times as he came in and out. He would be gone for months at a time, so I guess he had just slipped my mind. Ed's good thing was that he had an extensive fenced pasture around his home. Now that I was sure I wouldn't see him again, I wouldn't feel so rotten about trespassing.

"We can also check his house for supplies. He collected classic cars and stored them in his barn. I don't think any of them run, but I wouldn't hurt to check them, and for any gas he may have kept around. Hazel, are you and my parents, okay to hold down the property until the kids get back to help you? That leaves you with my parents, Kayla, Max, Dillon, and Jess. I have a feeling one of you is going to be on babysitting duty too," I said with a grin.

"We'll be fine; you just make sure everyone gets back here alive," she said with a grim set to her mouth. I could tell she wasn't liking the idea of being left here, but she and my mother were two of our best shots. If something happened while we were gone, they would have to take care of it.

While I was getting dressed, A.J. was putting together B.O.B.'s, or bug out bags. I dug through mine, adding a change of socks and a lightweight rain jacket. I saw he had added to the bags a couple of the freeze-dried meals we take with us when we go camping and hiking, a plastic bottle for water, and our life straws. He had also added some fire making supplies, but I didn't see how we would use them. I tightly braided my now shoulder-length hair back and tucked it under a cap.

The weather was warm today like it had been yesterday, but that didn't mean it wouldn't snow tomorrow for all I knew. I checked my bag's weight; it was as small and light as the bag I had taken to town when I went after Max and the kids at the high school. I swung the bag over my shoulder and headed out the door. Everyone making the trip was geared up similarly to me. A.J. was already wearing that damn gillie suit. I just rolled my eyes and swung my stuff into the beaten up old truck. This poor truck had been a hunk of junk when Max bought it off Craig's list. He had worked nights and weekends on the engine and whatever else was under the hood. It had only been running this well for a few months now, and Max was so proud of it. The outside of the truck was kind of blue, but mostly a dull color of rust. He had saved all summer for the new tires we were riding on now.

I gave hugs to everyone that was staying behind. I hated to have any of them out of my sight after fighting so hard to get to them after them E.M.P, but at least I knew they were here and together if anything happened to us.

My mother held me for a long time before letting go. "You don't need to do this for me. It's too dangerous and not worth your life, or any of the lives here," she said, looking into my eyes.
 "It's worth it to me," I said, squeezing her hand.

I climbed up into the truck bed with A.J., Jalyn, Max, Dillon, and Jess; the others were sitting in the front and making plans. We all waved as the truck rolled down the drive, where Hazel and my dad had pushed the cars aside just enough to get us through, and took off down the road the two blocks to Jess's family ranch.

The first thing we noticed when we pulled into the drive to the gate was the front door open. A.J. once again disabled the gate and pushed it aside for us to drive through. As we whined down the drive, I looked around for the horses but didn't see any. All the barns looked fine, no fires or blood as far as I could tell anyway. I couldn't see the entire pasture from here, but I was getting a bad feeling.

"Jess, will you and the guys stay in the truck for me?" I asked as I hopped down out of the pickup bed. Jess just nodded; I had a feeling she was getting the same vibes as I was.

A.J. was already ahead of me as I came up to the window of the truck. I think it was the first time the guys were even noticing something was wrong. Keith turned the engine off and tossed the keys to Max. The motion made it clear to Max that he would get the rest of them to safety if something happened. Out of the corner of my eye, I saw Max and the others taking positions to watch from all directions. Smart, I thought. A.J. and I walked up the drive as Brandon, Jacob, and Keith started to fan out around the house.

Nothing moved, no loud yelling or banging like the first time we came here. Just silence, too much silence. A.J. rounded the door ahead of me and stopped, causing me to slam into his back.

"Ouch, damn it," I whispered at him.

"You don't have to whisper; that guy isn't going to wake up," He said, walking further into the room.

In front of me, lying prone on the entryway floor, was a grey and swollen corpse. I could see the same dirty t-shirt and piss-stained pants that Jess's dad had been wearing last time we were here. What I did notice was different was the giant fucking hole in his forehead.

When we were making our way up the drive, I had smelled something horrible but had just shrugged it aside, thinking it was horse crap or something. I had never seen a dead body that hadn't been in a funeral home. This man looked nothing like that. What was left of his face was grey and waxy looking. His tongue was swollen huge and hanging out of his mouth. I had no idea how long he had been dead. The only thing I knew about decomposition was what I had seen on *Law and Order*. After I ran outside and threw up over the porch, I walked around back to find the guys. While they went inside to see if anything could be salvaged, I made a slow walk back to the truck.

"Jess, honey..."I started, but she cut me off.

"He's dead, right?" she asked, her face set with a look of indifference. 'Can you tell how, was it the booze, or withdrawal or something?"

"Uhm, no honey, he was shot. I'm afraid I don't know when it happened. Will you boys go ahead and go look for the horses, please?" I asked, looking at Max and Dillon. Jalyn and I sat with Jess for a while. She didn't move, just sat there perfectly still.

Max came around the corner of the barn about ten minutes later. "Mom, can you come here a second?"

I didn't want to leave Jess, but I knew the look on Max's face. I had seen that look on his face when he shot the prisoner in town, and it was sheer horror. I jogged down to Max, but right as I got to him, he pointed down behind the house. Horses, dead horses. Someone had killed the animals the same way they had killed the man inside. They weren't going to be used for transportation or food.
"Who the hell would be this damn short-sighted? I asked, kicking a rock by my foot. Sadly, I was pissed off more about these animals' loss than I was about the man in the house.

Jess came around me then and stopped dead, dropping to her knees. "I only see 7 horses; we have 12 here right now," she sobbed. Jess stood up and started running towards the barn. Max tried to catch her arm, but she outran him and pushed open the barn door. I saw Max stop and feared the worst, but he smiled.

"What the hell..?" I thought, walking over. Inside the barn eating at a huge hay wheel, were 4 large horses and one tiny baby pony. "Why wouldn't they have killed all the horses?" I wondered out loud.

 "I'm guessing they couldn't find all of them. I'm always having to saddle up a horse to go find these guys at dinner time. They always wonder together and way over in the pasture," Jess said with a watery smile.

I left Jess and Max to deal with the horses. I had only ridden a horse a couple of times, and those times had always ended up with me on the ground, and the horse is walking away.

Brandon walked out of the main house, carrying a bag over his shoulder. "Is that food?" I asked, walking up to him.

"No, these are some of Jess's things. I thought she might be more comfortable at our place if she had her clothes and toiletries.

Where are the kids? I'd like to get going; it's going to be a long couple of days." He said, tossing the bag into the back of the truck to Jalyn. I pulled him aside and told him about the horses dead by gunshot at the back of the house.

"Jesus, what the hell is wrong with people! It's only been a week, and people have gone crazy!" he said while we walked back to the house.

Jess and Max came out of the barn on horseback, all the other horses wearing saddles with blankets strapped down on them. They rode up, all the horses tied together with ropes to keep them from running off on the ride home, I guessed.

Dillon jumped down out of the truck and looked at the horse's kind of the way I do. "Do I have to ride one, or can I just walk along the side of you guys and hold a rope?" he asked, slowly reaching out to touch a horse on its nose.
The horse snapped its massive head up and away from Dillon. This made Jess giggle for the first time since we got here. I was guessing this day would come back to her in her dreams for years to come. At least we hadn't let her see her father. I handed up a walkie and the clothes Brandon had taken for her.

"You guys get moving. We'll come back for hay or anything else we need as soon as we get back from town. Radio the house when you get close to let Mam and Tupaw know you're close," I said.

The kids took off back to the house then. The cute baby horse jumping on its lead rope like a puppy does on its first try at a leash. Dillon stayed closer to the pony, talking to it. I could hear him saying, "It's okay…you don't want to kick me…" as they left my range of hearing.

The rest of us spent the next 30 minutes, loading up anything we thought we could use. Whoever had shot Jess's dad had taken any food that may have been in the house, but we managed to find a couple of old lanterns and lamp oil, as well as some flashlights and batteries. I hated the idea of leaving the bodies here. The thought of leaving the house without calling 911 just freaked me out.
"There is no 911 anymore," I thought to myself as we loaded up in the pickup. We are truly on our own now.

Chapter 13

The trip to Jess's farm had taken almost an hour. When I had spoken to Alicia this morning to let her know we were headed her way, I had told her we should arrive at about 9:00 am; by the time we switched up our back roads again and got to her house. I had also asked her if she would please go up to the main gate and talk with the old man watching it. She had said several of her neighbors had been by the house in the past week after they could not start their cars and had asked to borrow her old Chevy since the EMP didn't affect it like all newer. Others from the neighborhood had been arriving all week long with horror stories of the outside world. Some had had to even steal boats to get across the lake the community was built around. There had been talks about keeping out any outsiders that came by. I had to admit this was a good idea. They were in a securely gated neighborhood, and after the things I had seen in the past week, I couldn't blame them. I was hoping that with her speaking to the guy at the front, they might let us in, but it was anybody's guess.

We had only been on the road for about 15 minutes when we saw the truck. There were tons of abandoned cars and trucks on the road, but this one had smoke coming out its tailpipe. It was running. Brandon picked up speed, clearly seeing the same thing I did.

"Shit! It's following us. Yell at the guys in the back," he said as he sped up while weaving in and out of the abandoned cars.

A.J. was already turning. His gun pointed down the road behind us; by the time I got the words "behind us" out. Jalyn raised her rifle and began looking for a way to brace herself to start taking shots. The bright red truck was larger than ours, by a lot. I had no idea what kind of truck it was, but it had a deer guard on the front and sat upon giant wheels.

The shooting started as soon as I turned around for my gun. The glass window I had just been yelling out of only a half-second ago exploded, raining glass down my back. Brandon was hunched as far down as he could go and still see over the dashboard. Keith was trying to work the old window handle to get the window down, and I was almost sitting on the floorboard within a matter of about 2 seconds. I heard A.J. and Jalyn returning fire from the back of the truck. They must have been having a hell of a time because their shots weren't coming as fast as the red trucks. By the time

Keith had the window down and was leaning out, it was over. A.J. had managed to shoot out one of the big truck's tires. I looked up in time to see the giant truck swerve violently into the side of some little electric car. The truck smashed it like it was no more than a soda pop can, pushing it off the road and down into the ditch.

"Do you think those were the guys that killed Mike?" I asked as I looked back to see if A.J. and Jalyn had gotten injured. Jalyn was grabbing at A.J.'s arm. Blood was pouring down his arm and pooling in the bed of the truck.

"Brandon pullover! A.J. is hit," I shouted as I grabbed at my bug out bag.

I had tons of medical supplies I had planned on leaving with Mary for her baby's birth. Coming to a stop in the first driveway we could find, the three of us hopped out of the truck. A.J. looked a little paler but was sitting stoically and allowing Jalyn to remove his shirt. The bullet had gone through his arm, just above the elbow.

"It's fine; it's just a flesh wound," he said as he tried and failed to get his arm away from Jalyn.

"Okay, let's have a look at it. We can patch it up until we get to Michael and Alicia's house. Michael can put in some stitches," I said as I pulled my gear out and began to clean the wound. To A.J.'s credit, he didn't even flinch as I cleaned the wound.

"Do you think that's the guys that have been looking for us or just random jackasses? It seems like the guys looking for us are getting close. I hate to leave my parents and the kids out there alone. The guys in the truck just now are going to know what our truck looks like and report it back to someone if they have a larger group," I said as I wrapped the wound and taped it off.

"I'm not sure what to do," Keith said as he paced the side of the drive. He was rubbing the back of his neck as he paced. He looked so pale and thin.

"What do you mean? We have to get the medications we need. Plus, if we can find any more resources or people, we might just make it through this," I said, walking up and putting my hand on his shoulder.
He looked at me with sorrowful eyes. There seemed to be more he wasn't telling me. Brandon came jogging up to us just then.

"I saw those guys walking this way, and I don't think the truck is hidden well enough. We might have to fight," he said as he checked his weapon. A little more than a week since the end of modern life, and we were fighting and killing.

"The apocalypse sucks," I whined as I checked my ammo. This earned a snort of laughter from A.J.

The truck was half-ass hidden off the side of the road in the drive next to us. Anyone paying even a little attention would notice it.

"Hey, that's their truck!" I heard a voice say.

"Do you think those were the pilot people John was talking about?" asked a tall man in the group.
The guy was filthy. Not just a weeks' worth of filth either; this guy had started the apocalypse looking like that. He had reddish-brown ~~color~~ hair and a bearded face and neck to match. This man looked rough; his clothes were dirty and stained with what looked like all sorts of gross stuff I didn't want to think about.

"How the hell would I know?" answered one of the other guys.

He wasn't tall or short. Average and forgettable was the only way I could think to describe this guy. Brown hair, brown eyes, a brown shirt with jeans. Not ugly, but not pretty either.

"Boss said to find the group driving a blue truck. That was the only thing that old drunk guy could remember. I'm still pissed he wouldn't let us take any of those horses. We could have eaten them at least, but Nooo, the boss, wanted to send a "message," the tall guy said using air quotes.

Well, shit, I thought. We, but more than likely, I was to blame for the death of Jess's dad. I had worried at the time about the planes being seen when we came back from town that third day after the bomb went off. One plane gets people looking, but two planes got them searching. Why didn't we think to fly around and not straight to our home where our family is? Brandon leaned in over my shoulder and whispered too quietly. I almost didn't hear him.

"What are we going to do? They'll see us at any second," he had no more finished the sentence before A.J. popped up and shot the tall guy in the head, and the average guy in the thigh, dropping them both.

The average guy let out a loud wail of pain as he fell to the ground.

"Why are you looking for us?" A.J. asked as he leaned over the average guy.

"I was only supposed to find the pilots!" he squeaked as he held his leg; a tear was streaming from his fear-filled eyes.

"Why?" A.J. yelled in his face while gripping his shirt. The rest of us just stood there, still stunned.

"The boss wants the pilot to take him to somewhere in Texas where his girl is. That's all I know! I promise!" the guy yelled.

A.J. dropped him back to the ground and looked at us. I guess the look on everyone's faces looked about like mine. "Come on, guys, do you think when they got as close as the truck, they were just going to keep walking? They would have opened fire any second," he said with a roll of his eyes.

"I agree; if it wasn't for A.J., I would have done it. At least we have more information now on why the jackass is looking for us," I said, leaning over the man.

"What is your boss' name, and where is he?" I asked, getting down close to the man's face.

"I don't know his real name; we only call him the boss. He just got out of jail in Guthrie when the lights went out. He was a friend of my cousin," he said, looking over at the tall man on the ground.

"Where is he now?" I yelled as I shook his shirt to get his attention back to my face.

"We've been living in the Cash Saver store with our old ladies. Boss said we could control the town if we had control of the food," he replied.

"What about all the cops and the sheriff's office?" I asked.

"We kilt a few of them, and the rest ran off. I don't know where," he said.

"Well shit, at least we know where they're holding up. I'm guessing they will have the women from Mike's camp in the store with them," I said, standing up and walking over to Brandon.

"Tara, we can't let this guy live, and I'm not comfortable leaving him in the middle of the road to bleed out," Brandon said.

I understood this. Shooting someone trying to kill you and shooting a dying man lying on the road were two different things, though. I looked over at A.J., it had only been a week of living together, but A.J. and I had developed a weird sort of brain synch. A.J. pointed his gun at the guy's head and whispered,
"This is for Jess," as he pulled the trigger.

The rest of us headed for the truck while A.J. and Brandon pulled the bodies into the high brush off the road. We didn't want the "Boss" looking for the guys. Their truck was not running and would have to be hidden and dealt with later. For now, we needed to get to Alicia's, get some stitches put in A.J.'s arm, and get moving towards the lake.

"Do you think we should make the run to town before we go to the lake to warn Mary? If we go to the pharmacy first, we might be able to find stuff she'll need once she has the baby," I asked Brandon and Keith when we were finally in the truck and driving again.

"Hell, I worry either way. If some of the women wanted to go with us, it might be best to hit the lake after picking up Mike," Brandon said as he frequently checked his mirrors, now looking for any sign of trouble.

"Okay then, let's stick with the plan we have," I said, looking over at Keith, who was already asleep against the side window. "Babe," I said, nudging Brandon to look over at Keith.

"He has no business being out on this trip. Jacob told me yesterday was the last day on his main medication. He has some holistic medications left, but they don't seem to be helping," Brandon whispered so he wouldn't wake Keith up.

The rest of the trip was smooth. Hell, anything was better than what we had already dealt with this morning. I looked down at my jeans and T-shirt; I had blood in large spots drying on my clothes. I felt the splatter hit my face when A.J. had shot the second guy. We all looked a little rough today. A.J. had put his gillie suit back on and was pointing his gun out the back of the truck. He seemed okay.

When we pulled up to the gate, the same crazy old man stepped out, this time in a purple tracksuit. He looked pretty snazzy, even for the apocalypse.

"I'm guessing you've come back to see the Sawyer family?" He gave us all a look of disgust at the blood covering our clothes. "Mrs. Sawyer said she was expecting guests today. She didn't mention they would be so…… unclean. Open the gate and go straight down to her house. Just because she will put up with you people doesn't mean the rest of us will."

"Dude is an asshole," I heard Jalyn whisper to A.J. behind us.

"Thank you, sir, we won't be long in the neighborhood," I said in as sweet of a voice as I could muster.

"Let's hope not," he muttered as he walked back into his home.

A.J. and Brandon got the gate open, and we drove down to Alicia's. Once again, as we got close to the front door, Sean yanked it open before we could even knock.

"Aunt Tara, do you have a boo-boo?" He asked in his sweet little voice.

"No, but my friend A.J. has one on his arm. I'm going to ask your daddy to fix it up for him," I replied.

"Is A.J. the guy dressed up like a tree? My mommy won't let me wear my Halloween costume all day. Only at Halloween. How come he gets to?" He asked as he pointed at A.J.

I couldn't help it; I busted out laughing and picked him up for hugs and kisses. I could hear laughing behind me. This kid could make anyone smile. Alicia, with baby Joe on her hip, and Michael right on her heels, stepped around the corner then. The smile Alicia was wearing fell as soon as she saw the blood.

"Sean, why don't you take your brother to your room and play cars," she said as she scooted Sean and Joe toward his room.

"But Momma, it's Aunt Tara and Uncle Brandon..." he said as he pouted off down the hall.

"Come in, guys. Michael, go grab your medical bag," she said while pointing us to the kitchen table.

Chapter 14

We spent the next thirty minutes talking about our trip to Jess's house and our run-in with the guys on the road while Michael put stitches in A.J.'s arm. Thankfully the bullet had been a through and through, and the damage wasn't too bad. It would have been a lot worse if Michael had had to dig the bullet out. As it was, he didn't have any painkillers to help with the pain of getting the stitches. A.J. had taken his belt off and was using it to bite down against the pain.

After Michael was done with the stitches, I saw him looking Keith over. Keith was slumped down in one of the kitchen chairs.

"Hey, Keith, do you care if I look you over? You're not looking so good," Michael said as he took out his stethoscope. Keith just shrugged and tried to sit up straighter in his chair. The rest of us left the room to give them some privacy.

"Alicia, I'm thinking maybe we could let Keith stay here with you while we make our run to the pharmacy. The cancer is bad; today has been his worst day yet. He can't keep living like this. Our world has gone from normal to complete shit in just over a week," I said.

"That's fine; he can get some rest in the guest room until you guys get back from town. I'll ask him to write down the names of his medications so you'll know what to get," she said, going to a desk drawer and pulling out a pen and paper.

We walked back into the kitchen just as Keith was pulling his shirt back on.

"I've talked to Keith, and we both agree he should sit out on the run to town," Michael said, standing to face us.

"Great minds think alike, honey," Alicia said while handing the pen and paper to Keith.

After Keith had listed off the medications he needed, we just had to wait for Michael to gather up anything that he might need to deliver a baby. I walked into Sean's room and laid on the floor. Sean came over and put his tiny hand on my face.

"It's going to be alright, Aunt Tara; my Mommy and Daddy can fix people," he said as he leaned down and kissed my cheek.

Being only two, Joe started driving his cars up my legs, making sweet little purring noises that I guessed were supposed to car sounds. How were these precious babies going to grow up in a world like this, I wondered. All of us would die to protect the kids, but what if that wasn't enough?

Fear gripped my heart and squeezed; this world sucked, and we were going to have to someday explain to all the kids the things that we had done to keep them safe. Would they think of us as monsters for the things we've done already? We have killed people! Looking into Sean's eyes, I felt shame. This beautiful boy thought the world of me. Would he still think that way if he knew about my "look" to A.J. telling him to shoot the guy on the road? Would it matter how many people we tried to help if he knew I was a killer? Would he be scared of me? That thought hurt the worst. Tears leaked out of my eyes, and I gathered the boys in my arms and cried. Sean patted my back, and Joe ran his hot wheels car in my hair until it got stuck there.
After a trip to the bathroom with some scissors and returning the slightly hairy truck to Joe, I set off for the living room.

Everyone seemed to be talking at once. "What the hell?" I asked, coming around the corner.

"Michael wants to make the trip to the pharmacy with us for supplies. I think because he's the ONLY doctor we know, it would be safer for him to make a list and let us get what he needs," Brandon said, tossing his arms up in frustration.

"Michael, he has a point. Hell, I'm scared to leave Alicia home alone with just the boys and Keith while we take you to the lake to help Mary," I said.

"Damn it, guys, I'm coming along, and that's final," he said, snapping his bag closed. I saw Alicia sigh with resignation out of the corner of my eye.

"We're going to have to walk from here. We can't leave the truck in plain sight of the road once we get to the lake, and the gates there were chained with huge locks. We're going to have to go in and out on foot. It's probably better to leave the truck here while we go to the pharmacy too. The last thing we need is to get it stolen, or a tire shot out," A.J. said.

I hugged Alicia, and those boys like I would never see them again. For all I knew, I might not.
As a group, we headed for the front door to give Michael and Alicia some privacy. I'm sure it was going to be a tough goodbye.

We did weapons checks and made sure our packs were comfortable with the new medical supplies we had distributed between us for the possible baby delivery. For all, we knew the baby could already be here.

Michael walked out of the house, and we set off walking up to the front gate. Something told me we wouldn't be welcome walking through the neighborhood armed to the teeth.
It was a short walk, but none of us were in a hurry to get to the lake campsites. Not only would it take time to find them, but none of us were looking forward to telling Mary and the others about what happened at their last campsite.

The weather had started to warm up when we were approaching the main gates to the lake campsites. In Oklahoma, our trees looked like we lived in Chernobyl until about March. I always thought it was weird to walk around in a bleak winter landscape while sweating my ass off at the same time. It had to be around sixty-five degrees today. I looked over to see that even A.J. had taken off his gillie suit and had it slung over his shoulder. My fat ass was dragging. In the past week, I had gotten more cardio than in the last couple of years combined. Working behind a desk all day, you tended to get soft, and by the end of the day, my brain was so tired all I wanted to do was fall over.

I wasn't the only one huffing and puffing in the group; we sounded like a herd of elephants tromping through the grass. As a group, we were going to have to up our game because, at this rate, we'd either have heart attacks or be discovered by the enemy before we even got close.

We all took our packs off, tossing them over the gates, then began to climb. They were sturdy metal gates but were still easily climbed over. Once we had all landed safely and collected our bags, I immediately started looking for any signs of life.

"I'm going to guess the ladies we dropped off are deep into the woods surrounding the campsites," I huffed while readjusting my pack for the umpteenth time today.

"I can probably track them if we can find the spot they went off of the main trail," A.J. said.

For the next hour, we searched. The lake's campsites are set up like a giant horseshoe. There are three of those horseshoes the same size. The first one is for the R.V. type campers, campers that require full use of their air conditioning and bathrooms. The second camp is for the "I like the idea of camping, but not the reality of camping, campers. These campers come prepared with tents but still like to have power and water from a hose out of the ground. This area was where I liked to camp unless my dad was with me, then he would put us into the last kind of campsite. It was for the "I shit in the woods and start my fire using only sticks" kind of campers. I always went camping anytime we could swing it. It was a blast to sit around the fire, drinking beer and telling dumb jokes. What wasn't fun was the hike up to the second campsite area to use the communal bathrooms in the middle of the night.

"Got 'em," A.J. muttered, suddenly verging off the path.

We followed him as silently as possible, which is to say like a smoker on a mountain top. A.J. was following some kind of path I didn't see. Shit, for all I knew, we could be chasing a rabbit. By the time I heard the first voice in the distance and looked up, I also heard the cocking of a shotgun.

"Ladies, my name is Tara," I wheezed out. "My family and I brought you here in the back of our old blue truck last week. First, I brought Dr. Michael Sawyer to check on Mary or anyone else who needs any kind of medical help. Second, I need to tell you what happened at the other camp with the rest of your family and friends."

"You know why they haven't made it?" A lady off to my left said. She was well hidden behind the trees and the brush, but I could see dark hair. I could remember her face, but not her name.

"Yes, after leaving you here at the lake entrance, my family and I went to Dr. Sawyers to check on him and his family. Once we left there, we drove back the way we came and saw your camp." I paused, not knowing how to tell them the next part.

"Your group had been attacked. Everyone except Mike was killed, and Mike was gravely wounded with a gutshot. He passed away while we were there." I said, bowing my head.

"What the hell!" Mary burst into the clearing then. Her small daughter perched on her chest in one of those back carrier things. This was the first time I had seen the child without the snowsuit on. She was adorable with blonde ringlets and pink cheeks. The little girl smiled and waved at all of us.

"Mary, we took the same road home after stopping at my friend Alicia's. This is her husband, Dr. Michael Sawyer. We will try to get into town to find some medications we need for my mother, neighbor, and grandbabies. I wanted to stop in and tell you what happened to Mike and the group and offer medical help," I said.

"You came here to tell me my husband died a week ago! I have been waiting for a week with NO word Tara!" she yelled, flailing her arms.

"Mary, in the past week, we have dealt with bandits and horse thefts of all things. We have been in high-speed chases and shoot outs. It's not like I've been sitting at home on my ass," I said, really starting to get pissed.

"Fine, do you know who killed our families and why?" she gritted out through her teeth at me more than spoke.

"Yes, but we only got that information today. Mike said, your group was shot and killed because they couldn't tell them where the pilots lived," I slumped down on an overturned log as I said this. If they were going to shoot us, it would be after I said the next few words.

"Mary, we are the pilots they were looking for. A friend of mine and I both flew from Guthrie to our home the third day after the blast. I had flown into the Guthrie airport and walked to the high school to get my son. The guys we spoke to today after our high-speed chase and shootout told us a man is calling himself "The Boss," and he has set up shop in one of our old town grocery stores. He saw us in the air and has been looking all over the countryside for anyone that may know who we are. I honestly think they attacked your camp for the women who stayed behind. The women were taken from the camp to the grocery store, and all the men were killed. I'm sorry," I said.

Mary sank to her knees. "Those women are my sisters, and those men their husbands. They stayed behind to help the guys get all our stuff here to the lake."

Tears now ran down Mary's face. The lady holding the shotgun was shaking when I glanced over at her. I could see she wanted to kill us just for being kind of involved. The lady's long brown hair was in a tight braid, pulling her face into a fierce facelift kind of configuration. Her eyes were so dark brown; they may have been black. If I had to guess, she was from one of our Native American tribes in the area. The dark-haired lady squatted down in front of me then.

"What did you do with the men that told you this information?" She asked, getting into my personal space.

"We shot them in the head and dragged their bodies into the ditch," I said with my fierce look.

"Good," she said. She stood up and walked away. I don't know what I was expecting, but that hadn't been it. I hate to admit it, but I was kind of scared of her. I had to guess she was a hard lady before the bomb had dropped. Just a couple of weeks ago, not many people would have been happy to hear we killed someone in cold blood. These were different times.

Michael reached down and pulled Mary carefully to her feet. "Mary, are you okay?"

"If you want me to, I can check on you or anyone in your group. It's why I decided to come along today. If not, that's fine too. I brought you some supplies you'll need when you deliver your baby. I will leave them and some other first aid supplies and go," Michael said in his most calming 'doctor voice' while carefully steadying Mary on her feet.

"No, please stay. One of our kids has a cough that I'd like you to listen to. I'll think about letting you check me out after that," Mary said, quietly turning and leading us into her camp.

Her camp was deep into the "shit in the woods" horseshoe of the lake. I guess now that we had no power or water, all of the campsites were the same. I looked around to see only two large tents for several people. If anyone did get sick, it would pass through the group quickly. Kids had a knack for sneezing and coughing into your open mouth. God only knows why, but kids are natural-born cootie carriers. Mary's new baby would be in danger from the elements and any kind of illnesses that went through the camp. The thought of having a baby in this unique dog eat dog world scared me to death. Max had been looking at Jess with googly eyes. The idea went through my head to find all forms of birth control I could get my hands on at the pharmacy.

The Native American woman offered us all water and introduced herself as Sue. Sue had been living a few houses down from Mary when the bomb had gone off. Before that, she had been a corporate lawyer with one of the significant oil and gas firms in Oklahoma City. It just happened she was taking the day off to see her niece's school play when the lights went out. Another ten minutes, and she would have been on the highway.

Sue was also an avid hunter and had taken down a deer on her first night here. The group had been eating on it ever since. Hunting was great for now, but what happens when people start sniffing around out there looking for food too? People were going to start getting desperate soon. People are dangerous, and hungry people are worse.

Chapter 15

My family sat around on tree trunks the women had found and drug into their camp while Michael checked out the little boy with the cough. It sounded horrible, like bronchitis or something. Turns out bronchitis was exactly what it was. I heard Michael tell the lady he needed antibiotics to kill the infection. When we packed up at Michael and Alicia's, we hadn't packed any medications. There just wasn't enough. Alicia was like me, horrible at finishing prescriptions. She had bottles all over the house of halfway taken medications. Unfortunately, none that we would give to a small child. It was the first thing on Michaels's list to grab if we could find any at the pharmacy.

"Hopefully, the group will find the antibiotics he needs. If they can't, we may end up dealing with Pneumonia. Try to keep him warm, and make sure he has warm liquids to prevent dehydration," he said, walking out of one of the tents.

He gave me a look with a small head shake. I knew that look; if we couldn't find the medication he needed, the boy would die.

"I'm coming with you to town," Sue spoke from behind me, making me jump.

"That's fine with us. We need all the help we can get." I said.

Michael looked over at Mary then. "Have you decided if you'd like for me to check on you and the baby while I'm here?"

"You might as well. This baby should have already come by now. I wasn't this overdue with Jordan," She said and waved him into the other tent. Michael followed her in and zipped the flap.

Nobody liked random strangers up in their lady business, but carrying a baby overdue and sitting on your bladder will make you reconsider your modesty.

We had no more than resumed our conversation when Michael comes flying out of the tent with wide eyes. He was soaked from the waist down with what had to be her bag of water. He held the shirt out in front of him with his fingers.

"Jesus, what?" I asked him.

"Her water broke while I was checking her. She's already five centimeters; she is having this baby now!" He said before finally giving up his fight to not vomit.

"Gross. Okay, you've delivered babies before, so deliver that one," I said, pointing towards the tent.
Michael just blinked at me then, before dodging back, bind the tree to vomit again. "Men," I said with a roll of my eyes.

"You're right; I've done this several times during my residency, but that was in a hospital, Tara! I had monitors, medications, and nurses to help me. This is the woods in the middle of the apocalypse," he panted with wild-eyed panic.

"Dude, you need to chill the fuck out. Okay? Now, Michael, what do you need? I'll be your nurse. I've had three babies and was at the birth of both of yours." I said, leaning down to check a pot of water.

"Okay, Tara, go in the tent and put down those things you called puppy potty pads when we were packing. Have her lift up and put them under her. Sue, can you please boil some clean water to have on hand? Brandon, Alicia packed some towels and blankets for the baby in your bag. Give those over to Tara, please," he said. The initial panic seemed to have passed, and Michael was doling out orders and truly in "doctor mode."

We scattered like cockroaches then. From the sounds of the cries Mary was making inside the tent, it didn't sound like it would be too long. Brandon leaned around the tent's side and just chunked the towels through a hole in the tent door. I'm sure Mary loved being slapped in the face with towels while trying to push a human out of her lady business. I rolled my eyes at his fear of seeing blood or a naked lady. I had no idea which.

I unzipped the tent enough to climb in. The tent wasn't huge, maybe an eight-person tent. It was about the size of the one I have.

"What asshole just hit me with towels? "Mary yelled as I entered.

"Oh, that was my husband. He was scared to look in and see any lady business." This made Mary laugh as I had her lift to place the absorbent pads under her. "Mary, how long was your labor with Jordan?" I asked, moving her hair away from her forehead.

"Only about two hours once my water broke," she said between her increasing contractions.

Michael entered the tent then, wearing a face mask, gloves, and goggles now. He tossed me a set as he knelt to Mary. "We need to minimize any chance of infection while delivering this baby. I've got Sue boiling clean water now, so it will cool down enough to bathe the baby once it's here."

It looked like we were ready to get down to business. I held on to Mary's hand for what seemed like hours. A woman in labor is like sticking your hand in a vice grip. I tried to remember anything from my Lamaze class, but I had taken that class when I was pregnant with Kayla twenty-four years ago, and nothing was coming back to me. Mary and I settled into a quick, panting noise that seemed like as good of a plan as any to me.

"You need to slow your breathing Mary. If you don't, you'll end up hyperventilating." Michael said, giving us a demonstration. "He He Ho," he repeated over and over. I was starting to think he was trying to calm himself down as well as Mary.

"Okay, Mary, you're completely dilated. We're going to start pushing now. Tara, hold her up the best you can. Mary, I need you to hold your legs behind your knees and push," he instructed.

I lifted Mary into an almost sitting position by putting one leg behind her and bracing her against my chest.

"Okay, on the next contraction, I need you to push and hold it while Tara counts to ten. Okay, Mary?" He said, looking like he was ready to catch a football more than a baby.

"Here we go 1-2-3-4-5-6-7…" I counted out loud for her.

"Stop pushing; the head is out. Give me just a minute to suction out the nose," he said, using what we in our house referred to as the snot sucker. "Okay, Mary, I just need one good hard push. The baby will be here. Tara, grab one of those towels and put it on Mary's chest," he said.

I reached over to the discarded towels Brandon had thrown in and grabbed the biggest one. I covered her chest with the towel the same way the doctor had done for me when I had my kids. As soon as I got it spread out, Michael placed a red screaming little boy on her chest.

"Mary, he's beautiful! Congratulations. Do you have a name for him yet?" I asked.

Mary lovingly stroked the baby's back and cooed to him. "His name is Lucas."

Lucas had settled down and fallen asleep on his mothers' chest by the time Michael had delivered the afterbirth. Alicia had sent some baby clothes she had leftover from Joe, but they would be too big for now. We had also put him in a cloth diaper Alicia had used as a burp cloth.
I left Mary and Lucas to get some rest and get cleaned up myself. Even with the puppy pads, there was still quite a bit of splatter.

I walked up next to Michael, where he was trying in vain to rinse out his shirt. "You did amazing, Doctor Sawyer. Baby Lucas looks great."

"It went better than I thought it would. I've never been a fan of traditional medicine. Too many fluids involved." he said with a shudder.

I just laughed. Would this damn world be like this every day? This morning we killed two men, and this afternoon a new baby was born in a tent. I just shook my head as I walked up and kissed Brandon. Shit, this world was crazy.

We had only been sitting in the glow of triumph for about ten minutes when A.J. walked up and sat down next to us. "The ladies have made a path that goes down through the woods and pops out almost behind Michael's neighborhood. It will let us stay off the main roads and get Michael home safe. We need to get going on our trip to town. I think if we go into the pharmacy in the dead of night, we might have better luck," he said, repacking his supplies and passing out granola bars. We all just sat there, chewing and tired.

"He's right," Jacob said, "I think going in in the middle of the night is our best option. We have a lot of stuff to find, and we need to get going. I'm worried those guys might find our place. Jess's farm was damn close to our house and the airstrip. We need to get back home and warn everyone at the airport; they might be targets to this guy."

"Let me run in and check on the baby and Mary again, then I'm ready," Michael said.

Brandon picked up my pack for me and helped me get it adjusted on my back. I felt like I was going to fall over asleep any minute now. He held me in his arms while we waited for the others to pack up.
We had decreased the weight of our packs by dropping off the medical supplies. At least that was something.

We walked single file on the path through the woods, Sue leading the way. It was late afternoon, and it was starting to cool off again. If we were going into the town in the dead of night, we would have some downtime to rest, I hoped.

It was dark by the time we reached Alicia's gate. I didn't see the usual crypt keeper that stood guard up here in his fancy tracksuit. He either turned in early or decided he just didn't care anymore; either way, I was glad. We had a long night ahead of us, and I just wasn't sure I could do confrontation anymore right now. I could see into Alicia's window at the glowing fireplace; it looked so warm and inviting. I wanted to stretch out on the floor like an old dog and sleep. We were met at the door with a very enthusiastic Sean.

"Daddy, you're home! I miss you!" He squealed, taking a run at his father before coming to a stop a foot away. "Daddy, you stink!" He put his hand over his nose and mouth and ran away.

This made all of us crack up. Michael did stink; the smell had been getting stronger as it dried. Alicia walked around the corner then.

"I'm guessing you delivered a baby today? How many times did you throw up?" She asked, suppressing a giggle. Michael sighed and walked down the hall to clean up.

Alicia led everyone into the kitchen where Keith was sitting. He already looked better. His color was back, and he was coloring in a book with Joe. Alicia had made dinner for all of us.

"It's those freeze-dried meals we bought years ago during the crash. We might as well eat them. The package says beef stroganoff, but it looks kind of grey to me," she said, setting out plates and silverware.

Alicia had always been the domestic goddess type. On the other hand, I managed to light myself on fire three times in the last year before the blast. I'm not sure what it was, but I just wasn't good at anything in the kitchen. In the previous five years, my cooking had caused so much damage the entire family asked me to "please, just stop." I looked down at the plate of rehydrated stroganoff to see that, sadly, it still looked better than when I had tried to make it homemade. I could do other stuff. I kept a clean home, except for Max's bedroom. Teenage boys had their idea of what was accepted in everyday society. According to Max, if his dirty clothes did not fall out of the hamper onto the floor and walk themselves to the laundry room, it wasn't time to do any washing. I've seen him pick a shirt up off the floor, sniff it, frown, and put it on anyway. I had always been more comfortable out in the workshop. I loved carpentry and all forms of power tools. Not precisely "girly" activities, but I loved taking a piece of scrap wood and turning it into something useful.

We ate in silence, other than to praise Sean and Joe for their color pages. If I had to guess, everyone has the same misgivings I was having about going into town tonight. I thought back to my little town and the things I had seen while flying over it the day after the blast. It had been utter chaos. The city we were going into tonight had about four hundred times the population of my little town. Edmond, Guthrie's nearby city, was known for its constant bumper to bumper traffic, no matter what time of day it was. It was a town of means. I wondered if people would still be sitting in their fancy cars trying to guard them against vandals or if they had tried to make the walk home. Edmond was a big town. It took upwards of an hour to get from one side to the other during rush hour.

"We have about four hours to get some sleep before we start tonight. Alicia, have you been taking turns doing patrols?" Asked Jacob, standing up from the table.

"No, we haven't seen any reason to watch for anyone. We know all the people on this street. None of them would try to steal or hurt us," Alicia said as if that was the stupidest idea she had ever heard.

"It might be that way now, but not everyone prepared beforehand as you did. I know all those people are your friends, but desperate people do desperate things. It might be a good idea to start keeping an eye on the house," Jacob warned.

"Okay, since all of you are going out tonight, Michael and I will keep watch while you sleep. I can use Tara's watch to tell you when it's been four hours," She said, hand out to me.

Before I could sleep, I walked into Alicia's office, where she kept her ham radio. "Hello, is anyone at home?"

"This is home. Are you guys, okay? Your mother has been worried, sick!" My dad answered back.

"I'm sorry, it's been a rough trip. I'm guessing Max filled you in on what we found at Jess's house?" I replied.

"Yes, you guys should have just turned around and come home. You are taking way too many chances," he said.

"I know, but I promise, after this run tonight, we will be able to stay home. You know how important that stuff we're looking for is," I reminded him.

"I understand that, Tara, but I'm terrified for all of you. Even the weird guy," my dad said with a chuckle.

"I love you, please tell everyone I love them. I'll see you tomorrow when we get home. Keep an eye out for us and any trouble on your end. The guys that hit Jess's farm are getting closer. We had a run-in with two of them today. They gave us a lot of information I'll share with you tomorrow," I signed off before my dad could ask the questions I didn't want to answer.

Chapter 16

Brandon and I flopped down on Alicia and Michael's bed. I had no idea where everyone else was going to sleep, but I was exhausted. It felt like only minutes had passed before Alicia was shaking me awake.

"I'm worried about this trip Tara. It's a long way into town from here, and you guys are doing it all on foot. Do you think it's safe?" She whispered.

I could tell she was keeping her voice down as not to wake up Brandon. "No, I know it's not safe. I'm also not a fan of any kind of "looting," but we need those medications. Keith will go downhill fast without them, and my mom……," I choked out. "I can't lose my mom, not now. Plus, we have a two-year-old with asthma and no inhalers. We don't have a choice; we have to do this," I said.

I turned and shook Brandon awake to avoid talking about the trip anymore. Brandon and I had never undressed. This wasn't the world to be caught with your pants down. All we had to do was slip on our boots. A.J. hadn't gotten the same memo the rest of us had. I looked over through the giant window to see him in nothing but boxers and boots taking a piss in Alicia's yard. In his defense, indoor plumbing was quickly becoming an issue. Before long, we would all be out pissing in the yard.

After everyone was dressed again, we repacked our bug-out bags. Alicia had practically forced us to pack more food and water, even if it was just a day trip.

"You just never know what could happen out there," she kept saying to us.

Then it was time. We hugged each of the Sawyer family in turn. Sean and Joe had no idea what was going on, just that we were leaving. To the boys, we had always come back before, why wouldn't we do it again. Alicia hugged me until I couldn't breathe.

"Damn woman, this trip will be worse with broken ribs," I gasped out. I pried her off me and moved her over to hug Brandon. The look on his over squeezed face made me giggle.

The weather was cold but not uncomfortable as we made our way up to the gates of the neighborhood. A.J. pushed them aside and closed them behind us. The night was quiet, just the usual night animals doing their thing. They grew silent as we passed by, then picked up again as we got further away. It was so dark out here. In large cities and towns like this, it was always brightly lit, no matter what time of night it was. Now it was just dark and still. At least I hadn't heard any gunshots. That was something. Oklahoma was an open carry state, which meant almost every citizen carried a gun either in their car or on their person. That was a lot of guns to try and walkthrough. If we stayed on the roads and out of the neighborhoods, maybe people wouldn't bother us. I guess we were about to find out.

It took us a good hour of walking to get a couple of miles between Alicia's country neighborhood and into the town proper. The constant walking and hiking in the days since the bomb had dropped were helping with endurance. I was still slow and out of breath but getting better about it. It would take us another hour to an hour and a half of walking to get to the pharmacy. It was a chain store. Either the owner was guarding the store and could be bartered with, or the store was abandoned, and we could just pick through what was left. I had brought a couple of silver bars with me that Brandon and I had purchased during the 2008 crash. At the time, the price of silver was $33.00. The last time I looked, the "precious metal" was only worth about $15.00. I had one box of 9mm ammo and a small bottle of whisky. More than once, I had been tempted to drink the whisky. I had added it to my pack after getting my nose broken. My nose was healing well now, but it hurt like a son of a bitch at the time. Thankfully my bruised eyes were starting to yellow.

We were trudging along the main road when we heard a twig snap up ahead of us. We all froze instantly. Climbing down into the gutter, we hid and waited.

"Did you see where they went?" I heard a small voice say.
"No, you were ahead of me; why didn't you watch them?" an obvious teenage boy said. Every other word was cracking.

"Austin, I can't see in the dark, ya know," the small voice said.

"Dang it, Julie, what if they saw us. They'll take our food," the boy screeched.

"Guys, we don't want your food or any trouble. We're just passing through. We're going to stand up now," I said, holding up my hands.

"What in the hell are you doing?" Brandon hissed at me.

"Those kids could blow your head off before we even stand up," he said, trying to catch my arm.

"If I stand up, will you shoot me?" I asked

"Will you shoot us?" The girl who I guessed was Julie, said.

"Nope, promise," I said.

"Okay, us too," said Julie.

I stood the rest of the way up, holding my hands at chest level. I was brave, not stupid. I wanted to be close enough to my gun if these kids tried to draw on me. I had no intention of hurting them, but I would scare the shit out of them if I needed to.

"Hi Julie, I'm Tara. This is my husband, Brandon, and our friends. We're just trying to get into town to see if we can get some medicines. We won't hurt you; we just need to get by you, okay?" I asked.

Julie nodded, and the rest of the group stood up. Austin wasn't happy about our newfound truce but seemed to be sticking to it so far.

"Hi, I'm Julie, and this is my brother Austin," she said.

"J-u-l-i-e, Austin drawled out. Now they know our names," he said, stomping with frustration at his little sister.

"It's okay, Austin, we are headed that way," I said, pointing my finger.

"What do you need the medicines for?" Julie asked.

Julie was a small girl, maybe ten years old, if that. She had a slight frame, and a cute pixie cut hairdo. The haircut made her look like she could be a fairy instead of a little girl. The boy Austin was taller but just as lean. If I had to guess, he was about 14 or 15. Brown shaggy hair hung down in his eyes.

"What are you guys doing out here alone in the dark? I'm an adult, and I'm scared to be out here," I said. This made Julie laugh, a cute little tinkling sound.

"That's none of your business!" Austin barked out.

"Oh, stop being such a butthead," Julie said, walking up to us.

"So, why are you looking for medicines?" She asked again.

"Well, I have a mom that needs heart pills, a neighbor who needs cancer pills, a doctor friend who needs antibiotics, and a grandson who needs asthma inhalers," I said.

"Wow, you have a lot of sick people at your house," she said.

"Yes, Ma'am, I guess I do," I said with a giggle of my own.

"Julie, Austin, it was nice to meet you, but we need to get going. You two stay safe, okay," I said, adjusting the straps on my pack for the millionth time.

"We're alone. Our mom never came home from work, and our daddy lives in Texas now," Julie said to me.

I froze. Alone after this many days? That wasn't a good sign for the kid's mom. "How far away did your mom work? Maybe it was just a long walk."

"She works in Oklahoma City," she said, worry evident in her sweet little voice.

Shit, depending on what part of the city the mom worked in, it would be a hazardous walk. The problem with Oklahoma City was that for every nice area, there were multiple dangerous areas. Not to mention we had a major prison downtown. That would put hundreds of really pissed off prisoners back on the street.

"That's still a long way away. Without cars, it will take her at least a week to get home, plus she probably had to stop and sleep," I said.

I glanced up at Austin. He had his head down. It had to be hard to take care of himself and Julie. He looked tired and hungry.

"I live out in the country with my family and friends. If you want to, you can come with us," I said.

Brandon came up behind me to whisper. "Babe, these aren't stray dogs you can just take home. These are someone's children. What would you have done if you got to Max's school, and he had gone home with someone else?"

I pulled Brandon further away from the kids, so our whispering wouldn't be overheard. "Honey, if those kids are alone, what kind of person would I be for not helping them? Those kids are scared and alone. Would you want Max, scared and alone?" I hissed back at him.

"Okay, guys, here's the deal. If you want to wait for your mom, I understand. I have a couple of camping meals in my pack that I'll leave you with. If you want to come with us, you can meet us back here after going to the pharmacy. It will probably take us a while. Write your mom a note, tell her you're okay. I'll write down directions to our house. She can come and get you when she gets home. I'll leave it up to you,"

"If you want to meet us back here and go with us, meet us here about 7:30. That should give us enough time to get our stuff and get back." I said as I pulled a notepad out of my pack.

I spent the next few minutes giving detailed notes on how to get to our house. I handed Austin the meals, paper with the directions, and then we walked on. Nobody mentioned me giving food to the kids. I hadn't thought they would, but I was ready. My four hours of sleep had only been enough to make me cranky.

We made a great time getting into the central part of town. Edmond was dark and quiet. We crept around the backs of buildings and shopping centers until we got to the end of the CVS pharmacy.
I took a shot and knocked on the back door.

"What are you doing?" A.J. and Jacob hissed at me in unison.

"If someone is holding up in there, I don't think breaking in will buy us any goodwill to barter with. Do you?" I said. That shut them both up.

"Who's out there?" A voice from inside yelled.

"I need medications, and I brought things to barter with. The medications I need are life and death. I do not require any pain killers," I said at the door.

"I have a shotgun, and I'm not afraid to use it," the voice called back.

"Sir, I'm not here to hurt you or steal from you. I just want to barter for some medications. I need asthma inhalers, blood pressure meds, and a med my neighbor takes to help with his cancer. Oh, and some antibiotics for a small boy with bronchitis we met this morning," I replied.

The door cracked open. I guess a heavyset blonde wasn't all that terrifying because the man waved me in.

"Just you! I don't want everyone moving stuff around," he said, glowering at the rest of our motley crew.

"That's fine, sir, thank you," I said, making my way through the door.

The pharmacy was in shambles. Food and random medications littered the floor. I almost slipped and fell in some spilled laundry soap. The man grabbed my arm to steady me.

"Wow, what happened? I'm Tara, by the way." I said

"The night the lights went out, a truck smashed through the front door. They cut all the locks off my pharmacy shelves and robbed me blind. I'm just lucky I wasn't here. I had run home to check on my cats," he said as we carefully picked our way to the back of the store.

"Okay, for swap, I've got a couple of things. I have silver, bullets for a 9mm, and whisky. Do you have any interest in any of that?" I asked while handing him the list Michael and Keith had made for me.

Jalyn and my mom had already filled out their needs before we left, so I handed him their list too.

"Let's see what we can do for some silver," he said, making his way behind the counter.

I stayed on the other side of the counter. I didn't want to do anything to spook the man. I kept my hands on the counter while he searched.

"Okay, I've got everything but the cancer medications. I'm going to put a different pill in there, which might help with his side effects. You know if he's on this high a dose, he doesn't have long. I'm sorry. I wish I could give you some medications to help keep him comfortable, but those were all stolen within hours. Damn stoners," he said, filling a bag.

"Are you going to be okay here?" I asked him.

"Now that the damn stoners are gone, it should just be normal folks looking for stuff like this," he held my bag up.

"I'm going to get in my bag for the silver now," I said. I took my pack off my back and began pulling things out to get to the bottom, where I had hidden my silver in the bag's lining.

I took out two silver coins and handed them over. "Is that enough? I also have the whiskey."

The man just laughed. "No, thank you, Ma'am, I've been sober for twenty-five years now. I don't want to start that up again. The silver will be fine. Thank you for not trying to force your way in here. It's nice to see a normal person again," he said.

I took my bag, shook his hand, and made my way back to the door. Brandon popped up off the ground as soon as I opened the door. "Are you okay?" He asked, looking me over.

"I'm fine. I traded some of our silver for the medications. Let's get back to Alicia's, drop off Michaels' stuff, and pick up Keith. I'm tired and ready to go home," I said.

"Wow," A.J. whispered as we walked away. "That was really anti-climatic."

"Jesus, let's not jinx it. Thankfully the whole world hasn't gone feral…just most of it," I sighed in reply.

We spent the walk back to where we had seen the kids in silence. Jacob and Brandon were leading the way, Jalyn and I in the middle, and A.J. is bringing up the rear to watch our back. It was so dark out tonight-the moon must be small and covered by clouds. It gave our walk a sinister feel. The trees swayed in the cooling breeze giving me goosebumps. I wasn't sure if the goosebumps were from fear of my surroundings or the dropping temperature. If the weather was in the sixties today, tonight had to be in the low forties.

Brandon reached back and silently grabbed my hand. The physical aspects of the apocalypse had been challenging on all of us, but I was dragging. I gave him a grateful smile and continued to move one foot in front of the other.

As we approached the area where we had met the kids, I looked around for any sign of them. I whisper yelled for them but never heard as much as a twig snap. I looked at my watch and saw it was only five minutes from the 7:30 when I had told them to meet us if they wanted to go out to the airport with us.

"I want to give them five minutes. They still have time to get here if they decide they want to go with us. If not, we can go on," I said, planting my ass on the curb.

"God, I hate to leave any kids alone in this world," Jalyn said, looking at me.

"I know, kiddo, but all we can do is offer to help and hope they take us up on it," I said.

After the five minutes came and went, we slowly started moving again. We still had miles to walk to get back to Alicia's neighborhood. It was so late at night that we decided we could cut through the communities on our way back. It was a risk but would save us time, and miles, to walk as the crow flies.
We were only about a block into the first neighborhood when we heard footsteps behind us. Loud steps. Whoever was coming upon us was definitely not trying to be stealthy. We all jumped down along the side of a driveway in a rain ditch to try and make ourselves as small as possible.

"Are you sure they even came this way, Austin?" Julie asked, out of breath.

"I don't know, it's not like they're leaving bread crumbs," Austin said, exasperated.

"Hey guys, it's us. When you guys didn't show at our meeting place, I thought you decided to stay home," I said, standing up from the ditch.

"Somebody had to pack her entire bedroom," Austin said, pointing at Julie.

"It's not my fault you don't have nice things," Julie said, walking towards us.

After the group all introduced themselves, we all started the long walk back to Alicia's house. It was cold now, and we all shivered as we walked, even though we had all packed a jacket. I could smell the cold coming in. Leave it to the Oklahoma weather-today was sixty, tomorrow was snow. Sometimes I really hated living in Oklahoma. Thankfully for our family at home, Brandon had been able to get the wood stove hooked up. It would produce a lot of smoke, but the smoke was better than freezing to death.

Chapter 17

We were coming to one of the more dangerous parts of our trip. We had to cross the highway. As we approached our bridge, we saw a group of men standing in the middle. They had found a large barrel and made a fire in the middle of the bridge. With the help of the firelight, I could clearly see they were all armed with something. A couple had shotguns, but most had crowbars and tire irons from their cars or trucks. I was taking a guess, but since we were close to the large truck stop, these guys were probably long haul truckers.

"The way I figure it, we can trade passing on the bridge for some food. If they don't have any food, we just shoot em and take what they do have," random guy number one was saying. He had on jeans that hung off his large rear end and a coat and jacket that had ridden up to give him a belly top. He wore a large ball cap on his head with a truck logo stitched on it.

Random guy number two was nodding, like guy number one was preaching the gospel. This guy was extremely slim. He reminded me of a weasel. He had greasy hair that I couldn't make out the color of in the firelight. What I could see is he was wearing the ever-classy F.B.I., federal body inspector, t-shirt, and dirty jeans. Looking at this kid of about nineteen or so, I had to guess the only body he had ever inspected was his own. He had a large cop-style flashlight and was sweeping it back and forth over the cars below.

A couple of other guys were sitting along the bridge, paying no attention to random guys one or two. They looked more interested in visiting or napping.

"Pull back," Brandon said to me as he let go of my hand to get a better grip on his weapon.

As a group, we slowly and quietly moved back into the wooded area off the road. I was happy the night was as pitch-black as it was. There was no way they could see us from our position.

"Okay, what now?" Jalyn asked in a whisper.

"We're going to need to double back and cross the highway in a different spot," Jacob said.
"I agree; I'm tired and really not in the mood to deal with these dumbasses," Brandon said, nodding at Jacob.

The rest of us followed as quietly as we could and walked back the way we had come. To cross the highway, we would have to expose ourselves to a line of cars as far as the eye could see in either direction.

"I figure we'll need to move about half a mile down the road to avoid their flashlights," Jacob said.

I heard a small groan from someone in our group. I didn't blame them. None of us has slept more than a few hours in the past couple of days.

"I know, but we don't have any other options. Even if we gave them some food, I doubt they would let us pass, especially with women in our group. I don't want to kill someone just to make our walk shorter. It wouldn't be right. I'm not losing my humanity to this damn apocalypse any more than I already have," Jacob said.

I knew what he was referring to. Jacob had saved us in Guthrie when he and I had flown in to get Max. I remembered the look on his face after he shot one of the prisoners that had escaped from jail the first day of the EMP. Not only had we had to kill two human beings, but our flight was the reason we were being hunted.

"I'm fine with that. Let's find a spot to cross and get out of here," I said to Jacob.

We slowly made our way along the highway side. The highway had been cut down into a valley of sorts. We were easily eight feet above the highway as we walked. It gave us a vantage point to see all the cars below. It had been long enough that nobody had stayed in their vehicles. If I had to guess, everyone had either hiked into the wooded areas around the lake or went into town to take their chances.

One by one, we came down to the cars on the road. It was deadly silent. I could hear my heartbeat in my ears are we slowly picked our way around the cars. I was just stepping behind a large van when I heard a small cry.

I tapped Brandon on the shoulder and leaned in. "Did you hear that?"

"Hear what?" He asked

"A cry, like a baby crying," I said.

When Brandon and I had stopped, the whole group had stopped with us.

"There, did you hear it?" I asked. I heard the cry again; it was faint, but definitely a cry.

"Shit, can you tell where it's coming from?" Jalyn asked.

We walked along with the cars, crouched down to make sure we wouldn't be seen by the flashlight if the random guys actually left the bridge to check out the noise.

After going car to car, peaking in all the windows, we saw him. I should say we smelled his father in the car. It looked like he had been shot point-blank in the head. The body was swollen, but he still looked like it had only been a day or two. In the backseat of the car was an infant carrier. The type that looked like a little bucket with a handle. Inside the seat was a small baby. He looked to be about two or three months old, and he wasn't in good shape. Whoever killed his father had left this little boy to die in his car seat from dehydration and starvation. I was so pissed off. This poor little bald baby was dying.

I reached over and quietly unhooked the car seat from its base. Looking around to make sure the coast was clear, I slowly lifted the car seat out of the car. Brandon reached over and grabbed what had to be the baby's bag. Hopefully, it would have some formula in it. If the child had been breastfed, we were out of luck. The baby protested weakly about being moved, but his cries were so faint even up close that I knew the guys on the bridge couldn't hear them.

As we reached the highway's far side, we saw a beam of light coming towards us from the bridge direction. There was no way the beam could go this far without one of the men leaving the bridge to walk over and investigate. We were seven people and a baby now. They must have heard our noise while we came across the highway.

The beam ran over the cars we were hiding behind over and over. Whoever was shining that flashlight knew that we, or something, was in this area. We waited, hunched down. The baby made little noise, but still, his cries could be heard from a distance.

"It's just a baby in one of the cars," one of the random guys called back towards the bridge.

"Come on back, we don't want no baby," another random guy called.

That was, of course, the moment Julie let out a sneeze. Not even a quiet sneeze. We all looked back at her with wide eyes. "Sorry," she mouthed.

Her brother rolled his eyes and looked at the random guy. We all looked over at the guy. He was making his way through the cars closer to us now. It was the skinny weasel looking, kid. He was swinging his flashlight around, looking for the source of the noise.

"Would you come on? I thought I heard something on the other side of the highway, and I'm hungry," a guy yelled from the bridge.

Weasel sighed and turned to walk away, then stopped. He just stood there. He let out a large and loud fart and walked away. We all stayed crouched down for longer than we needed to. The last thing any of us felt like dealing with while half asleep and exhausted was an altercation.

We slowly make our way to the far side of the highway and up the steep hill on the other side. I had passed the baby car seat up to Brandon, and he was slowly climbing up the side while clutching the car seat handle. A.J. reached the top first and reached down, grabbing the car seat, while the rest of us helped each other up the incline. We were all breathing heavily by the time we reached the top. Without a word, we kept walking. We walked fast at almost a jogging pace until we could be sure we were safe.

Quickly I released the buckles on the car seat and removed the infant. He smelled horrible. I'm guessing he had been sitting in his own excrement for days—poor baby. I laid out his blankets in the grass and began to strip the baby. When I took off his diaper and removed it, I could see that he was bleeding from a diaper rash even in the dark.

Brandon handed me a bottle of water. I slowly rinsed the now screaming baby until the poop was washed away. I found one cloth diaper burp rag in his bag, an empty can of formula, a change of clothes, two dirty bottles, and a pacifier. Unsure what to do, I opened one of the bottles and rinsed it out. Filling it with water, I cradled the baby in my arms. He hungrily sucked at the water, only to pull away. I knew babies this age didn't need plain water. They get all the water they needed when it was mixed into their formula, but if this baby didn't get some fluids into his system, he would die.

I repeatedly tried until he finally latched on to the bottle and began sucking at the water. Brandon handed me a thick blanket out of the bag. The name Carson had been embroidered on the corner.

"Well, little baby Carson, let's get you to the doctor," I cooed at him.

Carson seemed much more content, having some water in his belly. I imagined it gave him a feeling of being full, even though it held no nutrition. We decided to leave his car seat behind. It was ruined by days of pee and poop. It was probably a miracle we had even found him alive. I had to believe we were meant to see Carson. Why else would we have had to detour from the bridge? It was fate.

Carson slept tucked down my shirt for the rest of the walk to Alicia's. He was so light I hardly noticed his weight as we walked. If I had to guess, he probably only weighed about eight or nine pounds.
Brandon was carrying his diaper bag, and Jalyn was wrapped up in one of his blankets, trying to keep the chill off.

When we got to the gate, the old man stood outside on sentry duty. He was wearing the best winter gear money could buy. He stood with a cup of coffee in one hand and a shotgun in the other.
"I see you made it back in one piece," he said, opening the gate for us.

"We did, but we had some close calls. We also found this little guy alone and dying in a car," I said, pulling down the front of my jacket to show him a sleeping baby Carson.

The old man paled. "Someone left him alone to die?" he said, choking up.

"They shot his father in their car and left him. I'm guessing his mother was taken, and the father fought the attackers, but that's just a guess," I said, covering Carson back up. 'If you know anyone who has some leftover baby formula, could you ask them to bring it over to the Sawyers, please? We're taking him down to get looked at."

"Sure, I'll ask around at the meeting later and see if anyone has any extra. We're meeting at sunrise, so I won't be too long. I'll let you know," he said.

"Thanks, I appreciate it," I said, but he just waved me off and went into his home.

Jacob knocked quietly on Alicia's door. It opened almost immediately. Alicia went to grab me, but I raised my hand and pulled down the front of my jacket to show her Carson. Alicia cried when we told her how we had found Carson. Michael was looking over the crying baby. His stomach was distended from lack of nutrition. Carson's skin was so pale in the light it was almost translucent. Michael was running his hands around him, checking for injuries, and checking his reflexes.

"Well, for all the poor little guy has been through, he's actually doing pretty well. I wish I had an IV I could give him, but we'll just have to give him fluids for now," Michael said, picking Carson up and snuggling him against his chest. 'Alicia, do we have any sweetened condensed milk?"

"Sure, what are you going to do with that? I've got a bunch of cans leftover from Christmas," she asked.

"We're going to dilute it with water and use it as a formula; for now, it can help him not only with fat content but also give him some sugar. Parents used to do it all the time in the olden days when they couldn't, or just didn't want to breastfeed," he said.

Alicia quickly disappeared into the kitchen and came back with the milk in a clean bottle. She had even warmed it up for him. Carson greedily gulped down the milk and gave a huge burp. The rest of us had collapsed on her couches and were trying not to doze off.

"The man at the gate said you had a neighborhood meeting at first light. He said he would ask if anyone had any extra formula they didn't need or just weren't using anymore," I said.

Alicia turned to me then. "Oh, you need to call your mom on the ham radio. Your parents are worried sick about how long you've been gone. I told them about everything that had happened with Mary and that you were on your way to town to get the meds." "Now that the baby is taken care of, would you like to introduce us to your new people?" Alicia said, looking over at Austin, Julie, and Sue.

"Sorry, these two kiddos are Austin and Julie. They're going to stay for a while until their mom gets back from her job in Oklahoma City. We left her a note, telling her how to get to our place," I said. Alicia gave me a knowing look but shook their hands.

"And this is Sue. Sue lives with the group in the lake campgrounds." I motioned over to Sue, and she nodded. Alicia walked over to the kids and shooed them into the kitchen.

"Sue, can I have a minute before you leave for the campsites?" I asked, motioning her to Alicia's entryway. 'I know you guys are happy where you are, but if the time ever comes when you're not, I hope you'll get in touch with us. If you come here to Alicia and Michael's house, they can reach me on the radio, and I will come to pick you up at any time. I don't have much to offer, but I can make a warm space, at least."

"I've been listening to your people talk; why would I put my people in danger? I know those guys are chasing you! Don't offer "help" for my people when it would only be adding numbers to yours for a fight! This group is women and children, not a trained militia," She snarled at me.

I stood there, taken aback. I hadn't really given my offer of help to bolster my own numbers; I was just trying to be nice. "Geez, lady, bitchy much?" I thought to myself.

"I didn't mean it like that. I think you know that about me if you really think about it! Did I rescue that baby so he could help me win an upcoming war? Does AJ only stay with us because we force him too? Fuck no, and fuck you for implying I would try to lure anyone into my fight. If you or your people want my help, fine, if not whatever," I said.

Sue grinned at me! Actually smiled at me like I was some small spitting kitten. What the fuck lady, that was about as fierce as I got after days of little sleep. I just stood staring at her, head cocked to the side like a dog.

"I wanted to make sure you were inviting us for the right reasons. If, and that's a big if, my people decide to join with you, I don't want you thinking you were getting an army. The women and children in that camp are just that-women and children, not trained fighters. I'll speak to everyone when I get back, and we will decide as a group what we want to do," she said.

With that, the crazy-ass woman grabbed her pack and walked out the door.

Over the next hour, as we waited for the sunrise meeting, Alicia, Austin, and Julie and made the rest of us cocoa. It was so strangely familiar. If that was even a thing anymore. AJ had managed to find a quiet place on the floor and was sound asleep. The rest of us sat around the dining table, sipping cocoa and whispering. There was a sharp rap on the door. We all jumped up. AJ suddenly came up behind me, scaring the crap out of me and making me jump.

"Sorry," he whispered and grinned at me.

"It's time for the meeting," a familiar voice yelled through the door.

Chapter 18

Jacob opened the door to see my favorite gate watchman on the other side.

"I'm not sure if I've ever introduced myself. I'm Glenn Thompson, and I live at the corner closest to the gate,"h said, stepping in the house.

Mr. Thompson had to be in his 70's. He was currently dressed up like the kid from the Christmas Story. He had so many layers of clothes on it was impossible to make out his shape. He had sharp gray eyes, and he always looked at us with suspicion until today. Today he seemed almost friendly.

"How's that sweet little baby doing? Is he going to make it?" He asked, looking all around the room for the child. Michael walked in with little Carson then. The baby had his eyes open and was cooing at Michael.

"It looks like he's found a new friend," Mr. Thompson said, walking up to Carson and softly rubbing the top of his little silky head. "I have four grandsons out there somewhere. I can only hope they get the same kind of help this baby did," He said with a watery smile to the baby. Almost as if catching himself, he stepped back and turned to the group.

"If you want to ask the group for help with the baby, one of Sawyers needs to come with me to the meeting. They usually take about an hour," he said, pulling his hat down further on his face.

"I'll go," Michael said, handing the baby to me. "I'll be back in a little bit," he said, leaning over to kiss Alicia before following Mr. Thompson out the door into the cold morning.

I snuggled little Carson to me. Alicia had given him a proper bath with the water they had stored when the EMP hit. He smelled so wonderful. I sniffed his sweet little head and sent up a prayer to ask God to let his parents know we would do anything in our power to keep him safe and happy.

I walked into the office and plopped down in the big office chair in front of the Ham radio. I had put off calling into the house until I knew more about Carson and what Sue and her group might do.

"Mom, it's me. Can you hear me? Over," I said as I depressed the mike button.

The radio burst to life within twenty seconds, with my mother's panicked voice at the other end. I had to guess someone was monitoring the radio. My mother's almost panicked voice came through the speakers startling Carson into a squeak.

"This is mom. Are you guys, okay? We've been waiting to hear from you. Over," she said.

"Everyone is fine, and we finished what we went for. Over," Carson was starting to fuss, and I yelled at Jalyn to come to grab him.

"What was that? It sounds like a baby. Are her kids okay? Over," she said.

"We found three kids, actually. One is thirteen, one is ten, and the baby you heard is about 3 months. Someone had killed his father, and his mother was missing. The killers left the baby in the car to starve to death. The Doc has given him a clean bill of health and is keeping an eye on him. The Doc is currently at a meeting looking for baby formula. We will be headed back your way in about an hour. I can fill you in on the rest then. Can you please make space for our newcomers? Over," I said.

"Yes, I guess. Over," mom sighed into her end of the mike.

Since I was a child, my mother had dealt with me, bringing home any stray and sick animal I could find. She had once helped me nurse a crow back to health. Unfortunately, in the middle of the night, it flew out of his shoebox. That bird crapped all over the house for hours before we were able to let him out. After spending the morning waving a broom at the crow while I screamed, I was never allowed to bring anymore injured animals in the house. I, not thinking this was fair, set up an animal hospital in my mother's gardening shed. Unfortunately, my next animal was a mouse. Mom had to call in the exterminator to deal with the infestation my sweet little mouse buddy brought on after he healed.

In a way, she was right. I always tried to help anyone or anything in need. This had gotten me into trouble too many times to count. Once someone knows you will still help them, they become dependent. I would never say that about a child, but I had dealt with it in adults. If I had to guess, my mother was currently cursing me under her breath and wondering what kind of menagerie I would be bringing home.

I wandered back into the kitchen and sat with the rest of the group.

"Is everything okay back at the house?" Jacob asked, coming to sit down next to me.

"Everyone is fine. My mom is making space for the kids before we get home," I said.

Jacob nodded at me and went back to the potable water discussion; the rest of the group was caught up in. A.J. had gone so far as to draw out diagrams by the time Michael got back to the house. I tried to focus but nodded off with my head on the table, mid-way through the discussion. Useful information, you bet, useful with no sleep?

Nope. Michael walked into the dining room and sat. "The neighborhood is closing up the gates. After today no outsiders will be allowed into the neighborhood, period." Someone tried to interrupt, but Michael raised his hand, shutting off all chatter.

"We knew something like this might happen. We've talked about it before. They also said our "guests" need to leave within the hour or move in with us permanently. The group thinks it's just too dangerous to be letting strangers go in or out, even with homeowner permission. Three streets over, a couple was killed, and their car was taken. Mr. Thompson had let them into the neighborhood because the dead couple had vouched for them. As for the baby formula, nobody has any. I did manage to round up some Ensure and condensed milk."

As soon as Michael stopped talking, the yelling started. It was all "how can they do this, and who do they think they are" type questions. Before long, the group began to quiet. There was nothing we could do. This wasn't our neighborhood, and these people were doing the best for their people that they could. It was the same thing I was trying to do for ours.

"Okay, let's start getting things loaded up. We need to get home anyway. Alicia, we can still talk on the radio and meet at the gate if we need to. It will be okay," I said.

"This is bullshit!" She ranted as she loaded up the rest of her condensed milk.

"Bull shit, bull shit, momma said bull shit," Sean sang as he danced around the kitchen.

Baby Joe thought this was hilarious and decided to clap and dance with his brother. This made me burst out laughing. What else could I do? It was so good to laugh again. Looking around the kitchen, I could see it wasn't just me. Little Sean had broken the tense vibe rolling through the house. Now we were all laughing and clapping with the boys.

I loaded up the last box into the truck and bent down to hug my sweet little nephews. I was going to miss these boys. I knew I would see them soon, but it was always hard to say goodbye. Alicia had dug an old car seat out of the attic for Carson to use for the trip. She had also included some kind of wrap I could use to strap him to my body and a host of other baby gear she had tossed up in the attic. Between all the people and the baby gear, it would be a tight ride back home in the truck.

Brandon drove while I rode shotgun, and little baby Carson was strapped down tight in between us. We went down Alicia's street with her neighbors, all staring at us like we personally had caused the EMP.
I looked into the truck's back to see what my group thought about the looks we were getting, only to see AJ waving with his best Queen of England wave. Jalyn had her face covered with her hand, and the rest of the group were between trying to grab his arm and laughing their asses off.

When we got to the gate, Mr. Thompson was not alone. Now a large man stood with a rifle in his hands. Mr. Thomson approached the truck with his usual no-nonsense demeanor. He was still wrapped head to toe in his winter best, but I could tell he was upset by his posture. The man reminded me of "The Rock" in his build, but not nearly as hot.

"You go and don't come back," He said way too loud for it to be only directed at our truck. "You guys be careful and take care of that baby," he whispered into our open window out of sight of the new gate guard. We nodded at him and drove out of the opening gate.

"I bet the entire neighborhood blames that guy for what happened. They were fine with letting an old man stand out in the cold," Brandon said with disgust in his voice.

"Looks like the new gate guard means business," I said, playing with Carson.

"We need to come up with another route home. I really don't want to use any of the same ways we've taken before. Whoever "The Boss" is is going to be pissed when he finds his missing guys. I'd rather be home on our turf before having to deal with any more of them," he said.

"What do you think will happen when they find us? I hate the idea of a bloodbath period. Max is already in shock after the guy in town. I really don't want to have to ask my son and his friends to shoot people," I said.

"I know he's freaked out, but this is life and death. I hate the idea too, but what choice do we have? The sheriff killed a bunch of those guys, but like attracts like. Assholes will naturally attract other assholes. The same way this group got together. There's no telling how many people "The Boss" has now," he said.

"Would it be smarter to go do some recon? At least that way we could get an idea of how many people they have with them. I'd also like to know how many women and children are trapped in that grocery store. It's horrible to think about what's going on in there," I said as I shuddered with disgust.

"I know, but that doesn't mean it's our job to burst down their doors and save everyone. Tara, honey, we just don't have the numbers. As you said, we've got the elderly and kids. Let's defend our land and OUR family," he said.

I couldn't really argue with him; I knew what he was saying was right. The injustice of it all just pissed me off. All we could do was train ourselves to be a fighting force. I doubted the kids would be screaming "Wolverines" a-la *Red Dawn* any time soon, but we just had to try. As soon as we got home and got everyone settled, I planned to talk to Jacob and my dad about training us. Both of them had been in the military and were our best chance if we were to defend our home and property.

I spent the next 20 minutes in silence playing with Carson. Brandon had taken us at least an hour out of our way, trying to avoid crossing any of our previous paths. The temperature was starting to plummet the longer we drove. I looked in the back of the truck. If nobody got sick, it would be a miracle. Our friends were all huddled together, trying to stay warm while they bounced around every dirt road in the county.

"Babe, you've got to get us home before they freeze to death," I said, pointing back at our friends.

"I know, I know. I'm just trying to avoid crossing the main roads. Give me 15 more minutes," he said.

It was cold in the cab of the truck with the shot-out window, but at least we had a heater blowing full blast on us. I couldn't imagine what it was like in the cold steel bed of the old pickup. As we rounded the final corner before our house, we saw a roadblock set up across the road.

"God, what now?" I whined.

Four men stood with their rifles pointed at our truck. We stopped a good hundred feet from them.

"Can we help you?" Brandon said, rolling down his window.

"Yeah, you can tell us what you're doing here," a tall man with an unruly amount a facial hair said.

Brandon leaned forward. "Ryan?"

The man got a little closer to the truck while lowering his rifle. "Brandon, damn, what are you doing out here?" Ryan asked.

Ryan, I knew that name. He was one of the pilots that lived at the south end of the airport runway. Brandon and Ryan had been on the same team while playing pool at our local dive bar.

"Trying to get home from a friend's house. The town has gone all to hell," he said. Brandon hopped out of the truck to fill Ryan in about "The Boss" and the danger everyone was in.

I turned around and sat on my feet. "Is everyone okay? We're almost there."

All I got was a few nods. It was so damn cold. I could smell water in the air. If I had to guess, the skies would open at any minute and drop either ice or snow on us. We needed to get indoors and get warm. I was worried about Keith. He had taken the drug the pharmacist had given us, but it didn't seem to be helping. I was just spinning around in the seat to yell at Brandon when he got back in the truck.

"Ryan said they've seen a couple of trucks driving by, but nobody stopped. He thought maybe it was just more of our neighbors. They set up the roadblock to try and keep strangers out of our area. The problem is we don't really know that many neighbors," Brandon said.

We pulled up to our stalled car entrance at the bottom of the driveway. Max and Dillon moved the cars out of the way for us to drive by. I guess we were really letting the kids do watch now. I had to remember that both of those "kids" were bigger and taller than me. Max could grow to 10 feet tall, and I would always think of him as my baby. Like before, everyone pilled out of the house to welcome us when we pulled in. I saw Austin and Julie tense up, then relax as my mom hugged both of them.

The house was warm and felt wonderful after the long trip home from Alicia's. I took Carson out of his car seat and headed to the kitchen to make him a bottle. My family was baby crazy, but none more so than my dad. Bill immediately scooped Carson out of my arms and walked off, cooing at him. I just rolled my eyes. When I walked into my bedroom, I did notice Brody and Ryler's old pack and play was set up in mine and Brandon's room. Babies were all fun and games until it came time for some sleep. Then it became a game of "not it."

I must have been sleeping hard. It was dark when I opened my eyes. I could hear the voices of way too many people as I sat up. I felt like I had a hangover. Going days with little sleep, followed by several hours of constant "on the go," always gave me the "hangover headache." I groaned as I left my dark bedroom and walked into chaos. My dad and Jacob were having an argument at the far end of my extended living room. Carson was crying while poor little Julie was trying to soothe him by bouncing him up and down. Austin was sitting at the table with Max and Dillon drawing something on a large piece of paper. All three were arguing and pointing at the paper. Kayla was painting her fingernails, of all things, and Jalyn was chasing two naked running kids. All the while, the dogs were barking. "Oh, what the fuck?" I thought to myself.

"See why Scratch and I sleep out in the workshop?" A.J. said, walking by me with a shit-eating grin to see what the boys were drawing.

Hell, at this point, I may need to join him in the workshop just for some peace and quiet. I walked into the kitchen, where my mother was making dinner. "Any idea what's going on?"

"Nope, the guys started talking about the best defense strategies, and all hell broke loose. Brandon is out on patrol with Keith. I was just about to take them some dinner unless you would like to do it?" She said.

"God, yes," I said.

I gather up what looked to be more canned chicken with rice and vegetables. It smelled wonderful. I had only tried to "help" with dinner once. After I lit my sleeve on fire, my father handed me a rifle and told me to go outside.

Chapter 19

I found Jess sitting on my porch steps. She had curled herself up into a ball. "Hey, sweetheart, are you okay?" I asked, sitting down next to her.

"I'm fine; I was just thinking about my parents. Is it wrong that I still miss them some? My dad wasn't always like that, a drunk. That didn't start until I was in 6th grade. We lived on a different farm then. The government came to our farm and wanted my dad to grow some kind of special corn. When he said no, they took our farm away. After that, my dad started drinking. When I was little, he taught me how to ride a horse. Mom used to get mad at him because we would be outside all day with the horses. In the last few years, he got really angry all the time," she said as tears made tracks down her face.

"Honey, it will always be okay to miss them. Always hang on to those memories of him. It sounds like he went into a depression after he lost his farm. Sometimes people with mental illness do things they don't understand," I said as I hugged her to me.

"I don't even know what happened to my mom. She used to have two beers a day. She said it made her a better mom. She didn't start the heavy drinking until we moved here to grandma's farm. Dad just made her so mad. They would fight all the time. I would have to stay in my bedroom with the radio turned up really loud, so I didn't hear them. My mom was okay, but she always called me a "daddy's girl," she said.

"I'm so sorry this happened to you. How about you and I take this dinner down to Brandon and Keith. We can make sure they aren't getting into any trouble. You know how guys are," I said. This made Jess smile as she straightened up, took a deep breath, and followed me into the night.

I found Keith first down by the end of the driveway. He was sitting in one of the stalled cars we were using to block the drive.

"Hey, I brought you some dinner," I said, handing him the warm plate.

"Thank you, your mom is one heck of a cook," he said as he lifted the foil.

"Cooking definitely wasn't a skill I inherited from her," I said, laughing.

"Oh, I heard all about you trying to burn your arm off making rice. Tell me, did you get further than boiling water?" He said grinning.

"Ha ha ha, funny stuff. Have you seen anything out here tonight?" I asked.

"I saw headlights about a mile up the road. It was probably just the roadblock, guys. Brandon said they had been patrolling this area," he answered, taking a huge bite.

"I hope so. We're going to take Brandon his dinner. Have you seen him?" I asked.

"I haven't seen him since we came out for patrols. I'm sure he's up in the pasture," Keith said.

I looked down at my belt only to see I hadn't brought one of the two-way radios out with me. Now I was going to have to walk the whole area looking for him. Jess and I walked in companionable silence for a good twenty minutes before we found Brandon perched up high on a rock.

"Hey babe, I brought you some dinner. It's probably cold now," I said. Jess and I moved back as he leaped off the rock about 5 feet down to the ground. "You had better be careful doing that. The last thing we need is for you to break something."

"I'm fine. I was just getting ready to head back. Your dad radioed a minute ago. He asked everyone to come to the house for a meeting. You got any idea?" He said. Brandon shoveled food in his face while we walked.

"Nope, my mom said there was some fighting about our security. Other than that, it could be anything. Our house is a crazy zone. Kids running, dogs barking. That kind of thing," I said.

"You wouldn't have it any other way, would you?" He said with his best shit-eating grin.

The three of us opened the house's front door to see everyone already gathered in the living room. I could hear kids and dogs off in one of the bedrooms but saw only Julie, Carson, and Jalyn's boys were missing. Max and Dillon were sitting in on the meeting. I hated the idea but understood the necessity.

"We need to wait a few minutes before we start. The guys from the roadblock are coming down to talk about how we can best secure our area," said Jacob.

"Tara, they want to put your kids into training with guns and teach them how to kill. I know Max did what he had to do after you left the school, but I think teaching the kids is going too far," Hazel said while giving Jacob the evil eye.

I glanced over at Max and Dillon. Max was head down, looking at the floor. "And what do the boys think of that idea?"

"I want to do it!" Dillon said, perking up.

"We live here too. If we have to fight, we should know how to. What if something happened to one of you?" He said, looking around the room.

We all knew this was a huge possibility. As a group, we have some skills, but we were definitely no Delta Strike Force team. One of us could die anytime we leave this house.

"Max?" I asked.

"I agree with Dillon. I asked Jess about it when we heard Tupaw fighting with Jacob, she doesn't want to fight, but she wants to learn," he said.

I looked at Brandon; I wanted him to say no, that they were too young. They were almost sixteen, sure, but not old enough to fight a war.

"Tara, this is a different world than it was even two weeks ago. The kids need to learn the skills to survive," he said.

"Okay fine, I guess the kids can train with us. I don't like it, but they need to learn," I said.

There was a knock on the door then. I looked out the glass to see nothing but hair looking back at me.

"Ryan's here," I said, letting him and a few other men in.

This was really the first time in a long time I had seen Ryan. I remember him being an attractive man under all that hair. I love beards, but Ryan was starting to look like an extra from a ZZ Top video.

Keith stood to take the floor then. "Ryan, did you see anybody else on patrols but us coming back from town today?"

"I saw a car drive by up the road from ya. Were you out driving tonight?" He asked.
"No, that means someone is out there besides us. Like we told you earlier, it's that guy from Guthrie looking for the airport. I think putting the planes in hangers and pulling down the sign may have helped us some, but it's only a matter of time before they find us. If I had to guess, we should be ready for an attack at any time," Keith said.

"How many of us are there? I asked.

"How many are okay with fighting; how many of us that are willing to help and defend the airstrip?" Ryan asked.

"What do you mean by "okay with fighting""? People hopefully understand we're dealing with the damn apocalypse here," I asked.

"There are two families down by my place that said they want nothing to do with any fighting," Ryan said, shaking his furry head.

"It's not like ANY of us like the idea of fighting and hurting people. I might think the same thing if I hadn't been out there and seen the things I've seen or known the guys that were coming for us," I said, slouching down on the couch.

"Regardless, it puts us at six people for the south end of the airstrip," Ryan said.

"Is that enough people to guard the road on the East and the South end of the Airstrip? We have fourteen adults down here, and I feel like we're still stretched trying to cover the road and acreage," My dad said.

"We just do what we need to do," said Ryan.

The next hour was spent going over and over plans for how to defend our area. After the first time I heard them repeat, I volunteered to go on patrol. I slung my gun on its strap over my shoulder, pulled down my beanie, and took off. I was almost to the end of the drive when I heard the whispering. I was walking on the side of the driveway in the grass when I heard it. I stopped, wondering if I was just going crazy or had actually heard it when it started again.

"We'll sneak up around the back of the house, and you come up the front saying you just want to talk to them about renting a plane. Then while they're distracted, you come in the back," a male voice said.

"But, "The Boss," said they have to be alive to fly the plane," another voice said.

I heard a smack like someone had been slapped in the face after that comment.
"Duh stupid, but they can't all be pilots. We take the women and kill all the dudes as long as they ain't pilots," the first male voice said.

I could hear an eye roll in that sentence as clear as if he had said it out loud. "Would you two idiots shut the fuck up? What good is it to sneak up on anyone if your dumbasses are going to talk the entire time? Geez," a much deeper and gruffer voice said.

I yanked my radio off my pants and turned it down as long as it would go. "Jess! Jess! I don't know if you can hear me, but we are under attack. I repeat under attack!" I whispered into my handheld radio.

I remembered baby Carson crying the whole time we had our meeting. I can only hope one of the kids was sitting next to the radio. Nobody answered me back. I was almost six hundred yards from the house now. All I could do was hunker down behind a giant bush. I nearly squeaked in protest as the thorns from the bush pushed into my body. I had to slowly make myself go into the bush. If I didn't, the guys might see me when they walked past me up the drive.
It was only another minute before the men got to my position. Two men came walking up the drive. I could see from my place in the damn thorns they were heavily armed. I could hear boots clomping around me but couldn't tell how many there were.

I kept looking at the house. I could see shadows moving around in the house, but I couldn't tell if they were in a hurry or just still arguing over strategy. As the men got further away from me and closer to my home, I tried Jess on the radio again.

"Jess, two guys are walking up to the door now, and an unknown number was planning to break in from the back. Please let everyone know," I whispered again into my radio.

"Of all the times for us to have a meeting!" I thought, almost slapping myself in the forehead. Why in the world didn't we have anyone on patrol while we did it? I was continually having to remind myself that we were not a trained military force but a group of out of shape adults, the elderly, and children.

I saw the two in the front knocking on the front door now, pistols tucked in the back of their jeans. I couldn't actually see they were there in the dark, but I figured from the way one of the guys kept his hand on his hip. It was a quick movement to reach back and draw from his waistband.

Light spilled out of the house, and A.J. stepped out on the front porch. I knew AJ had a gun on him; the man slept with a nine-millimeter on his pillow. I had asked him before if he would skip wearing it for meals. Brody and Ryler were always asking to "see" it. He had always told them, no, but I had worried about them getting a hold of it all the same. It was only after our first trip to Alicia's house that we all started wearing them. Brandon and I both slept with handguns on our respective nightstands. Now I was damn grateful. Every Adult and teenager in that house carried at least one gun.

Raised voices caught my attention back at the front porch. I had to guess whatever the guys were trying to pull over on AJ that AJ wasn't buying it. I watched the two men; when I saw one of the guys go for their gun, I yelled, "A.J.! Gun!"

The guy with the gun pulled it out only to have it knocked out of his hands, and the second guy was looking for me. There weren't exactly many places I could be hiding, but these two didn't exactly look like the group's brain trust. The idiot even looked up a few times.

I heard the report of a shotgun then. It was loud even this far away. If Jess was unable to hear my whispering over the radio, the people inside might be in trouble.

I glanced at the porch where A.J. was punching and rolling around on the porch with one of them. Max had the other one at gunpoint. The second guy was on his knees now, with his hands up.
Multiple shots started going off in the house. If they hadn't gotten my alert, they knew what was happening now.

Five-six-seven-eight, shots. I climbed out of the bush and started to make a break for the house. I was running as fast as I could to get to my family. My babies were all in that house.
Pain bloomed through my body and spun me in a circle. It was like a blazing hot knife spreading all through me. I stumbled, trying to keep myself up and moving, but the pain was so extreme. One second I'm running, and next, everything went black. I could hear a buzzing sound as I fell to the ground. Then nothing, as I followed the noise to quiet.

I woke up to arguing. I could feel multiple people around me. I was lying in my own bed. The next thing I noticed was the pain in my left shoulder. Oh my God, it felt like someone had poured molten lava into my shoulder.

"Holy crap, what happened?" I gritted through my teeth.

"You got really damn lucky," I heard a voice that might have been Hazel say.

I pried my eyes open. It felt like they were glued shut; they were so heavy. I opened my eyes to see Hazel and my mom sitting on each side of the bed. Little Ryler was sitting by my feet, patting my foot.
I tried to sit up, but the pain started in my arm and ran down my whole body. I had seen people in movies take bullets a million times and just keep going. Well, this was no action movie, and I was sure as hell no action hero. Hell, I wasn't even an A.J.; he had taken a graze in the truck on the way to Alicia's the other day. He just wrapped the damn thing up and kept moving.

"The bullet was a through and through to the fatty part of your arm. If we had to guess, which of course we are, it might have gone through some of the muscle. Without machines, we don't have; there's just no way to be sure," Hazel said.

"We radioed over to Alicia's to talk to Mike and ask him what to do. He walked us through the wrapping and cleaning part, and AJ stitched the holes closed the best he could. Alicia was freaking out.

I told her I would let her know as soon as you woke up," My mom said.

My mom stood to leave, but I stopped her. "Wait, was anyone hurt? What happened to the men that attacked us?" I asked. My mom sighed and sat back down.

"Max held the man on the front porch at gunpoint until AJ shot and killed the second man in the wrestling match on the patio. Then A.J. took some of Brandon's zip ties and restrained the guy. He's currently in the storm seller locked up until we can decide what to do with him. We think there were at least three men that tried to come to the back of the house. Jess came running out of the bedroom with Carson yelling how we were under attack just in time for Brandon, your dad, and the others to snap into action. The guys that came up the back used a shotgun to blow open the back door lock. They would have gotten into the house, but the dogs attacked. We know at least one guy got away because we saw him jump the fence to get away from the dogs and take off. If I had to guess, that was the one that shot you. The man with the shotgun and one other guy is dead," My mom said.

"What about all the shots I heard? That's why I came running towards the house without cover," I said.

"When the last guy jumped the fence and took off running, one of Ryan's people shot after him. We looked around all day today but didn't see anything in the way of blood. They must have had a truck or something hidden around here somewhere," Mom said.

"All day, what time is it?" I asked, trying and failing again to sit up.

"It's about 8:00pm. You've been asleep for almost 18 hours," Mom said.

I really looked at my mom then. She was pale with dark bags under her eyes. She looked horrible.
Hazel helped me prop myself up on pillows so everyone could come in and say "hi" over the next hour. I was already so tired it was all I could do to keep my eyes open.

Chapter 20

The next few days went by in a blur of activity. Jacob was running shooting drills with everyone who wanted to learn how. My dad was going over all the current defenses with Ryan and the other new guys down the airstrip. A.J. spent his time with Dillon and Max planning new ways to defend the area, and then there was me. I pretty much sat on my ass in the living room with baby Carson in my lap. Brandon had bound my arm down to my body, so movement wasn't quite as painful as it had been. Don't get me wrong, it still hurt like a bitch, but at least I could get out of bed now.

Keith, my dad, and Ryan had been down in the storm cellar, talking to the man who tried to invade our house. Our storm cellar "guest" had done very little in the way of speaking. They guys said he just sat in the corner crying. For now, we would just keep an eye on him.

Ryan and his guys came by last night to go over strategy for the millionth time in like three days. What had happened the other night had really shaken us to the core. It showed our weaknesses and gave us a good starting point for where to go next. Until the other night, we had just gotten lucky nobody had found us who wanted to start problems.

I asked A.J. what the guys on the porch had talked about when the shooting started. The man asked A.J. if this was an airport. He looked at a paper map, and it showed a small private airstrip in this area. A.J. had told him that he wasn't sure where the airstrip was located, but it wasn't here. I guess they argued back and forth a while before the shooting at the back door had happened.

Our big problem was the one that got away. If that one guy went back to "The Boss" and told him that we probably were the pilots he had been looking for, we would soon come under attack again. Not only would they attack again, but I doubted they would only bring a handful of guys.

I played with baby Carson after my conversation with A.J. when I heard loud stomping on my roof. "What the hell?" I said to an empty room.

Pulling Carson up into my one good arm using an inchworm type movement, I tapped at the door to my house until one of the kids opened it for us. "What are you doing?" I asked, looking up to see Max and A.J. holding what looked like small walls in front of them.

"This will give us the ability to shoot from the roof while still being able to stay behind cover," Max yelled down at me.

I would have asked more questions, but my voice was covered by the sounds of hammering. This, of course, made Carson start to cry. If being quiet was one of our strategies, we sucked at it.

"I can take him," Jess said as she bounced up to me.

"Thank you, honey. How are you today?" I asked.

"I'm good today; your mom has been showing me how to cook when I'm not having to work the radios. I love it!" She said, bouncing little Carson as she walked into the house.

She was in a much better mood than a few days ago. There had to be more of a reason behind it than cooking. Yuck, who got excited to cook? This thought alone gave me a shiver.

To the North of my home was where Kayla's trailer sat. Next to her driveway was apparently now our shooting range, from its looks. Dillon, Jacob, and a couple of guys from Ryan's group, I didn't remember their names, were in a straight line shooting cans off the fence. I did notice Jalyn standing behind Ryan. He turned around, placed the handgun in her hands, and then proceeded to stand behind her and help her line up her shot.

"Huh, I wonder what's going on there," I said to myself. Only to almost piss my pants when Austin said from behind me, "Is that her boyfriend?" I squeaked and spun around. Austin thought this was hilarious and ran off to join the shooters.

I walked about eight hundred yards to the bottom of our drive to find my husband deep in conversation with Keith.

"What are you guys doing?" I asked, strolling up to stand next to Brandon.

"Well, we're planting pipe bombs," Brandon said without really even looking up at me.

"Pipe bombs, what the fuck Brandon?" I asked. The tone of my voice made Keith start backing away slowly.

"While you were resting, A.J. came up with the idea to make pipe bombs. So we've been making them and setting them up here at the end of the road. They might not work at all, and even if they do, this is so far from the house that nobody will be injured," he said with a sigh like I was the one asking stupid questions.

"Listen, I don't give a fuck if A.J. is the original Unabomber! What happens if you get the mixtures wrong and blow your face off? Please get rid of that shit. We have too many people walking patrols at night to have them accidentally stumble into a bomb. I love that you guys are trying to keep us safe, but please look for a different way. I love you, and we've been through too much for me to lose you now," I said.

"Awe, that's so sweet, thank you. I haven't known you that long, but I love you too," A.J. said from behind me.

I turned on him, which made A.J. take a few steps back until he tripped over a downed tree branch and fell on his butt. "Thank you for trying this, but we have teens patrolling these areas. I'm sorry, but it's just not safe."

The guys had all broken out in loud, guffawing laughter while I was walking away. I rubbed my hand over my face. "Good Lord."

Hazel and my mother came around the back corner of our house. We had set a large water basin behind the house for clothes washing. We were using water from the pool. Our clothes were cleaner but still smelled like the city pool.

"Tara, what are you yelling about? I could hear you all the way from behind the house," my mother said, coming abreast of me.

"Mom, did you know that A.J. taught the guys how to make pipe bombs and that they are setting them at the end of the driveway?" I asked.

"Yes, we all talked about the bombs and decided it would be a good way to take out as many possible without posing any risk to us up here in the house," she said in her soothing mom voice.

"Fine, but when one of those guys blows their ass off, I don't want to hear about it," I said, spinning on my heel and taking my ass back in the house.

I walked into the radio room where Jess, Jalyn, and the boys slept. Carson was cooing at a singing Jess. They looked so sweet, I immediately felt all my crazy melt away. I got onto the bed next to the kids and just listened to Jess sing to the baby. I was just starting to doze off when the radio came on, and I heard Alicia's voice come over the airwave.

"Tara, are you there?" She asked, sounding pissed off about something.

I chuckled; with the radio, it was almost like old times. Alicia and I haven't gone a day without speaking for nearly 23 years. No matter where we were. Even on vacation, we called and checked in with one another.
"Yes, I'm here. What's up?"

"It's this new neighborhood watch! They got together and decided we should pool all our resources so they could be distributed "fairly," she said in a huff.

I could actually hear the air quotes in her sentence. "I guess you didn't know you moved into a neighborhood of socialists," I giggled.

"Sharing isn't the problem. I have no issue with helping anyone in this neighborhood; it's the fact that the head jackass has actually issued an order for us to do it. Oh! Jackass also wants to take my radio. He said the community needed it more than just one person. I told him anyone who wanted to could come and use the radio, but it's not leaving this house. I swear Tara, I actually saw him go for his gun before he stopped himself," she huffed.

"Shit, do you think things will get violent over there? That guy sounds kind of crazy. Is he a big military or cop looking dude? I kinda think he looks like The Rock, but less hot," I said.

"How did you know? Michael had been dealing with him before now. The guy actually came to my house. He said his name was Officer Jackson. Like we even have cops anymore. We can't really leave here. I've already got my plants started in pots, and I just have too much stuff I would have to move. That's if he even let us take our stuff. I can't exactly start a war with some guy over a years' worth of rice. Arg, he just makes me so damn mad!" She almost screamed into the radio.

Carson, who had just gotten to sleep, was now crying. "Sorry, Jess," I said, looking over my shoulder to a now glaring Jess. Jess picked the baby up and left the room.

"At least we put most of our food storage up in the attic. If they come now, all they would find is one bucket of each staple. That's something, at least," she said in a calmer tone. 'How're things over there. Is it driving you crazy not being able to do stuff with that busted arm?"

I spent the next several minutes telling her all about the crazy going on here with our new explosive experts. She got a huge kick out of that story. I also told her how Jalyn was getting closer to Ryan. Lots of gossip between our two homes, and we ended up talking for almost an hour before signing off.

The next few days were quiet. The group, which was more like a family, now spent the days in constant preparation and our nights on guard duty. We knew if people were coming for us, it would probably be at night. The waiting was making us all a little on edge.

Max came almost skipping into the house last night. While wearing a huge shit-eating grin on his face only to tell Brandon that, "The crazy redneck guy is gutting and skinning a squirrel on your pool table, dad." Poor Brandon looked like his heart might just stop. My husband had saved for that pool table for months and treated it like a newborn.

"Nobody gets next to the table with any kind of food or drinks," Brandon had said on the day it was delivered. I was pretty sure he had named it and was talking to it when he was alone.
I really figured he would flip out, but he just left the room to mourn the loss of his outdoor man cave.

On the sixth day after the attack, I felt much better and moved my arm some. I had called Mike on the radio to tell him the good news, only to be told it probably just went through fatty tissue. I ended that call abruptly. Thank God for flabby arm fat, I guess.

It wasn't until the seventh day when we were woken up to an explosion, that we saw any real action. The boom has loud, we came running out of rooms, still half asleep, and it was only about

4am. I had just gotten off guard duty with Jalyn and Max at 2am. Everywhere I look, people are trying to throw on clothes and load guns.

In the background, I heard the radio go off with a squawk, "False alarm! False alarm!" I could hear Brandon's voice coming through the speaker.

Everybody came running to the end of the drive to see what looked like pieces of deer hanging from the trees. Everything was covered in blood; the cars we parked at the end of the drive looked like a horror movie gone wrong. As karma would have it, Brandon and A.J. had been the two on duty at the time. Both of them were soaked in blood. Before Brandon could even open his mouth to defend himself, a chunk of Bambi fell out of the tree, hitting him on the head.

"My bad, my bad. I saw the deer coming towards me and panicked, thinking it was those guys again. Sorry," Brandon said while spitting blood and trying to wipe his eyes with his soaked sleeve.

"This is why I said NO BOMBS!" I told Brandon as I walked away. I seriously doubt he even heard me. He was close enough to the blast to look like a chain saw killer. He was coved head to toe in Bambi bits.
I looked over just in time for Jess to run behind the tree and vomit. Kayla and a few others didn't look far behind her. There was nothing left for me to do but throw my hands up and walk away.

Since I was clearly not going back to sleep, I decided to go down to the storm cellar and talk to our special guest. We had been taking down food and water for the past week and cleaning his uhm, bucket. This poor man was almost comatose; we really had no idea what to do with him. He picked at his food but just seemed to have lost his will. Today didn't look much different for him. I opened the door, and the stench hit me right in the face.

"Okay, that's it! You stand up and come out here," I said as I tried not to gag.

We had given him a washrag and a bucket of washing water. This man, however, had chosen not to use it. The man stood up and looked at me. "What was that? Did another bomb go off?" He asked, looking almost confused.

I just tossed a day pack at him. It had what he needed to get far away from here. "Wait, you're letting me go?" He asked.

"Yep, ya stink. I'm not just going to sit around waiting for you to either talk to me or die of asphyxiation because you won't clean yourself. If you want to go running back to your boss and tell him where we are, there isn't much I can do to stop you short of putting a bullet through your head. That wouldn't make me any better than your leader," I said as I covered my nose and backed away.

"That man was not my leader!" The man yelled as he fell to the ground.

"Okay, if he isn't your leader, what is he, your friend?" I asked.

"No! I was in the county jail for a DUI when the lights went out. Things happened so fast that day. I saw the guards all running, and they were yelling about a bomb. I didn't know what kind of bomb had gone off until later. One of the guys being booked into the jail saw a TV broadcaster freaking out, yelling, "they dropped the big one." The cop that was booking him in started to freak out and just tossed him in the closest cell. We sat in the dark for hours, all of us trapped behind bars. We had no idea where our families were or if they were okay. The guards wouldn't tell us anything, and I mean nothing. About the time the sun came up, the generators keeping the doors locked failed. It was crazy; the inmates killed all the guards that hadn't already run off and started stealing weapons before their bodies were even cold. The cops who ran off had taken some of the guns with them, so they were literally killing each other trying to get the best guns. I just ran; I had to jump over piles of bodies to get to the front door. When I got to the front, that's when I saw the mob running towards town. They started setting fire to all the buildings. I can only imagine what they did to the people in the buildings. I just wanted to get back home. My mom was supposed to pick me up that next morning, but I never saw her. I walked up and down the blocks looking for her car, I found it, but I never found her," the man looked up at me from where he was sitting in the grass. 'I got her killed. My drinking killed my mom."

"I'm sorry about your mom," I said, sitting across from him in the grass. I could feel people behind me, but I didn't want to break whatever spell that had made him talk. "What's your name, sir?"

"Beaux, my name's Beaux," he replied.

"Okay, Beaux, how did you get mixed up with the group you were with that came out here?" I asked.

"While I was searching the streets block by block for my mom, I ran into a couple of guys from the jail. They said everyone was meeting up at the grocery store. I was still hungover and thought he meant the townspeople. I know I sound like an idiot, and hell, I probably am. Once I got into the store, I found out real quick they did not mean the townspeople. I saw women and girls being herded to the store's back from the second I walked in. They were all screaming and crying. I walked to the back of the store to see if my mom was in the group. She wasn't, but the walk to the back of the store saved my life. Some of the guys in the store turned to walk out when they saw what was happening. They were shot and tossed out in the parking lot. I took a seat with the others; I didn't know what else to do! There was a man that came in then. He was this short little dumpy fat guy. He came in and started shooting this big shotgun into the ceiling. Then he started shouting out orders like he owned the place. I was about to get up when he pointed his gun at our group on the floor," Beaux explained.

Then the dumpy guy said to everyone there, "Are you guys going to fall in line or die like the other cowards in the parking lot?" He took turns, pointing his gun at us one by one. 'That was when I knew I was in real trouble." Beaux said, looking up at me.

Tears were now streaming down his face. "I never even knew his name; the other guys just called him "Boss." I saw some really horrible shit in that grocery store. Stuff I don't want to talk about. When Boss started putting teams together to look for some airplanes, I volunteered. Anything to get me out of that store and away from that guy. I thought I would run, but Boss sent one of his trusted "lieutenants" with every group that left. You know the rest of the story. We came here, and everyone but me died," Beaux said.

I decided not to tell him one of the attackers had gotten away that night by going over the fence and into the woods. "Okay, Beaux, what's next for you? If I let you go, are you going to run back to the Boss or go make a life somewhere else?" I asked.

"You would let me go after what we did?" He whispered.

"Well, you can either go look for your mother or another family to ride out the apocalypse with, or you can die in my storm cellar. Take your pick," I said, standing up and dusting off.

My mother must have known I would let him go because she stood behind me with a target sack with a blanket and some water with even more supplies.

Beaux stood and thanked my mother and me with a head nod. He slowly reached out for the target bag without breaking eye contact, I guess, in case we were going to kill him or something. Taking the bag, he turned and walked away.

"Do you think that was a smart move, babe?" Asked Brandon, who had come up behind me.

I just shrugged my shoulders and walked into the house. This day had worn my ass out, and I was ready to pass out.

Chapter 21

I slept through most of the day. I woke up the same way I always did, covered in my own sweat from another night of nightmares. Last night was my least favorite. I dreamt I never made it to the high school for Max and the other kids. The kids spent every day crying because I never came to get them, or some nights they even joined the gang in the grocery store. Those nights were the worst, followed by dreams of Brandon and Kayla being killed on their way home to me. I knew those dreams were crazy because we lived the absolute best-case scenario, but it didn't stop the screaming, I guess.

When I rolled over, I saw little Ryler giving me his big goofy smile. He moved so close we were almost nose to nose. "Hi Gigi, you no sleep now?" He asked in his cute little sing-song voice.

"Hi there, Mr. Curley, how are you today?" I asked as I poked him in the ribs with my fingertip. This always made him jump and squeal with laughter, causing his shinny blonde curls to bounce.

Jalyn came through my door while we were tickle fighting. "Ryler, what have I told you about letting Gigi sleep?" She said, giving me an "I'm sorry" glance in my direction.

"Gigi, no sleeping now," Ryler said in his most indignant tone, but he got up and ran to his mother, wrapping his chubby little arms around her neck to give her a kiss as they walked from the room.

With the early sunset, I was guessing it was about dinner time. I stood in my shower with a bucket of insanely cold water and attempted to wash the stink of fear sweat off my body. I felt gross. It seemed like no matter how many of these spit baths I took, I would never be clean again.

At my dinner table, I sat down to enjoy our usual meal of beans and rice with a side of some kind of flatbread A.J. had taught my mother to make. I was quiet this evening. Even little baby Carson looked a little morose this evening. If everyone was feeling anything like me, it was going to be a hard winter. Hard living, hard patrols, and hell, it was even hard to take a bath. We had all decided that we would heat our bathing water as little as possible to avoid running out of fuel except for the children.

When Brandon and I had made these plans initially, we really only thought we would be a group of about six, not the fifteen souls that lived in this house right now. Keith, Hazel, Jacob, and the two children we had found on our trip to town came in and out of our home the same way our group seemed to migrate towards their house when they needed some quiet. Even with a couple of people staying out in the garage with A.J., it was still crowded as hell in this house.

The group had had multiple conversations about moving some of our people into either my parent's house or Kayla's. The problem with that idea was that we would spread ourselves too thin to defend all of the homes if we split everyone up. The houses were just too far apart to take the risk, so we stayed together in one central location-overcrowded as it may be.

"Your mother and I have come to a decision," my dad said, coming to sit next to me at the table.

I continued eating; this wasn't the first time I had listened to the "we want to be at home speech."
"Okay, and what have you decided?" I asked as I shoveled food into my already full mouth.

"It's time, Tara. Your mom and I have already moved our things back to our house. It's only next door, and Connor is going to stay with us to help keep watch. It's been a while since we've had any raids on the property, and we're hoping the guy is going to give up and look somewhere else. There's no way this is the only place on earth with people who can fly a damn plane. Surely that guy realizes he is just wasting manpower. We've killed how many of his guys now?" He said. My dad stood, clapped his hand on my shoulder, and walked out of the house.

My mother just rolled her eyes. "I swear it's like we don't live right next door and eat all our meals together," she said as she was cleaning the bean pot with a shake of her head.

I just sighed. Who in the hell was I anyway to tell them to stay close. They were grown-ass people. With that last thought, I stood, taking my plate to the kitchen to wash. I kissed my mom on the cheek and grabbed my weapons to head outside.

"Damn, Damn, Damn, it's freezing out here," I squeaked at A.J. as I made my way off the porch.

Oklahoma weather was always a mystery, even when we had the news to tell us the forecast. Today was probably in the '30s, but it had to be down in the teens with wind chills. I made my way to the end of the road to see who was on watch duty. I looked around but didn't see anyone.

"What the hell?" I was just starting to raise my weapon when I heard Brandon speak. "Up here, babe."

"Up where? I don't see you..." then I did see them. Somehow today, in the freezing cold, Brandon and Max had built a treehouse looking thing. It was wrapped tightly with branches and cedar trees. It wasn't huge, about eight feet up in the air. It was just big enough for two people to sit comfortably.

"Wow, guys, aren't you freezing to death up there in all this wind?" I asked while shielding my face.

"Nope, we insulated it with pine needles and extra blankets. We have spots on each side to look out of so we can see all the way down the road," Max said proudly as he practically leaped his way down the side of the tree.

My husband followed next, but a hell of a lot slower. When he finally reached the ground, he turned to me with the biggest grin I had seen on his beautiful face in weeks. "Pretty cool, huh? A.J. helped us blend in so I wouldn't be seen unless you were looking for it. Aren't you glad now I never got around to clearing all the trees from our road as you asked?" His big cheesy grin on full display.

I just laughed. What else could I do? "Did my dad tell you they're moving back to their house today?" I asked when he was done patting himself on the back.

"Yep, he told me this morning. There was no arguing with him, so I helped him get his house set up. Dillon and Jacob chopped wood for the fireplace, and we moved the master bedroom bed into the living room so they could keep warm. I think with their dogs helping to keep watch, it should be okay," he said as he started to bounce with the cold.

Tonight was just Jess and me on this side of the property. Thankfully the guys, being all "manly" and shit, had decided we should spend the first night in the treehouse, as it had been dubbed. That was just fine with me. It was still cold, but between the insulation in the floor and walls and the thermos of hot water my mom brought to us earlier, it really wasn't that bad.

"It's not hot chocolate, but at least it's hot," I said, handing her a cup. Jess took the cup out of my hands and used it to warm her hands. She was looking down at the water and rolling it up and down in her hands.

"Are you okay, hon?" I asked, seeing something was eating at her.

"How long do you think this is going to last? Like how long before things go back to ya know, normal?"

I took a second to get my words together before I began to speak. "Well, I'm not sure if things will ever be like they were before the bombs dropped. I'm sure eventually there will be a new version of normality, I guess. I'm not sure, but I think this is normal for the next few years," I said.
"Well, we haven't really ever talked about it, but with your parents moving out now, I guess I will probably have to go too, ya know, I mean, I guess," she said.

"Okay, kiddo, let me stop you right there. I want you here. Not just now or until the lights come back on. I want you here until you turn like forty and decide it's time to get married. You're one of my kids now. That's just kind of how it's going to go," I was abruptly cut off when she threw her arms around my neck. This poor kid had taken my "spend the apocalypse with us" comment to heart. I felt like dog shit for not telling her she was stuck with us sooner.

Jess and I's watch shift was just about over when we heard the purr of an engine. It was a quiet night; living out here for the past forty-two years, I knew all the animals' familiar sounds and the trees scraping the window. This engine was coming down the main road and growing closer. Jess was on the radio calling all the troops by the time it got to our driveway and stopped.

I could see now it was a truck. It was full of men with guns. They made no move to get out but just sat in the back. They looked like they were half-frozen to death as it was. The door to the truck opened then, and a short, fat, balding man stepped out and walked to the end of our driveway.

My heart pounded like it was going to beat right out of my chest. I knew this man. This is the prisoner Jacob and I had run into on our way to get the kids from school. I remembered his sweaty face as he almost ran into us that day. We had actually talked to him.

I knew before I even heard the driver talking who this man was going to end up being. It was only a few seconds before I was proved right. "Hey boss, this is the drive. Do you want the guys to go up and bring them out to ya?" Somebody, I guessed the driver, said to the man.

The "boss" looked different this time. He was wearing a fancy suit like he was some sort of New York gangster. Not exactly the *"Mad Max and the Thunder Dome"* look I was expecting.

"No, if I had to guess, we all have guns trained in on us as we speak," he said, lighting a cigarette. 'No, this time I am going to ask for their help, and if that doesn't work, then we will just kill them all and be done with it. I am sick and tired of sending you idiots to find these people. It's become increasingly obvious to me that if I want something done, I need to come and do it myself," The "boss" said with a snort of derision.

"Gentlemen, what can I do for you?" My father said as he came walking into the driveway. No, No, No. I thought as I tried to extricate myself exceptionally slowly from the treehouse. Jess was grabbing my arms and shaking her head at me.

"Hello sir, my name is William Thomas. I have a problem that I am hoping you can help me with," William said as he dropped his cigarette to the ground and rubbed it out with his foot. 'Ya see, sir, I have some business partners I need to connect with in Dallas, and from the maps I've seen, you sir have an airport," he said.

My father started to reply, but William cut him off. "Sir, let's not waste each other's time. My men here have seen two planes fly into this area. I sure hope you're not going to insult my intelligence and say you didn't know you live on a runway."

The truck men laughed at this until William put a hand up to stop, and they silenced abruptly.

"No, I wasn't going to say that, but I will tell you the planes on this runway are old crop duster planes. Everything out on this runway, including the pilots, are damn near ancient. We have a running plane from the town airport to this one, sure, but it's in no way a plane that you could or should try to fly out of state. All of the pilots that live here fly crop dusters. None of these guys have ever flown anything bigger than a fighter plane, and that guy fought in Korea and is almost eighty years old," My dad said while he stood hands on hips.

"Oh well, you see, that's funny you would say that. I know for a fact that a blonde woman somewhere in her forty's or fifty's flying one of the planes that left the Guthrie airport. So I hate to call you a liar, but I guess I will," William then pulled a pistol from his long trench coat so fast I almost missed the movement.
He walked up to my dad and held the gun to his forehead. "Now, would you like to try again?"

"I will. That would be my daughter. She never finished getting her license to fly. She panicked once, almost crashed the plane, and quit. If I was ever going to have someone take me somewhere, it definitely wouldn't be her," my dad said.

I actually heard Keith from my spot tell someone, "boy, if that isn't the truth."

Guns began to chamber all around us; thank God the cavalry had come. As part of our preparations for this day, A.J. and Max had set up stations all over our property to fire our guns in relative safety. Jessie and I still held the best position possible in our treehouse. I was putting the jackass in my crosshairs when the shot went off. The bullet went wide and hit some guy in the back of the truck. If I had to guess with an aim like that, Max had just fired his weapon. I raised my gun to retake aim, but William had run to the far side of the truck. I started firing my rifle.

The sound of the guns going off was deafening. All I was able to hear anymore was a steady buzzing in my ears. I looked over to see Jess was on the floor of our treehouse, holding her hands to her ears. I was just about to leave my side of the treehouse and climb over to her for a better look when I noticed the blood.

I dropped my gun and started to feel around on Jess. She didn't even look up at me. She just held her hands to her ears. I had to physically pull her out of the ball she had wrapped herself in. She was so tiny, we had all lost weight during the past month, but this little girl didn't have any to lose.

It was her stomach. The blood was flowing out of a bullet hole the size of my thumb. I pulled off my hat and tried to apply pressure to the wound, but the blood flowed around my hat and over my hand. It was then that I saw her cough. I could see words coming out of her mouth, but I couldn't hear them.

Chapter 22

"Jess! Jessie, sweetheart, you stay with me! You hear me, baby girl, it's going to be okay," I shouted over the cacophony of gunfire.

I had no idea if she could hear what I was saying. Between the continued gunfire and my own cries, all I could do was keep repeating myself. Jessie was losing too much blood. I grabbed the radio off Jess's belt and tried to find help at the house, but I couldn't fucking hear if anyone was answering my pleas.

I laid my body over hers then and just held her. I could feel her shallow breaths on my face. I stroked her hair over and over until the breaths stopped, and just like that, she was gone. This poor child had suffered so much in her short life. I sobbed and told her how much we all loved her. This wasn't fucking fair! She was just a little girl.
I'm not sure how long I laid with Jess; it could have been five minutes or five hours. It wasn't until I felt a hand on my foot that I even looked up. I didn't care about the war we were fighting or the truck full of men. I turned all the noise outside and everybody off. It was Brandon touching my leg now. I looked up into his tear-streaked face; he had tear tracks running down his face too.

I let him pull me towards the small door of the treehouse. The sky was just starting to lighten off to the east. There was just enough light to see the blood and bodies lying on the ground. I tried to climb down the knots in the tree we used as a ladder but fell about five feet. I didn't feel the impact of the ground or the extreme cold that hit my body now that I was out of the warm treehouse. The blood that covered my body started to cool and act like ice water being thrown on me. I felt nothing. I could see in my peripheral people from our group walking around us. Some had blood on them from their own bullets or injuries.

I couldn't even make myself ask who won. I didn't care anymore. People had died today, a child had died today, and for what? Just because I didn't want to fly some fat fuck to Dallas? I was so pissed, I was pissed at myself, and at this damn apocalypse. I stood up and took my first real look around. The truck the men had pulled up in was shot to hell. Bodies laid on the ground around it and were draped over the sides. Blood covered the ground. So much blood, the coppery tang of it floated in the air along with the body's own releases after death. That was one thing the books and movies never talked about. After the body dies, it releases its bowels. I only walked about ten feet before I started to vomit. I was bent over, throwing up everything I had ever eaten when I saw them.

Hazel and Jacob were bent over a small body. I stood up, wiping the vomit from my face. "NO, NO, NO!" I said as I stumbled to their side and slid in the dirt. Keith was lying in the grass. I couldn't see where the blood was coming from there was so much damage to his middle.

"He took a round at almost point black range with a shotgun. The bastard just came out of nowhere," Jacob sobbed.

"The guy was headed right for me; I didn't even have time to get my gun up! Keith came out of nowhere and just jumped in front of me," Hazel sobbed.

Keith lay dead in the snow. It was the first time he had looked at peace since his wife passed. My brain flashed back to the day of his wife's funeral. He sat in the front row of mourners, wearing his best and sitting with their children. He didn't cry but just sat, letting the pain wash over him. I had checked on him every day after it happened. Keith would sit in his kitchen chair with his wife's cat on his lap for hours on end. It was over a month since her passing before he started to venture out of the house. He once told me it was like losing a part of your body; one day, you had an arm, and the next, you didn't.

I looked down at Keith. Hazel had closed his eyes; he looked like he could be sleeping. He had told me once that sleeping was the only time he felt at peace because she was always there, in his dreams. Now they would be back together forever.

The rest of the day was quiet. The men dealt with the invaders' bodies while the rest of us prepared Keith and Jess. It was a horrible affair. While we cleaned and dressed Keith and Jess, the guys took on the task of loading the destroyed truck with the other bodies. The truck was then rolled into a field in another part of the pasture and set on fire. A.J. had siphoned the remaining gas from the tanks and used it to douse the bodies before setting them ablaze. It was dirty and disgusting work.

Once the men finished with that task, they set to digging graves for our loved ones. This took hours, thanks to our mostly rocky ground. It was dark when we started the services. We all took turns saying nice things about our friends or telling stories about them. Hazel even sang Amazing Grace. I still felt dead inside. I could tell everyone was just trying to get through it. I looked over at Max; I wasn't even sure if he was there. His eyes looked a million miles away. I tried to go to him, but he just shook his head no and walked away.

I understood; I didn't really feel like talking all that much myself. I hugged Brandon and walked over to a fallen tree, and plopped down. I watched my friends and family sit around the graves of a large campfire we had built. Looking around the group, I could see all the sadness and anger. Anger at the world in general, anger at whoever had done this to us. What would this world be like in a month, or hell a year?

I was deep in my own thoughts when A.J. sat down next to me on my log. I looked over at him, pleading at him with my eyes to just go away and let me grieve, but no luck. "I know this probably isn't the right time to tell you this, ya know, with the funerals and all, but that "boss" guy wasn't in with the bodies," he said. I just nodded; that was a problem for tomorrow. Today I was going to mourn my friend and a child I thought of as my own.

It actually took three days for us to even broach the topic of William, "The Boss." We had spent the last couple of days shifting between watch shifts and mourning. Max had only left his room once in the past few days. My mother had been placing meals outside his and Dillon's door. The boys had only come out of their room for food and to take a shift on watch. The entire house was quiet. I spent the days either playing with Carson, Brody, and Ryler or on a watch shift. I needed to be close to the boys. Something about small children always made me feel better. All of the kids had been sleeping with Brandon and me for the past few nights. Jalyn had been helping with watch shifts down at Ryan's place. Nobody really believed they were watching anything, but who was I to judge the way somebody grieved.

That third night, the group met for the first time since the attack on the homestead. My mother had found some tea bags somewhere in my preps and had made up hot tea for the meeting. We sat drinking our tea and pretty must just staring at our feet until A.J. started the discussion.

"Okay, like I told Tara when we were doing the clean up after the attack, I noticed, "The Boss" guy wasn't in the pile of bodies. Did anyone see where he ran off to? By the time the shooting stopped, we were all too busy with, uhm, other things. I never even saw him running off," A.J. said, looking around the room, but everyone was just shaking their head. Nobody else had seen where the guy had gotten to either.

"Do we even know how many guys were with him on the night of the attack?" I asked, bouncing a very slobbery baby Carson on my lap. He was happily gumming my fingers and drooling all down the front of his t-shirt while making loud squealing noises. There was a chorus of "no" all around the room.

"There were eight bodies in the truck, but I'm not sure how many total. If I had to guess, what, we've killed about eight other guys of his in the past month. That's sixteen. Do you guys think he really has more than that?" My dad asked from his spot in the corner. I had tried talking to dad once about what happened that night, but he wasn't in the mood for talking like the rest of us.

"Maybe. That guy Beaux said he wasn't giving people a chance to say no. For all we know, he may have gathered up half the damn town by now. Tara, remember when we met, I told you what was left of the law was trying to get people to pack up and move into town to one of the schools? If the "boss" found some of those people, we could be looking for a small army," A.J. said as he sat down with a thump.

"Do we really think he'll come back? I'm sure he'll be looking for other people to fly a plane by now," my mother said with a huff.

The rest of us looked around our small circle. I made eye contact with A.J. but just shook my head. I knew if William "the Boss" came back out here, it would be to kill us. By now, I had to guess it was more about pride and less about a capable pilot.

The rest of the meeting was just a bunch of arguments about what we should do now. Should we move, wait here and fight, go there and fight, and so on. After about an hour, I gave up and took Carson into Jalyn and Jess' room, where the radio was still located. I sat on Jess' bed. I needed to radio Alicia and give her a heads up about what was going on, but I just sat there and rocked little Carson until I saw his little eyes close in sleep.

It had been almost a week since I had heard from Alicia. I felt like shit, I knew she had been dealing with her own issues, and I should have called before now. I laid baby Carson onto the bed and placed pillows all the way around his little body. He had started to roll around a lot more this past month, and I wasn't taking any chances he would roll off the bed.

I got a cup of warm tea and sat down at the radio. I had missed Alicia so much; we talked almost once a day for over twenty years. "Alicia, this is Tara. Do you copy? Over" I waited, and waited. Nothing. "Michael? Alicia? Are you guys there? Over." Dead air again. I was just about to give up and try again tomorrow when a familiar gruff voice came over the radio.

"This is Mr. Thompson; I live at the house on the corner by the gate. Is this the blonde woman? Over," he said.

I had to turn my speaker up. It sounded like he was whispering. "Yes, Mr. Thompson, this is the blonde woman. Why are you on Alicia's radio?" I asked. I was starting to get a bad feeling now.

"I don't remember your name, but Alicia is in trouble. That big stupid guy from the gate that day took over the whole neighborhood! They took my house! I have to sleep on the couch like some damn uninvited house guest," he said before the radio clinked.

"Mr. Thompson, I'm sorry to hear about your home, but how is Alicia in trouble?" I asked.

"Well, when they went to take this radio, she put up one hell of a fight and shot one of the new neighborhood policemen. Now they have her locked up in a spare bedroom in a house down the street from here. I heard them say they are going to give her a trial. They gave another guy a trial if you can call it that! The new cops are the only ones that even get a vote," he mumbled.

"What happened to the other guy Mr. Thompson?" I asked, a huge feeling of dread was winding its way into my stomach.

"Well, he was caught trying to steal back his supplies from the community store, so they cut his hand off," Mr. Thompson answered.

"Shit, how long before her trial?" I asked, trying not to cry or vomit.

"I'm not sure, but it's been a couple of days now, so probably not much longer," he answered.

"Mr. Thompson, any information you have or can find, I'd really appreciate it. I have to talk to the rest of my family to try and come up with a plan, but it will take time," I said.

"I'll keep an ear out, but ma'am, I don't think you have much time. Over," he whispered back. The airwaves went dead behind his last word.

I slid down the bedroom wall to the floor. I couldn't breathe or cry; I just stared at the wall in what used to be my guest room. It was only about a month ago when I was picking out a new bed for this room, but it seemed like years ago. Jess's stuff was all folded in neat piles with an old teddy bear sitting on the bed. I looked at that teddy bear for a long time. The beautiful little girl that probably snuggled with that teddy was gone. I saw her in my mind's eye when I looked around the room, or anywhere in the house for that matter. Was there something I could have done differently? Should I have just offered to fly that jackass somewhere? Would it have made a difference?

Now I had my best friend's life in my hands. If I failed, she died. If I couldn't get there in time, or if her family gets caught trying to escape with us, they died. That was more than I could take. I must have sat against that wall for an hour, trying to think of ways to help Alicia and her family against a trained police force. I couldn't lose anybody else to this God damned apocalypse.

I walked into the living room and really looked around at the gathered group. All I saw looking back at me were sad, tired faces of men and women who had no business playing apocalypse.

"Guys, I need to talk to you," I said as I waited until everyone had entered the room. It was a small group tonight. My parents were still here but had all their stuff loaded up to take to their house. 'Alicia has been jailed in her neighborhood by the police that took it over. She put up a fight when they came to her home to take her food and radio. She shot one of the cops, and he died. I just spoke with the little old man who lives at the house on the corner by the gate. They've taken over his home as their new office. So, according to the neighbor, Alicia will be put to death, and soon. It might happen tonight, tomorrow, the guy didn't know when, but he wanted me to know in case there was something we could do about it. He told me she's been locked up in one of the homes for a few days now. This was just the first time he's been able to use the radio without being seen," I said.

I flopped down on the couch next to Max and Dillon to let everyone take that in. The room was silent; all eyes were on the floor. Ryler took that cue to run buck ass naked from the bathroom, a tired and out of breath Jalyn right on his heels. Ryler popped up into my lap to give me a hug.

"I'm all clean, GiGi!" He used that moment to turn to his mother and stick his tongue out at her.

"I'm sorry, Tara, I was trying to keep the boys quiet and out of the way. I'm sorry for eavesdropping, but I heard that guy talking while I was giving the boys a bath," Jalyn said sheepishly, coming to grab her naked toddler.

"It's fine, honey; everyone should know what's going on," I said. I turned to the group. I looked at my parents in their 60's and 70's, the teenagers, the preteens, and everyone in between.

"Guys, you know I have to go. I'm not losing one more damn person to this apocalypse. We couldn't save Jess and Keith, but we can try and save Alicia and her family. I know it's been rough lately, and I know what I'm asking, but I'm going," I said, standing up.

"I'm in," A.J. said, getting to his feet. "You all took me in when ya didn't have to, and the doc and his wife are good people."

"We're in," Max and Dillon both said, standing up next to me. Max squeezed my hand.

Brandon stood and came to stand next to me. "You know I'm in," he said, kissing the top of my head.

"Okay, let's get some rest and plan on leaving about midnight. That will put us there just when the night shift is tired enough to be sloppy," I said, walking to my bedroom.

Brandon was still stripping off outerwear when I climbed into bed. The house was exceptionally well insulated, so it kept the heat in pretty well. It wasn't warm, but it wasn't uncomfortable. I rolled over and put my head on his chest like so many nights before this one. I listened to his strong heartbeat until I nodded off myself.

It felt like I had only been asleep for a few minutes when Max was shaking my shoulder to wake me. "Mom, it's midnight; we need to pack some gear and get ready to go."

Chapter 23

Max had grown up so much since the lights went out. At now sixteen, he had seen more firsthand killing and battles than I hoped he would ever see in a lifetime. I'm pretty sure he had even grown another inch or two in the last month. A month: a month was thirty days, a month was paying bills and keeping lights on and bellies full. Never did I think a month would be nothing more than continued survival. That's what the last month had been for us, just surviving, and for some of us, that wasn't possible.

"Thanks, honey, I'll wake up, dad," I said.

Brandon was snoring loudly next to me. How anyone in this house got any sleep was beyond me. It sounded like a running chainsaw trying to eat pavement or something. My parents could say all they wanted about it being "time to move home," but if I had to guess, they were sleep-deprived and just wanted a full night's sleep.

After waking the snoring machine, I went into my closet. The apocalypse had done wonders for my waistline. Between the lack of junk food and all the damn walking, I started to get my figure back. That would be great if I had pants to fit my new body. I had been the same size for twelve years. I hated diets; I always figured people liked me for me and, if not, who really cared anyway.

I pulled on some of my old black jeans and a black turtleneck. If I couldn't move like a ninja, at least I could dress like one; one, fat, blonde, and generally clumsy ninja. I pulled my now shoulder-length hair into tight braids that stopped at my shoulder and covered it all with a black stocking cap. I stood in my full-length mirror in my bathroom by candlelight. I looked pretty good for a mission I wasn't sure If I was coming back from.

Brandon snuck up on me in the mirror, making me squeak in protest. "Come on, Jackie Chan, the rest of the group is ready to load up," he said with a snort.

I turned to look at Brandon; he was in jeans and a University of Oklahoma sweatshirt with white dad tennis shoes. "Do you really think white is a good idea? We're trying to get in and out unnoticed in a neighborhood that's run by crazy cops," I asked him.

"If it's my shoes that screw up this job, I will personally let you use them as target practice when we get home," he said with an eye roll.

Walking into the living room, I saw everyone was loading up a 72-hour bag. We had no idea how long it would take, or if something went wrong and we had to ditch the truck, at least we would be ready. A.J. met me by the door. He was dressed in similar black clothes and even had grease paint on his face. I turned to give Brandon the "See? I told you so look." Again, all I got was an eye roll for my troubles. A.J. and I gave each other a fist bump; we knew we looked fabulous.

We loaded all our gear into the poor old and now beat all to hell truck. It was missing almost all the glass and making this crisp winter morning feel more like the North Pole. Max and Dillon piled into the back of the truck, both of them with rifles. They were going to be the lookouts for trouble behind us. A.J. stuck the muzzle of his shotgun out the passenger window. Brandon and I both had a gun in our laps and guns strapped into thigh holsters. A.J. made the holsters for us out of an old leather jacket he found in a pile of donation clothes that never made it to Goodwill. If nothing else, we at least looked like people not to be fucked with.

The drive was uneventful; I guess not even criminals wanted to be out and about this early in the morning. The sky was completely clear as we drove down the back streets, the ten miles or so to Alicia's road. There were so many stars out. The town's lights had always blocked us from seeing much from where we lived out in the country. This morning though, was beautiful. I had to feel this was a good sign for this mission. I know clear nights make us more visible, but they also let us see what we were doing.
We turned the lights off for about the last mile, using only the moonlight and the stars' light to see. We didn't want to take a chance on any lookouts seeing the headlights.

"Okay, what's the plan?" A.J. asked, turning to me.

"Uhm, plan? I guess we split up; one group goes to get Michael and the boys, and the other group finds Alicia," I said.

"Oh, good Lord, you don't have a plan, do you?" A.J. said, shaking his head.

"I guess you and *"Crouching Tiger Hidden Dragon"* over there should have worried a little bit more about how to get into the neighborhood and a little less about your outfits," Brandon said as he took off walking with the boys.

"Ass," we said, almost in perfect harmony.

That just earned me a grin. By the time we were a block away from the gate, we were all business. The joking, I know, had been a way to try and cope with the stress of what we were getting ready to do.

Our plan sounded simple enough. I was to take Max and Dillon with me to get Michael and the boys while A.J. and Brandon looked for where Alicia was being held. We would then meet back on the road about a block down the street. We would give Michael the keys to the truck so he could take the boys and drive away if the whole thing went tits up. If we all didn't make it back to the meeting point in two hours for some reason, the others would come to help.

I hugged Brandon and asked him to please be careful and come back to me. Max gave him the weird handshake hug thing that I guessed all men were born knowing how to do, and we left.

We split off into our two groups. My plan was simple, we only had to get over the large fence surrounding the neighborhood, then cross one street out in the open before we would be all in back yards. Thankfully for whatever reason, people in this neighborhood only seemed to have tiny designer dogs if they had them at all.

I wondered why anyone would want a dog that fits in your purse, but what did I know. I had always had large breed dogs. Brandon had always said if he had to have a dog, it had better be a working dog. He sounded stern, but he was the one that spooned our German Shepard at night when we went to bed. Brandon was always sneaking both of them treats and scraps of dinner off his plate. He even asked me once if they needed to wear sweaters when they were out playing in the snow.

We approached the fence slowly and quietly; the bars were almost far enough apart for a thin person to go through, but not us. At least we wouldn't have to lift the boys over the fence. They could just step through the bars. Max and Dillon both got down on one knee so I could stand on them to grab the top of the bars. It was going to be risky. The tops of the fence were done in that pointy metal that looked like a spear. I guess that was to deter people like us from trying to climb over it.

It took every bit of strength I possessed to pull myself up and over the fence. As I landed with an "oof," the boys already up and over, waiting on me to catch my breath. "I guess we need to start doing some strength training when we get home," I heard Max whisper to Dillon. I would have come back with a fancy retort, but I was still out of breath, and it may have proved Max's point.

We stood quiet and motionless behind a cedar tree and waited. If someone heard us at the fence, it was best to take care of it now and not be caught out in the open. The next part of the trip was all out in the open. The lots in this neighborhood were a couple of acres each, but they had large wide roads we were going to have to cross. The sun would be coming up in a few hours, we really didn't have the time to stand here and wait, but we did.
I'm glad we decided to; we were just about to step out into the road when we heard some talking from up the road. It was too far away to listen to what the people were saying, but we waited until they had gone before stepping out and onto the main road. We quickly crossed the road and ducked behind another grouping of trees. I'm not sure who thought they needed to plant a forest around this neighborhood, but I was sure glad of it.

Slowly and as carefully as possible, we made our way through back yards over fences, to a creek on the backside of the property. It was hard to know where we were going in pitch black, but I had known there was a creek running behind the neighbor's house. I had taken the boys down to look at it when I babysat a couple of times. They loved to poke at the frogs and stomp in the water.

I was just about to follow Max up the side of the creek bank when he sank down and put an arm out to stop me. "What?" I said only by shrugging my shoulders at him.

"Guy with a gun," he pointed them mimicked by using his thumb and index finger to make a gun sign.

"Michael?" I asked in an almost soundless whisper.

He shook his head, "No."

All three of us stood with only a little of our faces showing to access the new information. I guess it would make sense if Alicia was on trial for murder; they would want to keep an eye on her family to keep them from doing anything stupid. I looked to the sky; it was starting to lighten off to the East. It wouldn't be long before dawn would begin to lighten the sky, making it a lot easier to see us.

Max looked at me and mimed shooting his gun with a questioning look. "No," I shook my head. Not only did I not want my kid to shoot another human being, but the report of the rifle would wake everyone in the neighborhood.

Max, Dillon, and I all crouched down on the creek bank. Thankfully we hadn't had a lot of rain, so it was pretty much dry. "Okay, what are our options here?" I asked, my voice barely above a whisper.

"I can creep up behind him and knock him out. Then we can tie him up and let his guys find him when they come looking for Michael and the boys," said Max. Dillon and Max were both nodding in unison. I hated the idea of sending Max into any kind of danger, but it wasn't a bad idea. It was actually much harder to knock someone unconscious from what I understood than it looked in the movies. I guess we would see.
I let Max run down the side of the creek bank to a spot almost behind the house.

As I watched, the man on the porch paced and lit up a cigarette. He didn't really look like the guard type. He had a skinny and narrow build to him. His clothes looked dirty, like he had not changed them since the bomb dropped. I knew tons of people in this neighborhood had the "whole home" generators.
Alicia and I had talked to a couple of them when she and Michael first moved into the neighborhood. There was no reason this man should be in nasty clothes.

Now that I was really looking at him, he looked more gaunt, not just skinny. Like he had not eaten much. I thought the big cop guy was taking all the supplies for the good of the group. It looks like this man wasn't in his good graces.

Max was slowly drawing closer to the guy when the guy turned. The man immediately dropped his gun and put his hands up. "Please don't shoot me; it's not my fault," the man begged. He then proceeded to drop to his knees. Dillon and I climbed out of the creek and into the open then. The man saw the two of us and was actually trembling.

"Hey buddy, we just want to get to our friends. If you don't become a problem, we'll leave you here in peace," I said, walking up to him.

"There's no such thing anymore. Not here, not with these people," he said, starting to sob.

I knocked on Michael's back door until a sleepy Sean came and opened the door. "Aunt Tara, you came to help mommy!" He was almost screaming, so I scooped him up into my arms and went into the house.

Michael came barreling around the corner and almost smashed us into the wall. "Michael, it's Tara," I said quickly. To him, and I'm sure in the dark, I just looked like someone holding his kid.

"Tara, how did you get here? How did you get past the guard? How did you know how to come here?" He shot all these questions off in quick succession.

"Okay, one thing at a time," I said, turning to wave the boys into the house. They each had an arm of the still whimpering man. "Max, you two, please take him into the living room and keep him company for me while I talk to Michael," I said.

Max rolled his eyes at the mention of the man. "Mom, he smells terrible."

"Maxwell, what did I say?" Some days even in the apocalypse, you have to use the dreaded "mom voice," I thought to myself as I did my own eye roll.

I watched Max and Dillon deposit the man at the end of the couch. The man actually seemed to enjoy just being inside and warm by a fire. I really couldn't blame him, but I had a feeling the neighborhood was not the nirvana the cops that lived and ruled here had promised.

I held Sean in my arms and snuggled him while Michael made some tea for all of us, even his "guard."
"Okay, can you tell me what happened? Mr. Thompson was able to use the radio and call us for help," I said after Michael had delivered out all the teacups.

"It was a couple of days ago when we get a knock at the door. Alicia had started always carrying her gun in a holster on her hip. I opened the door, and several large guys came in. They said they were acting members of the new government and came to take our supplies for all the neighbors' good. We knew they might be coming for the food, so we hid several of the food safe buckets in the attic. The men took everything we had for food in the house then turned to our radio. Alicia and one of the guys got into a huge fight over it. When the man pulled a gun on her, she pulled hers and shot him in the chest. Everyone heard the gunshot.

The whole street came outside to see what was going on. The other guys grabbed her. She was kicking, punching, and swearing the entire way out the door. I stood up against the wall with both boys in my arms. The guys pointed guns at the boys, not me, and I knew if I moved, they would kill the boys. The boys were both screaming and crying. All we could do was watch," he said.

Michael looked rough. I could tell he hadn't had much in the way of sleep the last few days. He had dark circles under his eyes and a blank look.

"There was nothing you could do. Alicia knows and understands that. As a mother, I can tell you these kids are our whole life. We would do anything and give anything to them. You did the right thing in protecting them, Michael. It's what I would have done in those circumstances," I said.

"They're going to kill her, Tara," he said, choking back tears.

"No, we're not going to let that happen. I need you to pull it together and get these boys packed up. We're leaving now," I said.

"I can't just leave her, Tara!" He all but shouted at me.

"Nobody is leaving Alicia. Brandon and A.J. are looking for her location now. Once we have you and the boys out, we will create a distraction and get her out. Then we all go back to the airport. Got me?" I said, standing up. 'Now, let's get going. The sun is going to come up soon, and we don't have a lot of time. Where are the bug out bags? We will carry the boys and the bags out of here."

Michael just looked at me with those sunken eyes. "Michael, we'll get her," I said in a determined tone as I could muster.

Dillion stayed with our "hostage." I really didn't think he needed watching, judging by his gulping of tea, but hey, you never knew about people anymore. Max, Michael, and I loaded up everything we could carry and hid anything significant in the attic. The opening was hidden in the back of a dark guest bedroom closet. We had to hope no one would notice it. I knew they would come back here someday, and they would need supplies when they did.

The group could really use those supplies at home, but there was just no way the four of us would be able to carry the boys, their bags, and a bunch of heavy buckets. My family had helped Alicia's move into this house. It had taken several trips to the moving truck to lug all the food buckets into her new place.

In the last few years after the 2008 economic breakdown, Alicia and I had taken to storing food in buckets. Alicia and I had spent weeks sealing flour, oats, sugar, and the like. We had each spent several days hungry after the loss of our jobs that year; not having a scrap of food to eat for days at a time just added insult to injury. Making the food buckets, once we were back on our feet, had been cathartic. I hated to leave all that life-saving food here for strangers to find.

Chapter 24

Within ten minutes, we were packed and ready to leave. I was telling Michael the plan when the slim guy pipped up. "I can help with a distraction if you want," the skinny guy said.

"Why would you do that? Wouldn't it be better for you if I tied you up for whenever they come looking for you?" I asked.

"It doesn't matter. The men already killed my family. In the first couple of days, they went all crazy cop. They were shooting anyone who didn't willingly give up all their food. They shot my wife and her sister right in front of me. Then left me there with their bodies. I don't know how long I sat there. I just couldn't make myself move, ya know? I finally got up and went looking for where I could get some food. They told me I had to work for food. That was a few days ago. I've been here watching over this family ever since. They still haven't given me any food. The tea Mr. Sawyer gave me was the first thing I've had other than pool water in days," he said with his head in his hands.

"Well, shit!" Michael said while digging in his bug out bag. He pulled out two MRE rations and handed them to the man. "Eat one now and hide the other one. The others will just take it from you if you don't. Hell, they'll probably kill you for it, thinking you had it hidden," Michael said.

The man reached his stick-thin arms out and took the meals. "Thank you, sir. I..." he started, but I didn't let him finish.

"I need you to give us ten minutes to get Michael and the boys out of the neighborhood. Then I need you to tell him we took off to the other side of the neighborhood. Say we were headed towards the lake. Got me?" I asked, looking into his eyes.

I felt horrible for the man, but I didn't really know what to do. He had stayed here when he should have run. "Then get out of this neighborhood. Find a new place, maybe down by the lake. There's a group of women down by the lake. Maybe they'll let you stay with them. You have to get away from here if you want to survive," I told him.

With that, I loaded Sean into my arms, his little bug out bag over my shoulders. Michael carried Joe and his pack. Dillon loaded up Michael's gear, and we set off.

It started out a little rough, trying to all but crawl around in the creek bed until we reached a fence. We had to pass the boys back and forth while the rest of us climbed the fences. Sean was talking almost non-stop. We spent the entire trip, putting our fingers to our lips to try and keep him quiet. He was just at that age.

"Aunt Tara, what are we doing? Where are we going? Did you know I packed my superman toy in my bag?" he chattered.

We were almost in the home stretch when we heard talking again. It was the patrol. Michael and I shot each other looks, then looks at the boys. I could see Sean wanting to ask me another question, but I smiled and put my hand over his mouth like a fun game. This, of course, made him giggle.

"Hey man, did you hear something? I swear I heard a kid's laughter," I heard off in the distance.

"Quit being such a puss. You're just scared of the dark. Besides, who would be able to laugh in this shit show of a neighborhood?" Another man said with a loud laugh.

"Shut up, man, I seriously think I heard something. It sounded like laughing," the first guy said.

"Oh, then it was probably just your wife laughing at your micropenis while she waits for a visit from me," the second guy said with even more laughter.

When they had finally made their way out of site, we slowly crossed the main road and got into the bushes that lined the main fence.

"Aunt Tara, what's a micropenis?" Sean whispered in my ear.

It took everything in me not to burst into laughter. I put my finger back to my lips to keep Sean quiet.

Max went over first to catch all the bags and gear. Then we passed the boys through the fence. Like I thought, they were both thin enough to get through the iron bars just fine. Next, it was my turn. Dillon and Michael gave me a push to the top of the fence. I lost my balance, fell off the fence, and twisted my ankle. Looks like my coordination had just crapped out.

Once we were all outside, I told the guys to take the boys and get to the truck. It was going to be a slow walk for me now with a twisted ankle. Dillon stayed behind and did everything but carry me back to the truck.

Brandon and A.J. were waiting on us at the truck when I walked up. I was so glad to see they had gotten out without any problems.

"Now that the husband and kids are out, can we start the distraction and the rescue?" A.J. asked with what looked like a shit-eating grin on his face. I knew then what he was going to say even before he opened his mouth. They had brought the pipe bombs with them.

"You guys can't blow up a bomb! What about all the other people that live here?" I whisper yelled.

"Babe, we're going to set it off at the end of the fence. It won't be anywhere close to any of the houses. We even know where she's being kept. There were two jackasses we had to listen to talk for thirty minutes about how they were going to get to have a real firing squad," Brandon said.

"Oh shit, just do it and get her out of there," I said.

"I'm going," Michael said after depositing his son into my arms. "I won't just stand by and watch this time," he said.

I understood. I hated nothing more than inaction. I hated to wait, but it looked like it would be my turn to do so. I handed my gun with three full clips to Michael to load up his pockets. Brandon kissed my lips, and they all just walked away.

An intense fog had started moving in while we were making our way out of the neighborhood, and I watched as they all disappeared into it. The boys and I sat in the truck wrapped up in blankets we carried because of the busted out windows.

Sean had just stopped asking about my new horses when the explosion went off. I say explosion; it sounded like a straight-up nuke had blown up by the gate. I could only hope the guys were far enough away, and nobody was injured.

The boys both looked up at me once the noise of the explosion had passed, and just when I thought they might break into tears and screams, they both surprised me by laughing. Little Joe started clapping, yelling "Boom" over and over again. Sean just went back to playing with his Superman toy. I sat in the truck with the boys listening to Sean tell me all about Superman for what felt like hours. It had probably only been about one hour when I saw flashlights walking towards the truck.

The lights were still far off in the distant fog when I slid myself out of the truck door using the armrest to support my injured ankle. A.J. had unhooked the inside dome light from turning on when the door was opened, and right now, I could kiss him and that crazy-ass cat of his for it. I had given Michael my Glock but held onto my Smith and Wesson M&P. Looking back at the boys all wrapped up in their blankets, I had an idea.

"Hey guys, how about we go sit in the grass? We can play hide and seek with Mommy and Daddy when they come," I was saying this as I was pulling Sean out of the truck.

Hobbling around the truck's front and opening the truck's passenger side very slowly to avoid noise, I lifted little Joe out. When I turned around from lifting Joe out of the truck, I saw Sean had already taken off into the trees. Damn, he was fast for a four-year-old! I reached over and snatched up his blankets he had dropped while he ran. I came upon the clump of trees I had seen him running to, but no Sean. I tried to keep walking as far into the trees as I could, but the ankle was just about to give out by this point. I knew without looking it had swollen up inside my boot. I didn't dare take the boot off. I knew it wouldn't go back on.

I tucked Joe into his blankets and sat him down under a tree. From here, we could just see the truck, but I really didn't think anyone could see us. I was just getting ready to take off and look for Sean when I heard a "psst" from above me. Looking up, I saw Sean sitting on a branch a good ten feet above me. I waved and did the finger over the mouth thing to try and keep him quiet. Little Joe was cold, his cheeks turning red, even with all the blankets wrapped around him.

"Did you see anyone come this way?" A voice I knew wasn't one of ours asked.

"No, but it just makes sense anyone running would take the road, doesn't it?" A different voice asked.

"Dude, I'm freezing my balls off. Can we go back now? We haven't seen jack-shit." The first voice asked.

"The Major said to check the area, so we check the area. Don't be such a puss. Do you really want to go back and tell that crazy son of a bitch we got cold, so we came back? Dumbass." The other guy snarked back.

"No, but what if we just sit in this truck for a while, then go back?" The first guy asked.

"You can freeze your ass off walking or sitting around. What difference does it make?" Guy two said while lighting up a joint. The smell of weed filled the air. The guys both sat down on the tailgate of the truck and smoked their joint.

Joe had fallen asleep leaning against me. It was still hours before he was used to being awake. Sean was still sitting on his tree branch. I could almost hear his silent questions. The fact he had stayed quiet this long had to be a gift from God. I would still look up and give him a silent gesture. Sean had to be thinking this was the most boring game of hide and seek ever.

The wind started to pick up about twenty minutes into our wait. It was a deep bone-jarring cold. I tried to make Joe into a little baby burrito with the blankets, pulling them up over his head the best I could.
Sean had grown still up in his tree. When we had been getting ready to leave the house, we had made sure the boys were dressed in layers and wearing their heaviest coats, but he still had to be freezing up there.

I wouldn't be able to let this go on for much longer. The boys would get frostbite or hyperthermia or some other cold thing I didn't know about. I had a good layer of fat on me, and I was freezing my ass off.
I was just starting to move Joe's sleeping form when I heard shots in the distance. Both men jumped off the tailgate and took off running back to the neighborhood. One was so high, and in such a hurry, he left his gun behind when he took off. God, I loved stoners.

"Sean, baby, climb back down here for me. The game is over. We'll wait for mommy and daddy in the truck out of this wind," I said.

"I'm not a baby Aunt Tara; we were hiding from the bad men. Those were the bad men that took mommy," he said as he used his frozen limbs to climb down and into my arms.

I didn't know what to say to that, so I just nodded and took the boys back to the truck. It was 5:30AM, two and a half hours from when this started, an hour from the explosion that had gone off at the gate. I was going to have to start making some hard decisions soon. The boys needed to get warm. I could start the truck and run the heater, but it would give away our position if any more goons from the neighborhood came looking this way, or I could take the boys back to my mom and come back.

I started the truck and turned the heater on full blast. I would let the boys warm up some, then shut the truck off. If I had to, I would just shoot anyone who got close to us. The boys were huddled together like little puppies, both laying down in the seat and letting the warm air blow on their faces. I was turned in the truck seat with my gun pointed out the back hole where a window would have been.

Over the engine's sound and the heater blowing, I could just make out limbs breaking and cold grass crunching under what sounded like combat boots running towards our truck. I couldn't see who was making the noise, but I knew someone was coming this way. My plan was to wait until they were close enough to make eye contact with me, then I would open fire.

I would never be afraid to kill a man while I was defending me and mine, but I was scared of how the boys would see me if they watched me kill a man. They had not been in the room with Alicia when she shot that guy; they had come in the room when they heard the shot. Kids were weird. Would they be scared of me? Would they go into hysterics? I know Sean had watched his dad play Grand Theft Auto, I had never played, but I imagined there was some violence. Was he old enough to understand the difference between real life and video games?

Many questions were running through my head when Brandon came running out of the woods. The rest of our group hot on his heels. I could tell he was out of breath from the running; he was in about the same shape I was. The whole group came staggering out of the woods then. Nobody tried to get in the truck; they were just flinging themselves into the back of the truck, then reaching back to grab the next person. Once A.J. jumped into the back, he slammed the tailgate into place.

"Drive, Tara, go!" He yelled as he pulled his gun from his holster and pointed it towards the direction they had been running from.

I spun around in the seat, trusting everyone had made it into the truck and hit the gas. Since the engine was already warm, the truck pulled from the side of the road leaving only a vapor cloud behind us. I had only been driving for a few minutes when Brandon pulled himself up to the window.

"Are you and the boys okay? We had to hide when we saw some guys running from the way of the truck. You didn't shoot them, so I'm guessing they didn't make it out as far as the truck?" He asked, shouting over the wind.

"No, they made it alright. Two of the men sat on the back of the truck smoking pot while the boys and I hid in the trees. I didn't really want to shoot anyone in front of the boys if I didn't have to. You know?" I said.

"I get it; I used to feel that way about shooting someone in front of our kids before all this happened," he said, grabbing my shoulder before settling back down in the bed of the truck.

I took the most direct route home on the back roads. I didn't think any of us could take the cold much longer. The wind blowing in through the windshield had the boys shivering even with the heater pointed at them and on full blast. We really needed to find another vehicle for the rest of the winter. We needed a car or truck with windows. I had no idea where we could find something like that, though. It was bad enough we were only a few days away from running out of fuel for the truck and generators. The next day or two, another group of us would have to leave the homestead again and venture out into our new fucked up world.

I just sighed; the apocalypse was really turning out to be more than I bargained for. I had been reading apocalyptic fiction for years. Personally, I think the real thing sucks way worse than any book I've ever read. I'm not sure what country fired the nukes that took down our world, but I hoped we had troops kicking the shit out of them by now.

The radio had been quiet for weeks now. We still listened for it; we just didn't have anyone person sitting around it anymore. Since we lost Jess, nobody really wanted to. Even Jess had gotten tired of listening to it the last few weeks before her death. She told me it was like waiting for a boy to call. It was exciting at first, but then it just annoyed her. She spent hours on that radio calling out to people. People that had been talking to us out West were just gone. We didn't know if the radiation had got them or if they had just picked up and tried to move closer to the country's middle.

Chapter 25

The sun was up by the time I pulled the truck into the driveway. I could feel the bouncing as people were jumping out of bed. I was just reaching down to wake Sean when Alicia opened the truck door. She looked like shit; she had a busted lip, a broken nose, and a couple of black eyes. Alicia reached in and picked Joe up as he slept. I saw her wince and wondered if she didn't have a couple of bruised or broken ribs.

She reached over with baby Joe in her arms and touched my hand. After twenty-five years of friendship, that touch on my hand said it all. The family started running out of the front door to see the newcomers. Kayla ran straight for Alicia, putting Alicia and Joe into a big bear type hug. I saw Alicia wince at being squeezed, but she didn't say anything. Michael and Alicia underwent hugs and kisses from the whole group before my mother finally got everyone inside.

"Alicia, do you want to take a bath now or wait until you've had something to eat?" My mother asked while handing her a hot cup of coffee.

"If it's okay, I'd like to take one now," she said, looking down at her t-shirt. I was really only now noticing it was covered in blood. Whatever she had been through during her imprisonment, it hadn't been very nice.

Kayla took the boys into the bedroom to get them settled with Brody and Ryler before coming back to me. "Mom, can I talk to you when you get a minute?" she asked.

"Sure, kiddo, is everything okay?" I asked.

She nodded her head and went to help my mother heat water in the kitchen. I couldn't honestly imagine what was wrong now. I was so tired, all I wanted to do was flop down on my bed and sleep for a week, but of course, that wasn't in the cards for any of us. We had arrangements to make. We needed to find sheets and blankets and get Michael and Alicia set up in one bedroom. Space was getting tight, even with my parents and Connor moving back to their house next door.

I spent the next twenty minutes or so moving beds and blowing up air mattresses. When I had finally plopped down on the couch,

Freya immediately took that opportunity to jump in my lap and start licking my face.

"I missed you too, sweet girl!" I cooed into her fur. Bo took this opportunity to jump to my other side and get his share of love. I was trying to move a good hundred and fifty pounds of dog off my lap when Kayla flopped down beside me.

"Mom, Jalyn, the boys, and I are moving back to our place. It's only in the field next door. We've talked about it, and there just isn't enough room here. Also, Ryan, from down the road, will move in with Jalyn, and they, uhm, need their privacy. It would just be better for everyone," she said, finally running out of the breath she had been holding to get that whole sentence out.

"Well, I really wish you would have told me this before. I spent all that time trying to build bedding areas before you told me this, but I agree. You and Jalyn have proved your shooting skills to me, and I actually feel better having Ryan down there with you. One thing, though. I want you to take Bo down there with you. I'd feel better with you having a dog down there," I said.

Kayla just looked at me. I know she was ready for an argument and looked confused about why she wasn't getting one. "I get it; you guys want your own space," I said.

Our homes were set up in a baseball diamond pattern. I was home base, Kayla was first base, my parents at second base, and Connor's place at third base. I don't think anyone really noticed how we set our homes up until now.

I watched Kayla, Jalyn and the boys pack up their clothes and blankets for about twenty minutes.
Finally, I got what I had been waiting for, and Alicia opened the door to the bathroom. She looked thin; I was guessing, like the guy guarding her home, that she hadn't been fed in the past few days. Her face was drawn, and I could see black circles even under her black eyes. Alicia coming out of the bathroom must have been everyone's cue to go into the living room. We just sat and looked at her.

"Can you tell us what happened?" I asked.

Alicia accepted a mug of tea from my mom with a smile. "I'm sure Michael told you about the guys coming to the house. We had hidden most of our food by the time they got to our home. They were just going door to door, telling everyone to hand over their supplies or pay the price. Most people were standing in their yard, just crying about losing their stuff. Not me, I put up a fight. Michael tried to stop them from coming in, but they just busted through the door. It was a group of them, probably about five or so. They went straight into the kitchen and started loading up our food. Then they went room to room, looking for anything else they could find. I had tried to hide the radio under the bed, but they found it. I was so mad. I pointed my gun at the guy holding my radio and just fired. The radio fell to the carpet with the guy. I hit him in the chest Tara. It was awful; I could hear him trying to breathe. I guess the bullet hit him in one of his lungs. Everyone, including the guys taking our stuff, just froze and watched the guy die.

I knew a couple of the guys; they were from our side of the neighborhood. One was a cardiologist; he just watched it too. The shock, I guess. The next thing I knew, I was being thrown to the floor. I didn't know the guys that grabbed me. They might have been from a couple of streets over, or maybe even new people that came after the blast. I'm not sure. I saw one of the guys I knew put a gun to Sean's head. I knew him, Tara, you and I took the boys trick or treating at his house. I stopped struggling and just let them take me. We walked for a couple of blocks to one of the bigger homes in the neighborhood. I was taken by the arms and thrown into a basement with an elderly couple.

They had been thrown down there when they refused to let the new cops live there. It was dark in the basement, but I could tell they were in bad shape. The man talked to me some but mostly just sat and rubbed his wife's head. I think her leg had been broken when they were thrown down the stairs.
The men would open the door once or twice a day and throw a couple of water bottles down the stairs. Once, when I asked them for help for the elderly lady, they came downstairs. That's how I got the black eyes. They took the elderly couple that day. The elderly man was crying and begging them to help his wife. I heard two shots later that day, and I never saw them again. I could hear the men talking about how they were going to kill me. They went on and on about it to the point I just stopped listening to it; It wasn't until I heard the explosion, I thought that just maybe I could escape while they were distracted. I found a hammer in the basement, and I planned to use it to bust my way out of there. I had just started to really get after it when I heard Michael's voice calling out to me. He unlocked the door, and we ran.

I saw A.J. and Brandon with the boys firing their guns out the first-floor windows. We all took off together after that. Once we were outside, it was just chaos. Things were on fire, guns were going off everywhere, and people were screaming. We just ran and kept running until we hit the fence. That's when they told me where we had to go to get to you and the boys. Brandon and A.J. said it was too dangerous to walk down the road. We were going to have to run through the woods and double back to you. At one point, we had to hide in a giant cedar tree and wait for some guys to walk by on the road. We didn't want to shoot them and draw attention to the fact people were outside the gate," she said.

Sean and Joe came into the living room with Freya hot on their heels. Both boys climbed up in her lap.
When I heard Sean start talking about how he climbed the tree to hide from the bad men, I decided it was time to wash up myself. I would let him fill her in on everything she had missed in the last few days.

With Kayla, Jalyn, and the boys back at their house, that left us with plenty of room to bring in more people. I knew Alicia and Michael would want to go back to their home at some point; I only hope they gave it a while.

It was so lovely today. Baby Carson and I sat out on our porch, just watching people go to and fro and enjoying some hopefully fresh air. Carson was growing so fast. If I had to guess, he had managed to put on several pounds in the past month. I was still using watered-down condensed milk, but Ryan and his group had managed a trip into town. They had actually located some baby formula and gear. Michael had been giving all the children check-ups. Looking for any signs of radiation poisoning.

It had been two weeks since the night we went for Alicia and her family. The airport had established a new patrol schedule, adding Alicia and Michael to fill in for our lost friends.

A.J. had taken to taking all the children out hunting and foraging for edible plants. A.J. was adamant the weeds I had been mowing for years could be eaten as salads. So far, the Curly Dock plant was the only one I could really stomach. A.J. showed us all how to cook the leaves to remove an acid that is produced. He cooked soups made with the Curly Dock and some field garlic. When we first met

A.J., I had no idea that we would come to rely on his knowledge for survival. A.J. and the kids had so far brought down multiple turkeys and even a couple of rabbits hunting only with bows. We knew eating the animals feeding on the grasses, and drinking the water would be a problem. Still, cancer and radiation poisoning were taking a backseat to starvation at the moment. A.J. even had a plan for that, helping my mom in the greenhouse we had set up to grow spinach, turnip greens, and other vegetables high in beta-carotene.

While Carson and I rocked, the ground started to shake. "What the hell?" could be heard from everyone outside and inside the house. I was just starting to think it was an earthquake when I saw the planes' outlines, not only one or two jets but dozens of them.

"Oh, my God! The military is finally doing something," Kayla said as she and Jalyn were jumping around in the yard.

"Is it the Blue Angels?" Brandon asked, standing next to me and taking a screaming baby Carson from my arms.

I just shrugged my shoulders. The jets were all zipping by us; the noise made everyone hold onto their ears. I was scared it was going to break the windows out of the houses. I was watching all of them shake in their frames.

We boarded up from the inside, but I really didn't want to lose any insulation from the cold.
I was just about to start pointing at the windows when Jacob walked up behind me. He scared the shit out of me when he put his hand on my shoulder. Jacob hadn't really wanted to come out of the house after Keith died. Not even Hazel could get him to go to our group dinners.

"Tara, those are J-7 Airguard," he said with a solemn look.

This told me absolutely nothing. When the only reaction Jacob received from his comment was a slow blink, he started to move everyone into the house. Most of the kids stayed outside to watch the planes, and then a few dozen helicopters go by. All the adults gathered in my living room in front of Jacob. There was so much excited chatter in the room; it took several seconds for Jacob to gain everyone's attention.

"Everyone quiet, please, those are J-7 Airguard jets. Those are the jets of the Chinese military, not the Americans. Not only that, but those helicopters that followed the jets were the AS 350 Ecureuil. All of those aircraft are fighting and attacking weapons. Either the Chinese are here to help America, or they're here to invade it," Jacob said, dropping his upraised arms to his sides. 'I'm not sure it's a good thing they're here. If they're here over Oklahoma, they're were coming from Tinker Air force base. There's really no other place for that many aircraft to land and take off again."

The group was silent for several seconds before my dad spoke up. "America was in a trade war with the Chinese and Iran before the bombs hit our cities, but would that really have been enough to initiate an invasion? That just doesn't seem logical."

"Do you remember a couple of months ago when the U.S. Navy expanded patrols? Didn't they have some kind of skirmish with the Chinese vessels or something?" I asked.

"I don't remember, I think I saw something like that, but I really thought if anyone had dropped the bombs as they did, it would have been Iran. It seemed like we were pissing them off daily," my dad replied.

That was when the noise started again outside. "Holy Shit! What the hell kind of plane is that?" I asked nobody in particular.

Flying over my home was the largest plane I had ever seen. It was much higher than the attack aircraft had been. I was still able to make out a large round circle on the tail of the plane. Jacob stood next to me, looking up in awe like the rest of us. The planes were impressive in size and definitely a sight.

"I'm not sure what those are. It's definitely some kind of cargo plane," he said, yelling to be heard over the noise.

"That's a hell of a lot of cargo," I said, yelling back at him.

I didn't count the planes, but I'd say there were at least twenty of the behemoths. Walking back into the house with the others, I heard the backdoor explode with activity. A.J. came running into my living room, smelling like death. Probably because he had four dead and bleeding rabbits hanging off his belt.

"Get those dead animals out of this house! You're getting blood everywhere," I screamed at him. He stumbled back and landed on a shocked and now covered in blood, Austin. Of course, the dogs took this opportunity to grab his rabbits and run out the dog door.

"Fan fucking tastic! The world is falling even more to shit, and I'm living in a God Damn Chevy Chase movie." I said, pulling A.J. up off the floor.

"Did you see them? We're under attack; we need to bug out of here!" A.J. was screaming as he was now chasing my dogs, trying to catch his dinner.

Jacob and I ran after A.J. to try and wrangle the dogs. Freya had ahold of one of the rabbit's heads while AJ had its feet. I had never seen a rabbit stretch that far. A.J. was screaming bad words, and Freya was growling and tugging for all she was worth. In the end, Freya won the now unrecognizable prize and ran off to enjoy it in peace.

"Tara, we can't stay here if we're under attack. We have a ton of weapons, but not enough to fight off a damn army from China. You saw how many planes just went by. Now imagine if all of those planes are also carrying troops in them. We'll be overrun and speaking Chinese in like a week!" a now winded A.J. said.

"I get it, A.J., I do, but we need to find out some information before we do anything as drastic as picking all these people up and moving them. Even if we did pick everything and everybody up and left, where are we going? We have a baby, six little kids, and a couple of teens. Not to mention some people of uhm, advanced age," I said, giving a side-eye to Jacob. 'Let's just take a day or two to see if we can find out any information over the radio. Nobody has been on since they've just been trying to survive. Still, I'm guessing a full-scale invasion would start somewhere other than Oklahoma. They were coming from the South, so probably from somewhere in Texas. Texas avoided most of the nuclear fallout from the bombs. Give me a day or two to try and find out some more information. In the meantime, you start thinking of locations and how we're going to get everyone moved. We also need a plan for moving our food and any defenses we have set up. Deal?" I asked.

"Okay, I'll start checking the paper maps and looking for spots, but I mean it, Tara. I'm not going to sit around here and just wait to be shot by the Chinese or put into some kind of camp," he said, getting off the ground and walking back into the workshop.

"Shit, do you think he's right?" I asked as I turned to Jacob.

"Honestly, it doesn't make sense for the Chinese to invade. Plus, the odds of them just casually driving or flying by without an American rocket chasing them is slim to none. Even with the EMP that was detonated first, we wouldn't have lost all of our weapons and vehicles," he said.

Chapter 26

We walked back inside to be met by every set of eyes in the house. "What?" I asked.

"What, what the hell do you mean "what"? Do you think that A.J. is right?" Kayla asked.

"I'll tell all of you the same thing I told him. We need more information before we decide to do anything. I want a couple of people covering the radio around the clock and the rest of you helping A.J. develop a plan to bug out. If it is actually an invasion, which I really don't think it can be, at least we will have a plan B," I said to the group as a whole.

This seemed to appease the group for now. In my own head, I was freaking the fuck out. I calmly walked down the hall and into my bedroom, shutting the door slowly behind me.

I had no more sat down on my bed when my door burst open, and Kayla came in. "I KNEW IT!"

When I didn't answer and tried to give her my best utterly confused look, she started in on me again.
"I knew that was your "Let's be calm and talk about this" mom crap! You are just as freaked out as the rest of us. HA," she said, sitting down next to me on the bed.

"I am freaking out. The idea of losing American soil to any country is just unthinkable. I didn't lie when I said I really don't think it's an invasion by the Chinese. They're still our allies. If we had ended our relationship with them for some reason, we would have seen it on the news. Don't forget something big was going on behind closed doors in our own country. Whoever is behind this proved that when they assassinated the President and Vice President," I said.

"Who do you think could have dropped the bombs on us?" Kayla asked while flopping back on my bed. "Do you think it was really Iran like the new president said?"

"If I honestly had to guess, it would have been a joint effort between multiple countries. The US has too many satellites and anti-missile weapons. We have one of the best, if not the best, military in the world. Some random country couldn't have pulled something like this off without a major superpower behind them," I said.

"You mean like China?" Kayla asked in her best deadpan voice.

"Yeah, kiddo, like China," I answered.

The rest of the evening was spent making plans, fighting over the plans, then rewriting the plans. After a few hours of listening to the constant yelling and fighting, I took myself to bed. Brandon followed me within the hour. I heard him sigh as he came in and closed our door.

He sat at the end of our bed, holding his head in his hands. "This is a shit show. Everybody out there thinks their ideas are the only ideas. Ryan showed up with Jalyn after you went to bed. They want to send a team south towards the air force base to see if the Chinese have somehow taken over. A.J. wants to flee into the trees or some shit, and your dad wants to stay here and wait it out. It sounds like our group will be splitting up," He said, coming up to lay beside me.

"And what do you think?" I asked.

"I kind of want to know what's going on at the air force base. The problem is getting there. It's in the middle of the city, and it wasn't exactly in the safest part of the city, to begin with. I can only imagine what it looks like now. If we could fly.." he started.

"No way, even if one of the pilots wanted to go up, what happens if they run into one of those Chinese fighter jets? I will guess if they're here for bad reasons, they won't take kindly to small aircraft buzzing around. Regardless of what we do, we would have to hit a gas station first and use our pump to fill some cans. We need to do that anyway, and soon. The generators are running on fumes, and we still have at least another month of cold." I said.

"True, we'll do it tomorrow; for now, I just want some peace and quiet," he said.

Brandon was asleep in seconds. I had always envied his ability to just kind of turn his brain off. Neither of us had a watch shift tonight. It was rare that we both even got to sleep next to one another anymore. I was thinking of new ways to work our schedule to have more time together when I heard my door creak open.

"Mom," I heard a whisper come from the open door.

"What?" I said, kind of annoyed now.

"Kayla left with Ryan and Jalyn. They're about to take off to see if they can see the air force base in the dark," Max was stage whispering.

"Damn it," I groaned as I got out of bed.

I dressed in less than a minute and left my room to head outside. Ryan's hanger was all the way at the other end of the half a mile runway. How in the world he thought he would sneak off in a 1982 Beechcraft Bonanza was beyond me. That plane shook my entire house every time he took off. It was a much larger plane than I was used to flying. Keith's Cessna only held four passengers, versus Ryan's that seated six.

I knew he would have to come down to my end of the runway to take off, so I just sat and waited. It didn't take long before the plane came down the runway to ready for take-off. I held up my flashlight and flailed my arms around like an idiot until he cut his engines.

Growing up on a runway, the first thing you learn is to never walk around a plane with the propellers going. When I was a kid, a plane had come in for a landing. The passenger had to pee really bad, so she tried to jump out and run. She ran just a little too close and lost her arm. Once you see that kind of thing, you never walk up to a running plane, at least I don't.

Ryan popped open the window. "Hey, we're going to fly into the city and look around," he said.

"Do you think it's safe with the Chinese fighter planes around?" I asked, coming to stand under his window.

"They all flew north; since we're flying south, it shouldn't be a problem. I just want to look around," he said.

"Jalyn, who has your children?" I asked, looking past Ryan.

"Hazel kept them tonight. They like playing with Keith's cat," Jalyn said from the co-pilot seat.

"Fine, open up. I'll go with you," I said.

Kayla opened the door looking a little sheepish. "Sorry, I just didn't want you to wake you up," she said.

I just rolled my eyes; again, this was the loudest plane ever. I yelled over to Max and told him where we were going and to tell his dad. Brandon wouldn't be thrilled. I left him at home with all the crazy people, but I know he was just as curious as the rest of us about what was going on.

Once we left the ground, we rose to about three thousand feet. Some bullets could travel this high, but hopefully not from the general population. The night was beautiful tonight. Without all the lights from the city, all you could see was starlight. Thankfully we had almost a full moon tonight. Ryan was trained to fly by instruments or by sight.

We flew for about thirty minutes before we saw the light. It was the base, and it was lit up like a Christmas tree. It was beautiful and blinding at the same time. We stayed at a pretty good distance. The last thing we needed was to be shot down for entering the air forces' air space. Ryan had grabbed two pairs of binoculars we usually used while on patrol at the airport. I wasn't thrilled knowing we had left anyone at a disadvantage.

"Here, mom, take a look. Look at the aircraft that's parked to the side of the main runway," Kayla said after a minute.

It took me a minute to focus on the area she was pointing out. When I finally did, my heart dropped. Looking around the base, I didn't see even one American plane. It was all the Chinese air force planes like the ones we had seen flying around our place. People walked around the base, but I couldn't really make out what kind of uniforms they wore or what nationality they might be.

As we flew around the base's far side, I saw many white hummers with "UN" displayed on the hood. "It's the UN," I said. 'Maybe they are here to help."

"Tara, look a little further up the row of vehicles," Jalyn said.

When I did, I saw a row of darker hummers with the Chinese flag on them. Next to the hummers were three tanks, also bearing the Chinese flag.

"If they're here to help, why would they need tanks?" Kayla asked.

I just shrugged. What else could I do? I was wondering the same thing. We made a complete circle around the base but really only ended up with more questions than answers.

As we flew through the city, I saw small fires. It looks like all the crazy rioters and looters were done for the night if there still was any. At least I thought that until the small arms fire started.
We were flying pretty high, but I still swear a bullet whizzed by us. Ryan immediately began to climb in attitude just to be on the safe side.

The rest of the flight was pretty uneventful. With the plane's radios and headsets not working, we couldn't really talk. Small aircraft were so loud on the inside. Ryan had told me he was lucky his plane was in the metal hanger when the EMP had gone off. He thinks the hanger acted like some kind of Faraday cage. The metal was protecting the plane from damage, but the plane's headsets wouldn't work for some reason. It was okay with me not to talk.

We landed back at the Myrick Airport just as the sun was coming up. It didn't take long for people to start coming out of the houses. Ryan parked the plane in the hanger, and we all climbed out in silence. None of us quite sure what to say. I hadn't seen Ryan's plane in the light. He had painted new fancy red stripes down the side with "The Spitfire" in large red letters.

"Fancy," I told him with a grin.

I had only made it about a quarter of the way down the airstrip before I was met by Brandon. "What the hell Tara? Did you and those kids really jump in a plane and take off to an air force base in the middle of the damn night? Did you think, "oh, maybe I should wake up my husband," ya know, like in case you were shot down and I never saw you again?" Brandon was all out screaming at me now. He still managed to wrap me up in his arms. He was shaking, either with worry or anger, or maybe a combo of both.

"I'm sorry, honey. Max came in after you were asleep and said the girls had loaded up in Ryan's plane and were getting ready to take off. I just kind of made a snap decision. I should have woken you, but I didn't plan to get on the plane when I left our room. I just saw the girls on there and couldn't let them go without me," I said. This didn't seem to appease him at all, judging by the look on his face.

"Brandon, if you're done yelling at Tara, can we please hear about what they saw in the city?" A.J. said, walking up to the growing crowd. Brandon just rolled his eyes as we started the walk back to our house.

Along with Ryan and the girls, I spent most of the next hour going over every detail of what we had seen on the air force base. Nobody missed the fact we didn't see any American planes.

"Maybe they were just in the hangers? If Iran dropped the bombs, why are the Chinese here unless it's to help?" Max asked.

"Anything is possible, but I just can't see the government allowing that much of a foreign presence on an American base," my mother said.

"They brought tanks. Does that seem a little suspicious to anyone else? I still say we need to bug out into the woods and get away from the airstrip. What's to keep one of the Chinese choppers from landing right here in our back yard? Max, if I had to guess, China just waited for the smoke to clear before coming for the land assault," A.J. chimed in from the other side of the room.

There was a chorus of "Yeah" and "See? I told you" going all around the room. "Honestly, I still think we need to take a day trip. I need fuel for the plane. I was thinking about flying back into Guthrie airport. We haven't heard from that jackass in weeks. Maybe he decided to bother someone else," Ryan said with Jalyn perched on his lap.

"So we want to fly back into town and remind him why he started his crap in the first place? Besides, we had talked about making a run to the gas station today, and we only have one hand pump," I added.

"Okay, okay, it's just now dawn. Why don't we let Ryan and a few people fly into Guthrie airport to fuel the plane? After they get back, we can drive up to the gas station. We're going to need people to work the pump and fill the cans, plus a handful of people to be lookout and shooters if necessary," Brandon said, getting to his feet.

Brandon hadn't made eye contact with me since this morning when he was screaming at me. I don't think he had been this upset with me in our seventeen years of marriage. I watched him say good morning to the kids: they were all walking into the house for breakfast, then turning and heading to our room with a very resounding "slam" of our bedroom door.

The group, as a collective, turned to stare at me. "I know, I know, I messed up," I said as I walked through them to my bedroom door.

"Babe?" I said as I lightly tapped on the door.

"Tara, I'm really not in the mood to talk to you right now," came from the other side of the door.

I turned and walked away. This was going to take some groveling, but there was a lot of shit to do, and I needed to get started doing it.

Chapter 27

I walked out onto another, freezing March morning. In Oklahoma, winter really went anywhere from December to April before the heat and humidity kicked in to fill in the calendar's rest. I think Mother Nature decided we didn't need the rest of those pesky seasons, like fall and spring. One day it would be ninety degrees, and the next, it could be thirty with snow falling. Mother Nature was a bi-polar bitch around the south. The grass mowing season alone was April through November; that was why we always had so many gas cans full. It took two commercial-sized mowers and one large tractor to take care of the runway and all the acreage around it.

"Tara, do you want to hit the airport with Jalyn, Kayla, and I?" Ryan called from across the yard.

"I might as well, but let me go tell Brandon and see if he wants to ride along this time," I called.

I jogged back into the house only to be met by my mother. Apparently, Brandon wasn't the only one pissed off about last night. She didn't say anything to me but gave me her "mom look" while shoving some kind of flatbread covered in oatmeal at me. "Yuck," I thought but wisely kept my comment to myself.

I went down the hall to my room, opened the door, and walked in. I didn't want to give him the chance to tell me to buzz off this time.

Brandon was lying on our bed, arms crossed over his chest. "Do you have any idea how scared I was when I woke up, and Max told me you had jumped in a plane and flown away to see an airbase that had probably been taken over by invaders?"

"Babe," I started but was cut off.

"No, don't. Just don't. You scared the shit out of me! Not only did you do something that was incredibly fucking stupid, but you had OUR DAUGHTER and a girl I think of as my daughter in that plane! I could have lost two of you in the blink of an eye! Now that I'm done being scared, I'm just pissed. I just need some time. Can you just go, please?" he said.

"Okay, I really am sorry about last night. I came in to tell you, Ryan and the girls are flying to town to see if they can get some gas for the airplane. I came to see if you would go with me as a shooter while Ryan fills the plane's tanks," I said.

"Fuck, of course, you came in to say you were doing something stupid. Sure, load up; let's go," he snarked back. This was already turning out to be a great fucking day. Yeah me.

When Brandon and I left the house, my mother handed him some breakfast that looked much better than whatever in the hell it was she had passed me; everyone was ready to go.

Kayla and Jalyn were both decked out with rifles and handguns. Kayla could be a sniper; her aim was so good; Jalyn, though, jumped every time someone even cocked a gun. I walked over and checked both girls' guns to ensure the safety was on; it was more about checking Jalyn's weapons than Kayla's. Brandon and I took Kayla to the gun and rifle range from the day she turned sixteen and was allowed to enter. She had a God-given talent of aim. I'd seen that girl shoot happy face patterns into her targets at thirty yards since she was seventeen.

Before we could even get into the plane, we smelled smoke. I could kind of see some dark spots much further south, but I couldn't tell how far away the fire was.

The five of us loaded up in the plane. I decided since I didn't want to feel Brandon glaring at me, I would be Ryan's co-pilot today. I busied myself with pre-flight checks while everyone else got buckled. Thankfully the flight was only about ten minutes long; I could already feel his pissed-off glare on my back.
Ryan started the props, and we were off. Once we achieved altitude, we could see fires burning all over Oklahoma City to our south. Last night the city had seemed pretty quiet; today, it looked like the whole damn city was burning. The original plan was to fly straight into Guthrie airport, get fuel, and get back, but Ryan was flying us south towards the fires.

I was trying to see to the south, but there was so much smoke. It wasn't until Ryan started tugging on my sleeve that I saw the problem. Riots, there were riots in the streets. What looked like thousands of people were out in the streets burning down people's homes and the small-town shops. Most of these rioters had been purchasing their coffee and organic produce from those same shops for years.

I shrugged at Ryan; it was too loud to mess with much yelling. Banking the plane now to the north, we flew towards our own small town. Things on the highway looked different, like someone had come along and started pushing cars off the road and onto the shoulder. I had no idea who would undertake such a project, but I was glad it wasn't us. About two miles up the highway, we could see the highway clean-up crew. There were several dozen Chinese troops and troop transports pushing the cars to the side of the road.

Ryan's now persistent pulling on my sleeve made me look further over to see another large group. It looked like a group of rioters. The thirty or so rioters looked like they were headed for conflict.

The rioters started bending down behind the abandoned cars. Then the gunfire started. The rioters shot and killed some of the Chinese soldiers. The Chinese all turned as one and opened fire. The Chinese were using guns that from this height looked like machine guns, but I couldn't tell for sure. The men and women in the riot were being gunned down at record speed, their small handguns and rifles being no match for the much faster rounds of the Chinese guns.

Ryan banked the plane hard to the right. This caused us to almost do a full barrel roll. When we had first spotted the soldiers, we had slowed the plane's engines while we looked at them. A few of them had looked up, but none of them seemed overly upset about our plane being above them. None of them had pointed guns, and most didn't even bother to look up. Once we saw what was happing, it was all about the retreat.

Ryan was now pushing speeds of two hundred miles per hour. He also had pulled us up around six thousand feet from what I could see on his side of the dials. The air at this altitude was cold, so much colder than our usual three thousand feet. My hands, arms, and legs were starting to go numb. I opened all the vents to pull the engine's heat, but the outside temperature was still freezing.

I looked back at Kayla and Jalyn, sitting in the row of seats directly behind us. They were shaking. I'm sure some of it was from the cold, but the sudden crazy flying and the carnage going on below us didn't help.

Brandon was sitting in the third row of seats. I wanted nothing more than to climb out of my seat and go back to him. "I love you," I mouthed to him.

"I love you too," was his mouthed response.

Ryan flew the plane at this height for about five miles. All of us were shaking from the cold. I could see his hands shaking on the yoke as he began to slowly lower our altitude. With the lower altitude, the plane began to warm back up. I was still shaking, but at least I had regained some feeling back in my limbs.

We entered Guthrie from the far north side. I didn't really want this much exposure, especially near where the "boss" guy had his base, but we didn't really have a choice. It was either enter town closer to the Chinese and their large machine guns or take a chance of alerting "The boss" and any remaining men he had that we were back in town. All I could do was hope since the plane was different, nobody would put the pieces together.

The town looked pretty good. The fires that had been set in the first couple of days since the EMP had finally gone out. Most of the downtown shops had been lost to the fires.

As we flew over the town, I didn't really see many people out on the streets. Actually, I had only seen two, and they didn't seem bothered by the plane at all. As we approached the airport, though, things got worse. The tall grey tower we all used to communicate our landings and takeoffs was burned to the ground. The large metal hangers all down the main landing strip where all the local pilots came for maintenance were also burned. They had also pulled the planes out and burned them down to the frame.

We all looked down in stunned silence. This airport had been a home, a hangout, just generally a respite type of place for pilots all over the country. People would fly in on large personal jets to the smallest crop-duster. When I was a little girl, my grandpa used to fly us into the airport for fuel. While he was with the plane, I would go into the tower to get both a soda and some candy. I hated the idea that my kids would never get to see it in its glory.

"Seventy-nine God Damn years!" Ryan yelled and slammed his hand down on the yoke. The runway was five thousand feet long, but the burned-out planes littered the runway. There would be no getting fuel for the planes anymore, at least not from this airport.

The ride home was smooth. We gave the highway a large birth this time, flying a good ten miles out of our way to get back home. This would probably be the last flight for Ryan and the spitfire unless we could find fuel in the city. A city that was currently on fire, swarming with rioters and full of Chinese soldiers doing God knows what.

"What now, mom?" Kayla asked as she climbed out of the plane.

Ryan had gotten out and just walked off, Jalyn hurrying along behind him. He was going to need some time. Ryan, like myself, had grown up around that airport. I think I remembered him saying his family had even rented out one of the hangers to start their own maintenance shop. He had never mentioned where his parents were during the blast.

After my grandfather died, I stopped flying for years, one reason being I didn't have a license, but the other being, I couldn't stand being in a plane without him. It felt like cheating on him in some way. It wasn't until my mid-thirties that I started taking lessons. I just couldn't make myself enjoy it. I ended my classes with only two hours of training left. This had left my mother, speechless. She was furious that I would spend all that money and time only to get to the very end and quit. I couldn't make her understand how much it hurt to be in a plane without him.

"Mom?" Kayla asked again.

"I'm sorry, what?" I said in a dazed tone.

"I asked you what we're going to do now. If we can't get fuel for the plane, we can't use it to bug out. We only have one truck. Ryan has a truck, but it's a lot smaller. I'm not sure how many people it will hold even if we cram people in the back," Kayla said, now mildly annoyed.

"I'm not sure what we'll do next," I said, disheartened.

Brandon came over then and took my hand. We began walking to the crowd that had formed our family and friends. Brandon brought our joined hands up to his mouth and kissed my hand. "It will be okay. We'll figure something out. I hate the thought of leaving here, but the crazy redneck might be right about bugging out." I started to argue but was cut off. "Think about it, babe, we live on a runway. Someone or some army could come and land right in our back yard. We need to think about the group as a whole. We have so many children and animals here. It's going to be a nightmare to get all these people somewhere safe," he said.

I just kept walking, lost in my own thoughts again. Brandon was right; soon, we as a group would have to make some hard decisions.

The retelling of our trip went about the way I thought it would. There was a lot of yelling and a lot of cursing.

"Quiet!" my father yelled over the crowd of people in my living room. 'Listen, I hate to have to say this, but is it possible the Chinese fired on the rioters because they were fired upon? Would any of you stand there waiting to be shot? No, you would fire back. The kids said the soldiers were clearing the roads. That doesn't sound overly sinister to me," he finished.

Brandon stood then. "I think it's time to seriously think about moving to a new location. I talked to Tara after we landed. We have to think about how much has to be relocated. We can do it now before some Chinese soldiers land in our back yard, or we can wait until we're literally on the run," he said.

"I have an idea," A.J. said. 'What if we relocate to the lake? There is already a group there, but it's a big lake. It gives us access to fishing and hunting. The dogs are going through a deer a week for food. Eventually, we would have to expand our hunting grounds anyway. All of the same plants we've been eating grow by the lake, and maybe even a few more."

"How are we going to move all of these people into tents in the middle of the winter? Plus, not all of us have tents," my mom interjected.

The crowd was starting to all run together with their talking. I had begun to tune all of them out when I thought I heard the radio going off. "Shut up!" I screamed, probably a little too loud. Everyone stopped and turned. I could see they were getting ready to turn their anger out on me when we all heard the radio.

All of us rushed into the radio room, aka Alicia and Michael's room now. I sat down at the desk and cranked up the radio speakers. We had left the radio on pretty much all of the time. The battery the radio ran on was easy to charge, so we could get it on almost all the time.

This is WKLS bringing you a broadcast from the President of the United States:
I give this speech today in front of the remaining joint chiefs, congress, and all my fellow Americans.

For the last forty-eight days, America has seen a significant change. We have witnessed heartache and death, but we have also seen the American spirit that makes us who we are as a nation. I have seen Americans gathering together to help their fellow man. I have seen groups of people who have banded together to become a new kind of family in the last forty-eight days. Americans are fighters and survivors.

I know many of you have questions today, and I will try to answer as many as possible.
Iran dropped a series of bombs on the American people in retaliation for our attack on a known terrorist leader. Iran dropped these bombs on our major cities not only to end life but to end a way of life.

Be assured America is using every resource and every bit of intelligence to win the war Iran has started.

I'm sure you're asking how this could happen in a nation as great as America.

At almost the exact moment of the electromagnetic pulse, while our nation and military were scrambling to get our technology up and running, Iran launched its nuclear weapons. This was a window of around sixty seconds.

In response to this tragedy, America welcomed its allies to assist in cleanup and rebuilding.
Some of you might have already seen the large planes and naval vessels carrying vital supplies America needs.

The United Nations has sent help in the form of food, water, and personnel.

I am asking from one American to another to be patient with our friends. Help is being sent out to all major cities and will continue to spread until we reach all of the smallest towns.

American troops from around the world have been called back home. This was a considerable undertaking and still may take several months.

Workers from the United Nations started construction sites this last month to rebuild America's power systems. It will take at least eighteen months to three years to fully establish power in all previous areas. Special care is being taken to rebuild the grids that keep our nuclear power plants running. Again all systems will be restored, but I am asking you for patience.

I am asking all Americans, males ages eighteen to forty, and females without children or elderly to care for, ages eighteen to forty, to please come to your nearest military base. In this time of crisis, your help is desperately needed. This is not a reinstatement of the draft. This is a request for help from your president.

In the coming days, you will begin to see more planes, ships, and military vehicles. These vehicles will be bringing much-needed food and water to our population. If you miss a truck, don't worry, another one will be along soon.

I am asking all Americans to treat our new neighbors like what they are, our guests.

Thank you.

Chapter 28

"Is anyone buying that shit?" a now laughing A.J. choked out.

"Sadly, no. I can see maybe having the United Nations get involved. Still, there's no way a sitting President of the United States would ever allow foreign troops on our soil. It also seems suspicious our fallen President and Vice President would be killed off right before the Chinese came over to help. Their administration was tough on the Chinese. I mean, we were in a trade war before the bombs dropped. They, to me anyway, would have been the last country to come and help us and want nothing in return," my father was adding in.

"So, are we decided on going forward with our moving plans?" I asked the group as a whole.

This time around, there was no fighting or yelling, just grim nods of assent.
The group broke up and moved back into the living room. My dad started to pull out note pads and hand them out.

"If we're going to do this, we need to make sure we don't leave anything out. A.J., I need you to log everything that needs to be moved to the lake in the shop. Hazel, same for you. Anything we need from Keith's house. Jeri and I will do the same with our home. Kayla, take this pad and head down to your house. Tara, Brandon, and Connor can take this place. Everyone else, we need to use this time to find gas for the cans. A group needs to take all of the cans and the pump and go on the hunt. Try and find anything we can use for baby formula, too," he said.

We started to break up into our groups. Jalyn and Alicia, leaving the boys with us at the house, headed off to join everyone not stuck on list duty to gather the gas cans. I wasn't really excited that it was mostly our young people heading off on this errand. I watched out the window as the truck pulled out of the drive.

"Upset, you weren't on that team?" Brandon said, walking into our room with a smirk.

"It's not that I'm upset; I just don't like our kids going off without us to protect them," I replied.

"Tara, we have two adult children and one teen that is going to have to grow up now. I don't like it either, but that's life. Remember how upset you got when Kayla moved in with Carlos in the city? You freaked out and ran background checks on his whole family," Brandon said in a full snorting kind of laugh now.

"She was just a kid," I said.

"Tara, she was twenty-four," he replied. Brandon stepped up behind me at the window and put his arms around me. 'I'm scared for them too, but we can't hold them back from being the people they're going to be."

"I know that in my brain, but my heart just wants to keep them all home and safe," I said.

Brandon kissed my head and went on about his task of cataloging all our belongings.
I couldn't believe Brandon was taking the move as well as he was. He had built most of our home with his bare hands. Board by board, as he liked to say, and we were leaving it all behind.
It had taken Brandon and me six years to save up the money to build this house. After losing a home to the 2008 market crash, we were bound and determined we would never lose anything else.

2008 had been such a nightmare. I never dreamed of how much we would, or even could, lose.
Early fall of 2007, Brandon and I had decided to move from our family land to a house in the middle of town. We saved; we made damn sure that our mortgage was low enough so that even if one of us lost our job in the oil business, we would have no problem paying our bills. What we weren't expecting was for the entire market to crash. Within eight months, we lost our home. We moved back to our families' land and decided to stay.

Building the home was harder on both of us than either of us could have ever predicted. Brandon and I spent hours drawing the plans only to tear them up and start over. Once construction finally started, it was usually just he and I doing the work. We worked through the summer, sweating to death with no air conditioning, and the winter, when we were so bundled up, we could barely swing a hammer. This wasn't just home to us; it was years of saving and lost weekends all spent right here.

I sat down on my bed, feeling sorry for myself for about another ten minutes before pulling myself up and going to help the others. Walking out into the hall, I was almost run over by the children rolling baby Carson around in a stroller. The baby was squealing and waving his little fists in the air while the other children cheered and ran off around the corner.

"Sorry, Gigi, I didn't mean to run over your foot," Ryler's gorgeous blue eyes looked up at me.

I bent down and kissed his head and then baby Carson's head. "It's fine, but you need to remember Carson is just a baby. Slow down before he falls out of the stroller, or you run over someone else," I said.

"Can you take him, Gigi? I want to pack my stuff. If mommy does it, she might forget something," he said.

"Yep, you go ahead," I said, grinning at the innocence.

"Thanks!" he said, turning around and running towards his house.

Brandon walked up behind me, holding the baby's carrier for my chest. "You know he's going to pack every toy he has in his room, right?" Brandon asked, handing me the carrier.

"Sure, but that's a problem for his mother. Loving grandmothers can do anything they want," I said with a wink.

Baby Carson and I spent the next hour counting supplies and making lists, the sweet baby finally dozing off while strapped against my chest. My busted shoulder was throbbing from where the bullet entered. It had been almost a month since I was shot, but I didn't recover the way I used to.
Brandon and I spent the next few hours switching between carrying Carson around and letting the boys push him in a

stroller. I had forgotten how difficult having a small baby was. When Alicia had given birth to her boys, I would spend hours or sometimes the whole day playing with them at their house. The difference being I could go home when I got tired, and now there was no leaving. Carson, for his part, was a wonderful baby. He had even managed to gain a few pounds between baby formula we had managed to come up with, powdered milk, and sweetened condensed milk. He was happy and healthy from what Michael could see. All of the children were.

I really worried about how things would work moving to the lake. Would the kids be too cold? Would we be able to hunt the amount of game and forage for the right greens? I knew that was a silly concern. A.J. put on a crazy redneck front for everyone but the kids. I would walk into the shop to see all the kids sitting around him in a circle. At the same time, he showed them how to carve a cup or something out of a piece of wood while his crazy cat laid in the middle of all of them, allowing the children to take turns giving her pets. All of the children and the teens loved him. They spend most of their day following him around like he was the Pied Piper.

All of us would fight and die for every one of those children, but A.J. just had a special bond with them. When A.J. had first shown up, Jalyn had tried to keep the kids at a distance; it wasn't until they all started sneaking off to hang out with him that she just gave up.
I walked out to the shop to see just that. Brody, Ryler, Sean, and Joe all sitting around while A.J. talked to himself and made his list. I did notice out of the corner of my eye, Brody had packed and dragged two of his mother's suitcases into the shop. This made me smile; she was going to love that.

"How are we looking on supplies?" I asked A.J.

"Not bad, we could use more, but I think we have everything we need to live off the land. Our main problem is going to be housing all these people. We have two eight-man tents, one four-man tent, and a bunch of tarps. If we drag Connor's motor home, RV thing with us, we could use it to transport our supplies. This would take fewer trips and allow for a few people to live in the RV. We have what…twenty-two people and eight animals going? The tents we have will hold everyone, but it's not going to be comfortable. My main concern is going to warmth. We will have to make a large fire in the middle with the tents surrounding it, but that size of the fire is going to draw attention." He said, looking over a large pile of supplies he had gathered together.

"I'll talk to my dad. The RV is hooked up to the main septic system and uses power tied to my parents' house right now. It will all have to be taken apart. As for the tents, I know. Actually, I don't know what we're going to do about it. When we use those for camping, we feel crammed in with all our stuff in there. I guess we'll just have to make due until we figure something out. Keith! Keith had an old RV down in his field. I think it's been sitting there for like ten years, but it could be cleaned up and used," I said.

After going over the RV plans with my parents, A.J. and I headed over to Keith's. Jacob was outside chopping wood for the woodstove.

"Hey, guys, what's up?" Jacob said, setting the ax down and turning to us.

"That's what's up," I said, pointing at the broken-down looking RV out in the field.

"If it's in good enough shape to be moved, maybe we can use it as a shelter over at the lake," A.J. filled in behind me as we all started to walk.

I opened the door to the RV. The tires were flat, so it was really that high off the ground. This was a good thing since the stairs were missing from the front. The RV was musty. It smelled like maybe water had gotten in somewhere and leaked all over the carpet. We all three climbed the rest of the way in.

"Other than the leak and possible mold damage, it's not that bad," I said, turning to the guys.

A.J. was already walking around looking at the floor and ceiling; I guessed to see how much would need to be repaired. "It will take some work, but I think it's doable. We have some building materials in the shop and even some leftover laminate wood flooring. If we fixed the roof and treated the mold, it could hold maybe five people. That's five more people to be out of tents."

"Excellent! Even if we could get the small children into an RV and out of the tents, that would be a huge blessing," I said, excitement starting to well up for our plan. Jacob didn't look as convinced as I felt, but he didn't say anything. 'It's getting dark. Let's get back to the houses. We can sort all this out tomorrow." I said.

The darkening of the sky reminded me of how long the kids had been gone. Brandon had given Kayla a portable radio, but nobody had called in with problems as far as I knew. The radio only went about as far as our closest gas station, if that. If the kids got into trouble, they wouldn't even be able to radio in for help.

I walked back across the runway to my own home. I loved walking in, and having the warmth from the woodstove hit me. I wondered if I would ever get that feeling again.
My mom was standing over our wood stove, using the top of it to cook dinner. She was cooking some kind of soup that smelled heavenly. I could see chunks of some sort of mystery meat. Anymore almost all our meals were stews and soups; breakfast, some kind of oatmeal soup. Some days we got a treat of bread she made. Lunch was always random weed stew, and dinner was a meat stew with a little rice and random weeds that AJ and the children had foraged for in the woods. She may have moved next door back to her own home, but she still liked all of us to eat together.

We sat quietly, eating our dinner and letting the kids tell us all about the things they had packed for our move to the lake. Brody explained in great detail every toy he had packed and why. He even packed his floats and lake shoes for when it gets warm again. I made a mental list to pack life jackets for all the children. After dinner, I stood in front of the window, baby Carson asleep in my arms. It was dark now, and still no kids, Alicia or Michael.

"Honey, let's put the baby down and try and get some rest. Tomorrow is going to be a long one," Brandon said, coming up behind me.

"I can't. Not until the kids get back; they've been gone for like eight hours. What if something happened? What if they were attacked or the truck broke down? There are a million things that could have happened," I said, panic beginning to rear its ugly head.

"Or it could be taking longer because it's the apocalypse, and nothing ever seems to go as planned. Let's not panic. How many times have we been gone longer than we thought when we went out to do something?" He said, trying to soothe me.

I handed the baby to Brandon but pulled a chair over to the window. I must have dozed off because Brandon woke me to come to bed sometime in the night. The house was dark and quiet. Sean and Joe were snuggled up asleep on the couch. It wasn't the first night they had been away from their parents overnight, but I think even they were worried. Brandon and I slowly lifted the boys and took them to bed.

Baby Carson was in the middle of our bed, surrounded by the dogs. He was so peaceful I picked up an extra blanket and headed back to the couch. I laid in the dark until the sun came up. The house started to come alive with the arrival of my parents and Connor. Mom started on breakfast, and the smell of food woke up the rest of the house.

I gave up on trying to rest when the kids came running into the room. The living room had a wood stove, so the kids liked to hang out and play with their toys. My mother would always moan about stepping on their toys while she was trying to cook a meal. She never made the kids move, though. I think she secretly enjoyed the company. None of us knew how to cook anything. Alicia was an amazing cook, but she needed the modern conveniences of electric ovens to work her magic- not fire. I couldn't boil water before the apocalypse, now was not the time to try and learn.

The rest of the morning went by in a flash. Connor's RV was disconnected from everything and ready to move. We started to load the RV with all of the gear we were carrying, and it was a lot to cram in. We would be lucky if we only had to make two trips.

A.J., Jacob, and Hazel worked on Keith's RV. A.J. had managed to find the leak and replace part of the ceiling. He had also torn out all the old carpet to find a hole near the toilet. It was a composting toilet, which A.J. said was a hell of a find.

By lunchtime, we were all worried. The handheld radio sat quietly. We had tried calling out, but we got no answer.

"It's been twenty-four hours Brandon. Should we saddle up the horses and go looking for them?" I asked.
"Do you know how to saddle a horse?" he asked in return.

"No, but how hard can it be? You just put it on their back and tie it or something," I snarked back.

"I don't think it's that easy. Let's get everything finished; by the time we get ready to go, maybe they'll be back. I'll make a deal with you; if you wait a few more hours, I'll ask A.J. to saddle a horse for you. Chances are he'll know how to do it. That crazy son of a bitch knows how to do everything else," he said with a roll of his eyes.

"Fine," I said with a sigh.

Brandon put me to work folding blankets, sheets, and the like into trash bags. That was just if it rained or something they wouldn't get wet or damaged, he had told me. Personally, I felt like he was just giving me busy work.

By dinner time, a good ninety percent of what we were taking to the lake was packed up. A.J. had taken the four small boys and the preteens to check traps in the woods when the little boys had started asking where mommy was. I think the fun of staying with Aunt Tara or Gigi was beginning to wear off.

I had asked him if he would please saddle a horse for me. His reply was to ask me if I knew how to ride a horse. When I said no, he had declined. He promised if they weren't back by morning, he would go himself to find them.

The horses had been causing problems. Since we couldn't run to the store for hay, they only ate what they could find grazing in the field. Max and Dillon had taken over caring for the horses after we lost Jess. Once my dad had mentioned, maybe setting them loose to find other grasslands, and Max had lost his shit. Screaming and yelling about what Jess would want. I understood where he was coming from. I missed Jess every day. In the end, we took to moving them around the airport as much as possible to make sure they had enough to eat. They were still a massive pain in the ass, but it would be horses or walking if we lost the truck.

I sat on the porch with my parents and baby Carson. It was a mild night, thankfully. Brandon and Connor were out on patrol tonight, so it would be just the kids and me pretty soon. As I sat looking out down the driveway, Carson began chewing on my hair. This kid chewed on everything.

"I think we're about to have a teething baby on our hands," my mom said, cooing at him.

"Michael thinks he's four or five months old. I guess that sounds about right," I said while trying to dislodge my now tangled and wet hair from his chubby little fingers.

I was trying to pull my hair back out of his reach when I saw headlights coming up the drive.

Chapter 29

My parents and I all jumped to our feet and began walking to the drive. Kayla, Max, Dillon, Ryan, and Jalyn all jumped from the back of the truck. They looked tired but no worse for wear. Alicia was almost knocked over, getting out of the truck by an excited Sean and Joe. A.J. had brought the kids back just in time. Brody and Ryler ran to Jalyn while I ran to my kids. They smelled like they had bathed in gasoline.

"Wow, that is a powerful smell," I told Max.

"I really don't want to talk about that," he said.

"What you don't want to tell mom how you dropped a full gas can? Mom, it went everywhere. We had to drive around until we found some water. It splashed up into his hair and eyes. Thank God we didn't have any smokers with us," Kayla mocked good-naturedly. 'We also found a store with the windows broken out. It didn't have much, but I found some powdered milk, six cans of that condensed milk you feed the baby, and a couple of personal items."

"That's great, honey. I am so glad you're home," I said, relief washing over me at seeing everyone home safely. I squeezed all the kids until Brandon came up and pried me off them so they could get cleaned up and grab something to eat.

"So tomorrow is the big day, huh?" I asked.

"It looks that way," he said, both of us looking up at our house.

"I'm going to miss it," I said.

"Me too, but you never know. We could get to come back. I heard Alicia say they would sneak up to their old neighborhood and see if it's still run by those assholes. If not, they're going to move back home," he said.

"Shit, can you blame them? It's either their home with all their things or crammed in a tent with multiple other people," I laughed.

The house was full of excitement when we walked in the door. An exhausted looking Alicia sat down at the dinner table. She relayed the details of the group outing all while scarfing dinner down, partly to reassure me that they were okay the whole time but also to calm herself down from the adventure. Alicia was a talker and talking things out always relaxed her.

"Okay, so when we left here yesterday, I really thought we'd be back in a couple of hours. We went South, I know you guys saw rioters, but there's also more stores and gas stations that way. Gas was actually the easiest time we had. We had just finished filling up the truck when two guys walked around the corner. I guess they had been watching the truck with binoculars or something. When they saw we were able to get gas, they came to check it out. Well, Kayla and Max had guns on them the whole time they were walking towards us. Both of the guys had guns. You could see the outline of them under their shirts. They might have drawn down on us, but Dillon and Ryan came up behind them. They asked if they could please get some gas with our pump. Ryan held them both at gunpoint while Dillon took their can and filled it up. Then they just left.

We looked inside of all the stores. The windows were all busted out, so it didn't really feel like looting anymore. We found some bottled water and paper towels. Nothing too exciting. I knew we really needed baby food, so we hid the truck and went in on foot. We had to wait until it got dark so we could move around a little easier. We had to go to three stores to find anything. Most of the stores in town were burnt down or just completely empty. We were in the last store when the rioters came. They were screaming and chanting something about being left to die. You know, because the rest of us are doing so much better. Idiots. When they finally got done and had all ran by, we made a run for it. Town has just gone crazy! It's like scenes from that *Mad Max* movie. We went to a couple more stores and looked around. That's when we found the milk for the baby. We also found a couple of jars of baby food. Michael said he's old enough to start eating the mashed up veggies and stuff. We still have to find some kind of milk for him for another eight months, but we can hopefully supplement some mashed food. We also found a bottle of multivitamins. Michael thinks we can break them up for the boys and the teens. He's anxious about the baby not getting the nutrients he needs. I looked, but sorry, I never did see any diapers. Looks like we're both stuck with washing those dirty cloth ones. Yuck.

Anyway, by the time we got back to the truck, the radio was dead, so we couldn't even call you to let you know we were okay. Did the boys do okay while we were gone?" she asked.

Sure, they missed their mommas. All four of them kept asking when you guys would be back. Thankfully A.J. kept them entertained. He took them all out after lunch to "check traps," I'm not sure how much they really do out there," I said with a laugh.

The rest of us filled in the others on our plans and everything that needed to be done. "I know we really need my truck, but I can't leave the guys at the other end of the runway without any transportation," Ryan said, sitting down with his own bowl of soup.

"Do you think they would want horses?" I asked quietly where Max and Dillon couldn't overhear. The last thing I wanted tonight was a fight.

"I don't know, maybe. We're more airplane people and less cowboy, ya know," he said.

"I know, I know, it's just going to be really hard to get them to the lake. Someone is going to have to ride them there," I said.

"A.J. and I are going to ride them; I've already talked to him about it. Dad said we're going to be pulling RVs. That means the truck will be moving slow. We can just follow behind you," Max said, coming up behind me.

"What do you know about riding horses? The only horses you've ever been on were on a merry go round," I asked.

"It can't be that hard. I'll be fine, mom. Quit worrying about it," he sighed with an obligatory teenage attitude.

Brandon gave me a smirk and a wink. I gave him the finger. With that, I got up to help my mom wash some dishes in the sink.

"It's hard not having a place in your kids' lives, isn't it? You should try being relegated to 'food maker,'" mom said, using air quotes with food maker.

"What do you mean? You just started cooking when this whole thing started. I never said you had to be the cook," I said.

"No, but you've never included me in one of the outings. You've left the kids with me several times; you've never once asked if I wanted to go to Alicia's, or fly somewhere, have you?" she asked. She was giving me a hard stare now. I knew that stare. It was the "I'm about to flip my shit all over you" stare.

"Mom, I just wanted to keep you safe. I know you can handle yourself. Hell, you taught both Kayla and me to shoot a gun. Half of the stuff we can do is because you taught it," I said. "Tara, you can't protect everyone at the same time. Dad and I are just fine. You take too much onto yourself. Let people take care of themselves," she said.

"Okay, I know. Making sure everyone is okay is the only way I've been able to keep my anxiety under control. If I have something else to focus on, I don't have to think about how bad things are or how much more difficult they might get once we move," I said, feeling like shit for trying to protect my parents. My mom was right, though; both of my parents were badasses in their own way.

Morning came exceptionally early the next day. My dad had woken everybody up by 5:00am; he had us fed and ready to go by 6:00am. The man was like a drill sergeant today. He had even assigned small children jobs. All four boys and our young teens were in charge of an animal. Animals who were not thrilled they were being pulled around by those children. Joe and Ryler were both only two years old, so Joe was in charge of Scratch, the cat who was wearing one of Skeeter's body halters and a leash. The cat seemed to take the whole thing in stride. Instead of having a fit or scratching the baby, it had laid down in the grass and refused to move. Joe, who never detoured from his duty, pulled the cat along behind him through the grass. Ryler was walking around with my sixteen-year-old blind and deaf dog, Skeeter, behind him. Ryler was walking around, talking to the blind little dog. Telling him to "Watch the tree." Unfortunately, Skeeter's grasp of the English language didn't go much further than "Treat or Park" even before he went deaf. This left Skeeter scrambling behind Ryler, running into anything in his path.

Ryan had managed to attach his truck onto Keith's old RV after an hour of airing up tires and filling them with Fix a Flat. Jalyn, Kayla, and now the boys with their animal charges in the backseat. Both of the RV's were filled as full as they could get with supplies.

A.J. and Max had the horses saddled up and ready to go. A.J. was going over the finer points of horsemanship with Max. Who knew there were so many rules about riding horses.

"Don't climb on from this side of the horse, don't walk around the back, don't pull the reins too hard, and don't let the reins droop. No, you have to kick them harder to get them going, but never too hard, or they'll throw you to the ground," I could hear A.J. giving instructions to prepare for their roughly six-mile ride.

Brandon would be pulling Connor's RV with Sean, Joe, and two dogs. All the rest of us would be piled in the back of the trucks. We had briefly talked about letting people ride in the RVs. Still, if we ran into trouble on the road, someone in the back of the truck would quickly unhook the ball hitch to the RV's, letting us make a much quicker getaway.

With ten people and a handful of animals in each truck, we pulled away from our homes. Max and A.J. were bringing up the rear behind us. Both of them looking like old-time cowboys with a rifle on their backs and hip holsters with handguns. If we got into trouble for some reason, they were supposed to make a break for it. Running the horses in different directions, while the trucks did the same. We would all meet back together when it was safe at the lake site.

I had never really thought of a six-mile drive being long or frightening before, but today was different. Today I was in the back of a truck, guns loaded with six other people—all of us facing a different direction so we could see a full 360 degrees.

"Hey, Tara," Alicia said from my left.

"Yep," I answered back, not taking my eyes off of my direction. The last thing I needed was to miss something because I was visiting.

"Michael and I've been talking. I think when we get to the lake, we might sneak up to our neighborhood. We just want to see if the same people are in charge, or if maybe the night you guys started blowing things up changed things. I saw some of my neighbors running with guns the night you came for us. Maybe things are better. I was also thinking, if you wanted to, maybe we could take baby Carson. If we end up at home, that is. At least until the cold weather passes. I have a spare room and an office. Maybe your parents, Jalyn, and the boys could come too," she said.

"Sure, I guess. When we get set up at the camp, we can head over around the back and check it out." I said.

I had gotten overly attached to Carson. Since Jess had passed, I had spent nearly every minute I wasn't on a watch or out doing something stupid with him. Carson had also decided that he liked sleeping not in his playpen but between Brandon and me in bed with the dogs. If I woke up before him in the mornings, he would be either on top of Brandon or myself. How the little inchworm had pulled that off, I'd never know.

It was a cold morning today. All you could see of the kids were eyes and leashes from somewhere in a pile. I could hear growling and hissing coming from inside the truck, but I refused to turn my head. I'd let Brandon deal with the "Cat Dog" problem going on in the truck.

"Tara! Can you please take this God damn cat? Without windows, it keeps trying to climb out on the hood," Brandon yelled at me.

"Sorry, babe, you know Freya's back here with me, you know how she feels about that cat. Hand the leash through the window, and we can maybe tie it to something." I groped my hand around until I felt the leash make contact. I didn't really have anything to tie the cat's leash to, so I put it through my belt loop. God help me if I forgot that later.

We were about two miles into our back roads country drive when we came to a roadblock.
I wasn't looking in that direction, so when we stopped, I fell on my butt, almost knocking my rifle into my forehead.

"Damn it, Brandon, what are you doing?" I asked, trying to get back to my knees. I heard a hiss coming from the front seat.

"Tara, stay in the truck, please," Brandon said as he climbed out of the truck.

I could hear Ryan pulling up and stopping behind us. I very slowly pulled myself up to standing—the rest of the people in the truck following my slow movements. It was a dark-colored hummer that blocked our paths—a hummer with the Chinese flag on it.

Three miles, we had only made it three miles. Brandon passed me with a shake of the head, walking back towards Ryan's truck, and I'm guessing A.J. and Max. Within only five minutes or so, Brandon climbed back in the truck.

"Babe, what did they say?" I whispered through the shot out back glass.

"He told me to keep on this road, then get on the highway. I told him we were looking for a safe place. I got directions to a survivor's camp in the city," he said as he smiled and waved at the Chinese soldiers.

All of the soldiers stared at us with machine guns at the ready when we passed. I smiled while pulling my gun in while we passed.

"You told him we would go to a survivor's camp? Are you crazy…" I started.

"Honey, I would have said I would run there naked if it meant they would let us go on our way in peace. The last thing we need to do is piss off a group of guys with machine guns," he said. This made sense to the rest of us because none of us said a word in response.

When we got to mile five, we were met with another group of Chinese soldiers. Again, Brandon got out and spoke to them, telling them we were headed to the survival camps. The Chinese seemed to believe this. They really didn't know Americans well. We lived in a free country. The odds of any intelligent person actually going to an internment camp were slim to none. I couldn't really imagine anyone trading their freedom for some crappy MRE's, but I'm guessing a lot of those people in the riots will run right down there and sign up. I never understood the "I'm entitled to this or that" mentality. In my mind, you were entitled to what you earned and fought for, and only that.

We pulled up to the lake entrance. This was going to be A.J. and Max's job. A.J. would get rid of the lock, make sure all of us made it through, then relock the gate behind us with a new chain and lock. This lock we actually had keys for. Once we got done unloading, Michael and I would take an extra key over to Mary and her group.

We rolled through the gate and into the horseshoe on the other side of the lake from Mary's group. We had talked about the best place to set up away from them. We didn't want them to think we were trying to creep into their space or hunting territory.

It was about noon by the time we got both RV's tucked under trees. We were going to cover all the tents and RVs with brush and a few camouflage tarps we had. A.J. had said it would make us invisible from the air. Thankfully we hadn't seen any planes since the first day they flew over, but we all knew things would get much worse before they got better.

This camp would be our home for the coming months. We could only hope we would be safe here. Having the Chinese every two miles blocking traffic in the middle of small-town Oklahoma isn't a good sign for the future. I looked around at all my family and friends. Everyone busy and rushing around to cover everything that was out in plain sight.

My family had started the apocalypse separated by miles, but we were determined to end it together. I knew we couldn't stay hidden forever. Sooner or later, the fight for America would walk straight into this park, but we'd be ready to face it together.

Manufactured by Amazon.ca
Bolton, ON